OLGA SINCLAIR

◆

AN HEIR FOR ASHINGBY

Complete and Unabridged

ULVERSCROFT
Leicester

First published in Great Britain in 2004 by
Robert Hale Limited
London

First Large Print Edition
published 2005
by arrangement with
Robert Hale Limited
London

British Library CIP Data

Sinclair, Olga
  An heir for Ashingby.—Large print ed.—
Ulverscroft large print series: historical romance
1. Love stories
2. Large type books
I. Title
823.9′14 [F]

ISBN 1–84395–850–3

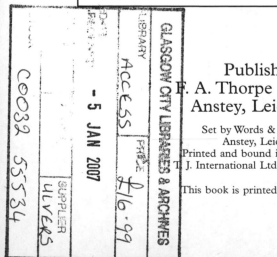

Published by
F. A. Thorpe (Publishing)
Anstey, Leicestershire

Set by Words & Graphics Ltd.
Anstey, Leicestershire
Printed and bound in Great Britain by
T. J. International Ltd., Padstow, Cornwall

This book is printed on acid-free paper

Olga Sinclair was born, and has lived, in Norfok all her life. She was a Justice of the Peace for twenty-seven years as well as serving in the A.T.S. during World War II. She is currently President of Norwich Writers' Circle.

AN HEIR FOR ASHINGBY

1812. America and Britain are on the brink of war. American-born Sarah Dunthorne is visiting her grandmother in London. Sarah is compromised when she assists her friend, Corinne de Vere, to elope with Forbes Thackstone. Corinne is the ward and heir to Colonel, Lord Wrenningham, who is now determined that the rebellious couple shall never inherit his estate at Ashingby. Physically attracted to Sarah, Wrenningham proposes, but she will not marry without love. Grandmama is furious and sends Sarah home on the same ship as Wrenningham, who is taking reinforcements to Canada. Then war is declared. As the couple journey on through danger and difficulties, will they find love?

1

London, May 1812

All fashionable London seemed to be crowded into Lady Guernsey's richly furnished house in Berkeley Square. Ladies in revealingly *décolleté* gowns, high-waisted, clinging to curvaceous bodies, hair, befeathered and piled high. Gentlemen were decked out in immaculate white stocks, rich velvet coats and tight pantaloons, the civilians desperate to compete with the richness of the scarlet, gold-braided jackets of the officers. The most decorated and splendid of them all, Harry, Lord Wrenningham, leaned against a pillar, idly watching the throng. Tall, lean and pale, the gaiety of his gold-faced tunic was in direct contrast to his sombre appearance.

The horror of that last battle against the French had scarred him deeply. It had made him think as never before, of his own mortality. The scenes of death, the mangled bodies, the screams and groans of his men had haunted him more than at any time in his military career.

His injury, though not the worst he had

ever suffered, had been slow to heal. But now he was almost fit again, hot blood should be coursing through his veins, yet none of the women he had encountered recently had held any appeal for him. He had toyed with the idea of finding an alluring little muslin and setting her up in an apartment, but he had found none to his taste. In truth he had lost the urge to bed any woman.

Although not yet thirty he had been in many battles, advances and retreats, for years Britain had been at war with France. Napoleon threatened to overrun the whole of Europe and now America was beginning to complain about the British attacking their ships. That was only a smokescreen, of course, what they were really after was the annexation of Canada.

Languidly his eyes lingered on a new-comer; he watched her as she danced, singling her out as different. Dressed in the height of fashion, her gown of flimsy cream gauze over silk had an enticingly low neckline. It revealed a tantalizing glimpse of firm breasts, and the tiny sleeves, puffed and slashed, complemented her becomingly rounded arms and she moved with a natural and unconscious grace that was seldom seen in the ballrooms of the *beau monde*.

He had noticed her when she arrived, in

the company of his feather-brained young cousin, the Honourable Corinne de Vere, they were followed by Lady Turley, Corinne's *duenna*. The newcomer, Miss Sarah Dunthorne, recently launched into London society, was the granddaughter of Lady MacKenna.

'Sarah, you really must help me,' Corinne whispered. Her large blue eyes were close to tears, golden ringlets bobbed around her pretty face. 'I'm desperate. Harry's been so unreasonable since he was invalided home from the Peninsular Campaign and I declare I'll die if I can't see Forbes — alone — just for fifteen — or even for ten minutes.'

Sarah sighed sympathetically. Etiquette was so much more complicated in London society than it had been in the small town in America where she had grown up. She kept her voice low so that her words did not reach the ears of Lady Turley, Corinne's *duenna*. 'You know I'd do most anything for you,' — Sarah's voice held a trace of American accent — 'but is it wise? You could ruin your reputation — '

'Bother my reputation. I don't give a fig for it,' Corinne said airily. She was so much in love with Lieutenant Forbes Thackstone there was no telling what she would do. Sarah's sympathies were all with Corinne, who had had become her closest friend and confidante since she had arrived in London. When

Corinne declared herself desperate, Sarah knew it was the truth, shocking though such wild talk was. Lady Turley would have a fit of the vapours if she overheard.

'All I ask you to do,' pleaded Corinne, 'is distract Harry's attention whilst I slip out to the conservatory.'

'But Lady Turley will be watching — '

'Fiddlededee, she'll never notice — especially if she's had one or two glasses of Madeira. It's my cousin Harry I'm worried about. It is odious to have a guardian who's so monstrously hard. It's impossible to please him. The brute has been watching me like a hawk since Forbes called upon him to ask for my hand.'

'And Lord Wrenningham refused even to consider an engagement, just because in his opinion Forbes is neither rich nor aristocratic enough to marry into his starchy, upper-crust family.' Sarah's tone was cutting.

Corinne had related the story of that unfortunate interview many times and Sarah was totally in agreement that such an arrogant attitude was unworthy of a real gentleman.

'He cares nothing for my happiness, for I am drowned in misery when I cannot see my dear Forbes.' Tears quivered on her lashes. 'But I am determined — just as determined as Harry is — and if you won't assist me, I'll think of some other way, no matter what scandal it causes. I shall — ' Her voice was beginning to rise.

'Hush, Corinne,' Sarah said soothingly. It made her angry when she thought of the power that man exercised over this sweet girl, who had no parents to guide her. 'Of course, I'll do as you wish, only I haven't yet met Lord Wrenningham.'

Corinne gave a light little laugh and squeezed Sarah's fingers. 'I shall introduce you this very evening.'

'Introduce whom? What are you scheming now, you minx?' panted Beatrix, Lady Turley. She was overweight and had been hurrying to catch up with her charges.

'Why, my dear cousin Harry, of course,' Corinne purred sweetly. 'I am informed that he will be attending this rout, especially as it is given by Lady Guernsey — with whom he is on very close terms.'

'Corinne!' Lady Turley had caught up with them. 'It is not becoming in an unmarried young lady to speak of such matters.'

'It is only what I have heard, that he has an eye for beauty and an appreciation of wit.' In Sarah's ear she whispered, 'His reputation as a rake is well known.'

Sarah was by no means shy or retiring, but

nothing she had heard of Wrenningham disposed her to think well of him. How on earth could she distract him? But she must keep her word, even though such deception did not come naturally to her.

Lady Turley raised her lorgnette and surveyed the throng. 'We shall sit there, not too close to the orchestra — but where we can both see and be seen.'

Sarah found the sophistication of the *ton* fresh and exciting; she gazed around, fascinated, faintly amused, but ready to participate to the full. As she paraded across the floor her arm linked with Corinne's she could not help being aware that they presented an agreeable picture of feminine elegance. Men made a leg and ladies inclined their heads in acknowledgement as they passed. Although she had been in London for only six weeks, already Sarah had a feeling of belonging. That was strange, because when she was at home in America she had thought of the English as enemies — a view that had been thrown into confusion since her arrival. What a contrast London was to the small town of Cassie's Rock in the north of New York State, where she had been born and raised!

Cassie's Rock had only two stores, three saloons, a hotel, a gambling shop, one dressmaker, a wooden schoolhouse and a doctor. The doctor was Sarah's father, a dedicated, hard-working man. She loved him dearly. In her estimation he stood head and shoulders above any of the rich, idle, dissolute aristocrats in Lady Guernsey's house that evening. The population of the small American township was barely one thousand — and she knew almost all of them. She had been brought up to a simple, natural, industrious life, among folks whom she loved. She had never even thought of going anywhere else — until her family suddenly took it into their heads that she must visit her grandmama in England.

Sarah had protested. Why should she leave the home where she was happy and busy? She had told her parents quite positively that they would find it difficult to manage without her. As the eldest of five children she took on much of the responsibility of running the house and looking after her younger brothers and sisters. She also assisted Papa in his work as a doctor, carefully checking the medical supplies in his black leather bag before he climbed into his one-horse buggy to set off on his rounds. From a very early age, he had trained her in nursing and dispensing. She took messages, handed out medicines and could dress minor wounds.

Papa often said what a wonderful assistant she was, and she'd been hurt when all that was brushed aside because of the letter that arrived from Grandmama MacKenna, with an invitation for Sarah to pay her a long visit. Enclosed were bankers' orders to cover the fare and equip her for the journey.

'It will do you a power of good, child,' Papa had said. 'It's time for you to learn something of your English roots, your heritage, to try being a grand lady — '

'I've no wish to be a grand lady,' she interrupted.

'Nonsense. Your mama has seen to it that you have the accomplishments required by a young lady of high class, as she herself is, and I'm assured you will enjoy yourself famously.'

'If England is so wonderful then why did you and Mama leave it?' she countered.

'You know perfectly well why we came here.'

'I do indeed! It was because Mama's parents objected to her marrying you, Papa,' Sarah said, accusingly. 'I never could understand why they felt like that. It just shows how unreasonable the English are!'

'It was only my Papa who objected,' Mrs Dunthorne said, soft voiced and conciliatory.

'And Grandpa never forgave you — even after all these years,' Sarah pointed out.

Mrs Dunthorne looked sad and Sarah wished she had not spoken in quite so brusque a manner. She was on the point of apologizing when her mama spoke again. 'However, that's past. I've corresponded regularly with my Mama.'

'Sending your letters via her friend, Lady Turley, so that Grandpa would not be apprised,' Sarah interrupted.

Mama bowed her head in assent and continued as if she had not been interrupted. 'Now that she is widowed and alone she would like very much to meet my children.'

'If Sarah doesn't wish to go, can I take her place?' Monica said. She was the next eldest and just sixteen.

'Certainly not, Monnie. You're far too young. But if Sarah's visit proves to be agreeable, I have no doubt your grandmama will invite you in a year or so.'

'It's an excellent opportunity for you, Sarah,' said Dr Dunthorne. 'Travel broadens the mind, and you will meet many more young men than you do here.'

'I'm perfectly content here,' protested Sarah.

'I know that, my dear — but there is more to the world than Cassie's Rock and its surrounds. To my way of thinking you've been seeing far too much of Seth Boyer recently.'

Sarah shrugged. 'Seth and I are only friends — just as we've always been.'

'I'm not sure if that's the way he looks upon your relationship.' Her papa was watching her keenly.

She blushed, remembering an incident a few days previously, when she'd been down at that secluded spot by the creek with Seth. It had been one of their favourite haunts since they'd been eight or nine years old — they'd paddled there and sailed toy boats. More recently, they'd just talked and listened to the water. Then last time, sitting close together, Seth had suddenly pushed her over on to her back — the sort of rough and tumble they'd enjoyed in childish romps — but this time he'd pushed his hand up under her skirts, fumbling beneath her petticoats.

'Stop it, Seth.' She'd jumped up immediately and moved away, smoothing her skirts down again.

'Didn't mean anything, Sarah,' he'd mumbled.

She had accepted that as an apology. He'd always been a bit impetuous and unruly but she was sure he would never hurt her.

'Race you back to the house,' she'd called, and they had been young and carefree together again.

'For goodness sake, Sarah!' snapped Monica. 'You must go. And do try to make a good impression, otherwise Grandmama will never invite any of us again, and I do so long to be launched into high society, as Mama was.'

Sarah sighed. They hoped she would reopen a relationship with Grandmama and that seemed a terrible responsibility. Would she be able to make a favourable impression?

'I have always hoped that one day you would go to England and meet my mama. I've taken care that you know how to behave in society and to speak perfect English. It is high time you made the acquaintance of your grandmama — you are her eldest granddaughter and she has never seen you!'

Tears came into her eyes, and she dabbed them with a lace-trimmed handkerchief. Papa patted his wife's shoulder consolingly and she lifted one delicate hand and clasped his. Their love remained warm and binding. Sarah could not bear to displease such good, kind parents, and she had to admit there was a great deal in the prospect that was alluring.

'Very well,' she said. 'I shall accept the invitation.'

'You'll be the belle of the ball, the toast of London,' exclaimed Dr Dunthorne. In that he spoke the truth.

Artlessly, being just her natural self, Sarah had taken the *ton* by storm. Her features might not be classically beautiful, but she glowed with good health that showed in her flawless complexion. Her head was crowned by luxuriant hair of a rich dark brown that in sunshine caught tawny highlights. Friendly interest twinkled in the depth of her deep blue eyes, and the pleasure-seeking world of London society found her youthful, open character refreshingly attractive. Added to which and even more importantly, her lineage was impeccable.

Sarah enjoyed the attentions of the rich, sophisticated gentlemen who gathered around her. She was aware that with their exaggerated protestations of undying passion, they were more in competition with each other than wilting with real feeling for her, but as they clamoured to dance with her, how could she help but enjoy herself famously?

So here she was, at yet another ball, pacing across the floor, Corinne's arm linked affectionately with hers, giving and receiving greetings.

Lady Turley approached an elderly gentleman, who stood up and kissed her hand. 'You know the Honourable Miss Corinne de Vere — ' she said.

'Of course. The cousin and heir apparent of

12

the notorious Earl of Wrenningham and positively enchanting, as always.' Mr Rawlingson bowed over Corinne's hand as she curtsied.

The man's voice had a cynical note, his face the pink, puffy look of debauchery, which Sarah found quite repellent. She was surprised that such a man should be on close terms with her grandmama's old friend.

'Sarah,' Lady Turley continued, 'allow me to introduce my wicked friend, Mr Rawlingson, the celebrated wit and the most feared cartoonist in all of London.'

'Dear Lady Turley, how you flatter me!' Mr Rawlingson drawled.

'You old reprobate! You adore the power your mischievous pen gives you!' Lady Turley, tapped him playfully with her fan. 'Be silent and allow me to present to you, Miss Sarah Dunthorne, the granddaughter of Lady MacKenna.'

He regarded Sarah with an almost insulting twist to his thick wet lips. 'The American gal of whose beauty I have heard so much. I am honoured to meet you.' He paused, then added, 'Damned troublesome country you come from, though. Far too big for their boots, those old colonials.'

'We've been free of the British yoke for many years now, Mr Rawlingson.' Sarah's voice was sharp. 'Contrary to your assessment, the trouble between our nations is caused by you British.' She spread her skirts and curtsied low as she spoke. Rising gracefully, she looked straight into the man's pale little eyes. They reminded her of one of the pigs on Seth's farm. Then she added, 'However, at the moment we are supposed to be at peace, are we not?'

'Certainly at this time and place we are,' Lady Turley interposed firmly. 'I know nothing of international politics and what is more I have no wish to be informed upon such matters. Let us sit and indulge in some pleasant gossip. Your cartoon of the Prince Regent has been the talk of the *ton*, Reginald. It's a wonder you're not locked up in the Tower.'

'It was quite effective, was it not, my dear Beatrix?' Mr Rawlingson beamed as he assisted her to a sofa.

'Come, Reginald,' purred that lady, fluttering her fan. 'I'm sure you've uncovered some fresh scandals and I'm just dying to hear them.'

He chuckled. 'You're a lady after my own heart, Beatrix.'

With their heads close together they embarked upon discourse of the latest capers of the *beau monde* and began to enjoy themselves mightily.

Corinne drew Sarah a little aside, her eyes searching the ballroom. Suddenly she tensed. 'There he is!' She caught hold of Sarah's arm. 'Over by the pillar — that's Harry.'

Sarah was disposed to dislike him in advance and at first glance he appeared to be both haughty and indolent, but he was undeniably handsome. With his straight-backed bearing he looked every inch a military man, one of the hated red-coats — and Sarah had grown up on tales from the War of Independence, some true, some biased, all lurid and horrifying. She would have distrusted him for that reason alone, even if Corinne had told her nothing more about him.

Then a new dance was announced. Sarah was swept off to join in a longways set. She loved dancing and the movements were much the same as in some of the square dances she'd enjoyed back home in Cassie's Rock, only lacking the exuberance to which she was accustomed.

The slow movements, meeting, parting and turning, gave her an opportunity to glance surreptitiously over to where Wrenningham stood. To her intense embarrassment she discovered that he was looking directly at her. His eyes met hers and held her gaze and she saw an indefinable sadness that wrenched at her most tender feelings. Momentarily Sarah forgot where she was — until her partner spoke and she realized she had missed a step.

'I'm so sorry.' She smiled her apology, and concentrated more fully for the rest of the dance.

Lithely and delicately she executed the remaining movements, and kept her eyes on the ladies and gentlemen who were in the same set as she. As the dance ended she dropped in a deep curtsy, then with natural vitality, sprang up, to place her hand upon the arm her partner offered her. Gallantly, he prepared to escort her back to where Lady Turley sat, but Corinne rushed up. 'Sarah — you must allow me to introduce you to my cousin.' Sweetly but firmly, she manoeuvred Sarah's partner so that he escorted both young ladies to where Wrenningham stood.

'Harry, dear guardian.' Corinne held out her hand and Wrenningham raised it to his lips.

'Your servant, dear cousin.' His voice was a lazy drawl. The bow he directed at Sarah's partner was coolly dismissive and that young man quickly withdrew.

Hastily, Corinne said, 'Allow me to introduce my dear friend, Miss Sarah Dunthorne, who has come from America on a visit to her grandmama, Lady MacKenna. Sarah — this is my cousin and guardian, Lord Wrenningham.'

Sarah was aware of the raking gaze of a pair of steel-grey eyes, as she dipped into an exaggerated curtsy, deeper than she would normally have performed. Wrenningham's bow was the acme of elegant refinement.

'Charmed to make your acquaintance, Lord Wrenningham,' Her voice, despite its polite formality, was tinged with sarcasm. 'Corinne has told me so much about you.'

'But little of it good, I'll wager.'

Since that was the truth Sarah decided it was more honest not to reply.

'Upon my soul, I cannot imagine why you should think that,' Corinne exclaimed. To Sarah's amazement she looked up at her cousin positively archly. 'You know I am the most dutiful of wards.'

'I am relieved to hear you say so.' His voice was dry. He ignored the coy glance with which she attempted to divert him. 'Am I to take it that you have reformed in some manner?'

He turned to Sarah, his eyes lazily hooded by dark-lashed eyelids. 'What is your opinion, Miss Dunthorne? Would you vouch for the truth of your friend's assertion?'

'Most assuredly, sir. I've always found

Corinne to be completely trustworthy,' she replied, staunchly.

'Obviously your experience differs from mine.' With that he turned back to Corinne. 'You will not wheedle me into changing my mind, young lady. Forbes Thackstone is nothing but a damned fortune-hunter.'

'Oh, Cousin Harry. I declare you will cause my heart to break.' Her voice sounded deceptively submissive, her eyes meekly downcast, though Sarah noticed the rebellious pout on her friend's pretty lips.

'Nonsense! 'Tis but a passing fancy,' snapped Wrenningham. 'You may put him out of your mind, for I shall never give permission for you to marry him.' Sarah could stay silent no longer. 'How can you know what Corinne's feelings are? If I were truly in love nothing would prevent me — '

Wrenningham interrupted her frostily. 'Miss Dunthorne, my ward has responsibilities. She is descended from an impeccable line of landed noblemen, she cannot indulge such whims, any more than I can. Nor will she be permitted to whilst she is in my care.'

'What will you do, my lord? Keep her under lock and key?' demanded Sarah.

'If need be.' Wrenningham spoke in coolly, measured tones. 'If that is the only way to bring her to her senses. Such a marriage would bring disgrace upon our family.'

'What right have you to brush aside Corinne's happiness just because of your own pride?'

'I have every right.' His eyes narrowed. He was watching her closely in a manner that disconcerted her. Sarah trembled as she remembered other items of gossip she had heard about him. An officer and a gentleman, he had rank, wealth, and elegance, but for all that, she decided he was positively inhuman.

2

Accustomed to having his least order obeyed immediately, Wrenningham was disturbed. He looked more closely at this girl, this friend of Corinne's who was challenging him so boldly. An American gal, even though she had British parents, stating opinions on matters she did not understand and which were no business of hers — he was surprised to find himself goaded into defending his action.

'My decision has not been taken lightly. I take no pleasure in making my ward unhappy. When she is older, she will understand why I forbid this marriage.' He snapped his mouth shut to indicate that he was not prepared to enter into further discussion. He was accustomed to commanding.

Sarah stared back at him, her anger increased and their eyes clashed. Then his dark-lashed eyelids drooped, and his expression changed — she knew he would not look at another man in such a way, but the message he was giving her sent a shivery sensation down her spine. Had she been alone with Wrenningham her instinct would have been to walk away, and even in the midst of that highly civilized society a tingle of apprehension coursed over her body. He was having the most extraordinary effect upon her.

There was menace in his eyes, yet she found it impossible to look away, and she had to stay with him, prevent him from noticing that whilst they conversed Corinne had moved away. One thing she knew was that men liked to talk about themselves. She smiled sweetly and said, 'I admit I know so little of the world. You must have had some extraordinary adventures — I should be enraptured to hear about them.'

'I would find it more interesting to hear about you, Miss Dunthorne.'

'You would?' Sarah said with genuine surprise. 'Perhaps you wonder how I come to be here in London?'

'Not at all.' He replied coolly. 'You are the granddaughter on your mother's side of Lord and Lady MacKenna, whose estate lies in Lincolnshire. And on your papa's side also from the aristocracy, though he had the misfortune to be the youngest son of — how many boys was it?'

'Five,' said Sarah.

'And not one single girl,' he remarked. 'Undoubtedly you come of admirable stock.'

Sarah bristled at this list of her pedigree, as

21

if she was a prize cow rather than a human being. Only the thought of Corinne prevented her from uttering the sharp retort that sprang to her lips.

'How is it you know so much about my family?' she asked.

'London may be a great city, but our circle within it is very circumscribed. Gossip spreads like wildfire, for what else is there to talk about except each other? But tell me, where did you live in America?'

'Cassie's Rock,' she told him. 'A small town, not far from the famous Niagara Falls. My father is the doctor there. He is loved and respected by everybody.'

'Including yourself, I observe.'

'Yes, indeed! Most certainly by myself,' she said earnestly, 'but by my mama and my sister and brothers too. When I was at home I helped in his surgery.'

'Your family must all miss you greatly. Was it difficult for you to persuade them to allow you to come to England?'

'On the contrary, they insisted I must! Papa thought I should have the opportunity to meet more people and my mama dearly wished me to make the acquaintance of Grandmama.'

Sarah saw Corinne passing behind Wrenningham, moving towards the conservatory.

For one dreadful moment she thought he was about to turn around, and quickly put her hand upon his sleeve to keep his attention focused upon her.

'You've been wounded — should you not be sitting down?' she enquired.

'My wounds are almost healed.'

'But you must not take risks, my lord. May I ask, what is the nature of your injuries?'

'Flesh wounds in arm and chest. Nothing compared with what some of the men suffered.'

The bleak expression that came into his eyes distanced him from her, taking him away from the elegant ballroom to a life that was hard, hostile and dangerous. A deep inner unhappiness twisted his face. Despite her distrust of Wrenningham and all he stood for, she could not help a surge of compassion. She had witnessed illness and suffering, death too, but she had never before seen such anguish as she read on his pale face.

'Do let us sit, my lord,' she repeated.

'As you wish.'

He placed a hand under her elbow and led her aside a few steps to a pair of satin-covered gilded chairs. Fortuitously they were beyond sight of the conservatory doors. To keep his attention she said, 'I hear the Duke of

Wellington is having a successful campaign in Europe.'

'He is. But Napoleon remains powerful. The war is not yet over and it's high time I rejoined my regiment.'

'You mustn't think of going until you are fit — '

'I should be with my men.' He paused and then continued, 'I sincerely hope the rumours of unrest coming from the war hawks in your country are unfounded. But I fear fighting will break out before long.'

Her heart plummeted. 'Then we shall be enemies,' she said.

He did not deny it. 'We do not make war upon women.'

'That is not what Seth says.'

'And who is Seth?'

'A friend. His grandpa was killed at Bunker Hill.'

'Such things happen in war,' Wrenningham said, grimly.

'Yet men go on fighting.' Sarah shook her head for the thought saddened her. 'And when they come home, people like my father struggle to heal their wounds.'

The earl was silent for a long time and his eyes slipped away to some pit of sorrow deep within him. His distress touched her. She forgot about Corinne and Forbes Thackstone.

She was oblivious to the merry rhythm of the orchestra, scarcely heard the chatter of the rich and fashionable world around her. Her attention was entirely focused upon Lord Wrenningham. His face was etching itself deeply into her consciousness.

She was jerked back to the present by the sight of Lady Turley bearing down upon them, the plumes in her hair waving, proof of her agitation. Wrenningham leapt to his feet.

Guessing the cause of their chaperon's consternation, Sarah began to move towards her, intending to lead her aside before Wrenningham could know of the problem. She had taken only one step when she felt the iron grip of his hand upon her upper arm. He held her back and advanced to meet Lady Turley. He addressed that agitated lady suavely. 'How delightful to see you looking so well. I apologize for detaining the charming Miss Dunthorne by my side.'

Only when Lady Turley was so close they could whisper, did he add, 'But I assume that it is actually some other young personage who gives you concern?'

'Corinne. The wicked girl has disappeared, slipped away when my back was turned — '

'And when I, too, was otherwise engaged!' Wrenningham said sharply. He turned to

Sarah. 'I imagine you know the whereabouts of my ward?'

Sarah stood her ground and held his gaze. She owed it to her friend to remain silent, convinced that Corinne's happiness was at stake. Only a few minutes previously she had felt drawn to Wrenningham, had experienced an inexplicable sadness that they had to be enemies — now she felt no such compunction. They were different in their attitudes to life, to personal liberty, to belief in love, and the treasure it could bring. Her own parents were living proof of that. They had eloped to Gretna Green, and although they had been saddened because Grandpa MacKenna had refused to forgive them, they had never regretted their runaway marriage. Sarah's eyes flickered in the direction of the conservatory. It was a totally instinctive reaction and she regretted it immediately.

'Ah!' said Wrenningham. He bowed to Lady Turley, offered his arm and said, 'Madam, Miss Dunthorne has expressed a wish to observe the collection of exotic plants in the conservatory — please be so good as to accompany us.' His eyes were as hard and icy as the voice with which he commanded, 'Come, Miss Dunthorne.'

She had no option but to walk beside him. His pace was measured, no one observing the three of them would have dreamed that anything was amiss. Yet Sarah's heart was thumping wildly within her breast and, unable to contain herself as they neared the wide double doors that led to the conservatory, she wrenched her hand from his arm and ran on ahead of her companions.

The huge, beautifully proportioned glasshouse appeared to be deserted, filled only with palms and the greenery of forests in faraway places, with bushes and creepers bearing flowers from the tropics, plants whose names were quite unknown to her. Nor, at that time, was she interested to learn. She made a great deal of noise quite intentionally, spinning around with her arms outstretched, clicking the heels of her dainty shoes, assuming a delight she was far from feeling.

'It is exquisite!' she cried out in a loud voice. 'Absolutely exquisite. I have never seen such beautiful plants — and such an elegant construction.'

Moonlight gleamed through the glass and made twisty shadows on the white-painted wrought-ironwork. The warm air was filled with perfume from a hundred huge exotic blooms. A movement drew her attention to the far end of the long building. Sarah continued her paean of praise. 'Oh, my lord, it is indeed good of you to suggest that Lady

Turley and I should see this magnificent conservatory!'

She glimpsed two fleeing figures, heard a quick scamper of footsteps. Seconds later, Corinne's guardian and their chaperon walked in but Corinne and Forbes were out of sight.

Wrenningham deposited Lady Turley at Sarah's side and strode impatiently away. The heels of his shoes rang on the mosaic tiles of the floor. Sarah offered her arm to Lady Turley and together they followed him to the far end, where a door that led to the garden stood wide open. He closed it.

'Obviously Corinne is not here,' said Sarah.

Wrenningham regarded her scathingly. 'I shall speak to my ward tomorrow.'

'I shall, of course, have to inform Lady MacKenna,' said Lady Turley.

'Surely no harm has been done,' pleaded Sarah. Neither of her companions made reply. They were already walking back towards the ballroom. One of Mr Playford's most intricate dances was being performed and Corinne and Forbes Thackstone were in the set nearest to the conservatory. The smile on her pretty face was brilliant as she swept by, her hand held with proper elegance by her partner. Sarah breathed a sigh of relief.

* * *

The following day, in the morning-room of her London house, Lady MacKenna listened gravely, as Lady Turley told her of the improper conduct of her two charges. Sarah and Corinne stood side by side, and Corinne's hand stole into Sarah's and held on tightly.

Lady MacKenna was as tall and thin as Lady Turley was short and fat. Both were dressed in morning gowns of satin and lace, and both were in their late sixties. Lady MacKenna's sharp eyes were so dark as to appear almost black and they shone as bright as those of a little mouse.

'Well, what do you have to say for yourself, Sarah?' she enquired.

'Grandmama, please do not blame Corinne,' Sarah said. 'She has to meet Lieutenant Thackstone in secret because her ogre of a guardian will never allow her to converse with him in the normal way of civilized society.'

'And why do you suppose that is, child?' There was a sarcastic note in Lady MacKenna's voice.

'Why, it's only because Lord Wrenningham has taken a dislike to Lieutenant Thackstone,' Sarah explained hastily. 'There

29

is no other reason.'

'Do you take me for a dunderhead, child?' snapped Lady MacKenna.

'Oh, no, Grandmama I know you are very wise and kind and you would never suggest that a girl should be married to some man for whom she has no liking.'

Lady MacKenna gave a snort, but her face softened a little. 'Maybe not, but nor would I give any encouragement to a gal to enter a disastrous marriage, for that is what it would be if Corinne married this — this soldier! He has absolutely no prospects. He could not possibly keep a wife in proper style.'

'I-I do not need to live in a grand style.' Corinne was stung into objecting forcefully. 'I would be content to live in quite a small cottage if I could share it with Forbes.'

'Nonsense!' said Lady MacKenna. 'Thackstone knows you would never be reduced to living in penury. He's counting on your money becoming available to you upon marriage.'

'That is why he is pursuing you so arduously, my dear Corinne,' Lady Turley nodded vigorously. 'Wrenningham is quite correct to oppose this union.'

'It's not true. Forbes loves me,' wailed Corinne.

'Dear Grandmama,' Sarah interposed.

'Remember how it was with my mama. I know you and Grandpapa were greatly opposed when she married my papa. They have never had much money, but I am sure you would not find two happier people on this earth.'

'And a deucedly hard time my poor Amy has had of it, I believe,' interrupted Lady MacKenna. 'But it was of her own choosing and cannot be altered now. Besides, I am of the opinion that your mama was made of considerably sterner stuff than this young lady. Not to mention that your papa had a training in medicine which enabled him to make a living, of a sort.' She gave a snort to convey that in her opinion his earnings were despicable.

'I-I am s-stronger than you th-think,' stammered Corinne. She was near to tears. Her voice shook, despite her brave words, making her sound even more vulnerable than she looked. Sarah squeezed her friend's fingers to give her courage.

'Question is, what's to be done about it?' demanded Lady MacKenna.

'Wrenningham is of the opinion that Corinne must leave London immediately and go to Ashingby,' said Lady Turley. She looked at Corinne sternly. 'She has already been told.'

Corinne sighed. 'It's abominable! I'm to be sent to the country like an outcast whilst the season is in full swing. But I shall endure it, even though the loneliness sends me into a decline.' She turned her appealing eyes upon Sarah. 'If only you would accompany me? But I mustn't be selfish. It's too much to ask!'

Sarah had no idea where Ashingby was, but she couldn't allow Corinne's plea to go unanswered.

'I'll be happy to go with you, Corinne, provided, of course, I am invited and my grandmama is agreeable.'

'I shall see that you are made welcome,' said Corinne, with surprising confidence.

'Have I your permission, Grandmama?' Sarah asked meekly, remembering her duty to her family. She could almost hear Monica whispering — 'Think of me — for heaven's sake, don't upset Grandmama any more than you have already.'

Lady MacKenna's face was thoughtful. 'What is your opinion, Beatrix?'

'I cannot see that it would do any harm,' replied Lady Turley. 'I would certainly appreciate your company, Primrose, for I am sure you would wish to accompany your granddaughter?'

Lady MacKenna inclined her head in agreement. 'I admit that a short stay at

Ashingby would not be displeasing to me.'

'I hoped you would say that, Primrose,' said Lady Turley. 'Harry is always a most obliging host — although his duties may prevent him from joining us.'

Sarah was somewhat disconcerted as she realized that Ashingby was Wrenningham's country seat, but it was too late to withdraw. Corinne squeezed her hand in gratitude and Sarah knew she had made the only possible decision. She hoped that Wrenningham's duties would keep him away for a consider-able time.

*   *   *

The vast estate of Ashingby was set in pleasantly undulating countryside. Heavily wooded, it included several farms, a small market-town and five other villages within its boundaries. The Hall, a huge Palladian house stood only three miles inland from the rolling North Sea, and there were vantage points from which views of landscape and seascape could be marvelled.

Sarah thought it delightful. Greatly though she had enjoyed her sojourn in London, the quieter pace of life in the countryside was equally congenial to her. Corinne, deeply in love, found little to please her in being so far away from all those places where she might hope to see her beloved. She sighed and day-dreamed and hungered for messages from Forbes, but days went by and she received nothing. Sarah tried to interest her in the beauty of the garden, suggested they should ride together, or drive down to the sea.

Corinne's answer was always the same. 'No, Sarah. I couldn't bear to go out today. There might be a letter or a message.' She sank down on the *chaise-longue* and closed her eyes.

Restlessly, Sarah moved to the window and stood looking out; though cool, the sun was bright and the weather spring-like. 'Please, Corinne — take a walk around the garden with me. You'll lose your looks if you stay indoors all the time.'

'I care nothing for my looks if I cannot marry Forbes.'

'At least take care of your health whilst you are waiting. I'm sure Forbes will manage to get a message to you before long.'

'Do you really think so?' Corinne asked eagerly.

'I am sure of it.'

'You know, Sarah, one of the most romantic stories I have ever heard was how your mama and papa eloped. How they met at a grand ball, fell in love at first sight and danced together the whole evening, even though it was extremely improper.'

Sarah smiled fondly. 'Yes. But my Grandpapa MacKenna had other plans for his daughter. She was told to put all thoughts of young Doctor Dunthorne out of her mind and never see him again.'

'You told me she was sent miles away to stay with an aunt,' Corinne prompted.

'Yes, but Mama contrived to send a letter to Papa, and at once he rode northwards, travelling day and night and within a few days arrived on her doorstep.'

Corinne sighed. 'And he dared not knock on the door!'

'Faith, no! That would never have done. But he managed to let Mama know he was there, and at once set about planning their elopement. He made friends with a young man who lived next door and persuaded him to hide a ladder in the grounds. Then one night, Papa set the ladder against Mama's bedroom window and she climbed down into his arms. He had a carriage ready just around the corner and in no time at all they were off and over the border and they travelled on to Gretna Green and were married there in the early hours of the morning.'

'Did no one pursue them?'

'Oh, yes. Servants were sent on fast horses to try and head them off, to stop their post-chaise, but they were too late.'

'It's such a wonderful story and I know exactly how your mama felt,' Corinne said. 'For it's the same with me. I am only happy when I am with Forbes, and so sad when we are parted. I really think I shall die if I do not get a message from him soon.'

'Time would pass quicker if you came out with me.'

'I'll be perfectly all right my own. I'll order a mount to be saddled for you, Sarah, and one of the grooms will accompany you.' Without raising herself from the *chaise-longue*, Corinne reached for the bell pull.

The joy of being in the saddle, out in the clear fresh air, lifted Sarah's spirits. She had ridden astride when she'd been a child, with freedom to explore the countryside around her hometown, but Mama had insisted she should also master the graceful art of the side-saddle. Lucy, her maid, helped her into the new riding-habit of soft midnight blue in which she had won many compliments when she'd paraded with the *beau monde* in Hyde Park. Grandmama had insisted she must be dressed in the height of fashion.

The groom brought out a pretty bay mare,

which Sarah loved on sight.

'Where do you wish to go, miss?' he asked.

'I believe the sea is not far away?' she suggested.

'A couple of miles, miss. That way.'

She delighted in the beauty of the countryside as they cantered over the parkland that surrounded the house, dotted with huge spreading trees of chestnut, oak and beech.

Soon they turned down a track that led through a stretch of woodland and, after about a mile, came out on to a narrow country road. They had gone barely half a mile when she heard a vehicle coming up fast from behind. As the road was narrow she drew her mount to one side, and glanced over her shoulder. It was a curricle, drawn by a perfectly matched pair of greys and driven at considerable speed. Handling the ribbons with masterly ease, was Wrenningham. Sarah's pleasure in the ride vanished. He was closing upon them fast, and appeared quite suddenly to recognize his groom. He reined in sharply and stopped the vehicle alongside the man who greeted him deferentially.

'What's this, Yallop — out with some of my best cattle?' he asked.

Before the man could answer, Sarah spoke

for him. 'My lord, your groom is accompanying me to the beach.' Wrenningham's eyebrows shot up as he became aware of Sarah.

'I was assured by Corinne that you would have no objection to my borrowing one of your mounts.'

'For once that young lady is correct. Most certainly I have no objection. On the contrary, it sounds a most commendable occupation for such a fine day.' To her surprise he then added, 'I shall accompany you.'

He handed the reins to his groom, jumped down from the whip's seat and stepped over to the man who accompanied Sarah. 'Take the curricle back to the stables,' he ordered, as he mounted the horse which the groom had been riding, and within moments was alongside her. She watched this manoeuvre with surprise — their last encounter had left her with the uncomfortable impression that his opinion of her was so low he would avoid her company as much as possible.

As they trotted forward side by side, she tried to gauge Wrenningham's present mood from his expression, but his face revealed little. His profile was thin, his nose hawk-like, brow jutting sharply. He had, however, lost a little of the pallor she had discerned previously.

'I trust you are well, my lord?' she ventured to ask.

'Well enough. The sawbones advises me to rest.'

'Then should you not take his advice?'

'I refuse to be treated like an invalid, coddled just because of a few scratches. I believe healthy exercise in the country air will be more beneficial.'

Undoubtedly he would do whatever he wished. They rode in silence for a short time but she found that oppressive and remarked, 'I did not know you were expected, my lord.'

'An oversight for which I apologize, Mistress Dunthorne.'

Of course he had no need to inform her of his movements. She glanced at him, saw him watching her and quickly looked away. She wondered why he had opted to ride with her, but could find no answer to that, convinced that he found no pleasure in her company.

Abruptly he asked, 'Has there been any communication between my ward and Thackstone?'

'No, sir. There has not.'

'You are quite certain?'

'Only this morning Corinne was saying how greatly she longs to hear from him.'

'I'm pleased to hear it.'

They turned off the road and traversed a track, wide and grassy, enclosed between high hedges.

'Corinne is very unhappy,' Sarah told him bitterly.

'Better a few weeks of unhappiness now than a lifetime of misery later.'

'She is deeply in love.'

'She may think she is, but this infatuation she has for Thackstone is no basis for a lasting marriage. Corinne is the daughter of my younger brother. Unfortunately, he and his wife both died some years ago. She will come into a large fortune when she is twenty-one and, apart from that, should I not marry and produce an heir, she and her offspring are next in line to Ashingby.'

'But if you marry — ' Sarah began boldly.

He cut into her words harshly. 'I am a military man. Many times in my life I've been within inches of death. Soon I shall return to my unit and I know not what battles lie ahead. I shall go with great concern if there is even the remotest possibility that Thackstone may inherit what I have here.'

'I am sure you misjudge him.'

'And I am sure I do not.' He spoke with a conviction that seemed unanswerable.

They breasted a sand dune and the

seascape was suddenly, magically spread before them. Beautiful as it was, she felt sad and dispirited. It was useless to continue the conversation. Nothing would make him change his mind.

He reined in his horse and she watched as he turned his head, leisurely surveying the scene, straight-backed, motionless in the saddle, lord of all he surveyed.

She wished him joy of it. For her there was no pleasure in the company of such a man. He epitomized all those characteristics she most disliked. He was proud and arrogant; he had not shown an ounce of tenderness or compassion for Corinne. Acting on impulse, she kicked her heels into the mare's flanks and urged the willing animal forward, fleeing from Wrenningham, heading with wild recklessness towards the sea. He infuriated her!

On the wide firm beach she gave the mare her head and allowed her to stretch into a gallop. The coolness of the rushing salty air, the exhilarating movement of the lively animal beneath her, and the distance she put between herself and Wrenningham helped to calm her. She wanted only to get away from him. She had nothing in common with him — he angered her, yet for some reason she did not even try to define, she cared that it was so. His face had haunted her since their first meeting, the manner in which he looked as if his mind was filled with memories too terrible to speak of. Against her better judgement, that had stirred her gentle nature — now it increased the rage she felt against him!

Since that night at the ball, her thoughts had turned to him over and over again. She told herself it was for no other reason than that she found him unusual. She couldn't understand him, yet she found him intriguing. Without realizing it, she'd been looking forward to the time when she might see him again, but his hard, unbending manner infuriated and upset her. Their dislike of each other was mutual. He would never understand her attitude to life, and most certainly she would never adopt his. They belonged to totally different worlds and so it would always be.

The mare slowed to a walking pace. Sarah did not urge her forward again. She had no wish to punish the willing little creature. Presently Lord Wrenningham cantered up alongside her.

'It's time we turned back, Miss Dunthorne,' he said. His lips set in a tight line.

Wordlessly, she turned her horse and followed him.

3

Wrenningham's presence in the Hall was evident in innumerable ways. Even though he moved quietly and was a man of few words, it seemed to Sarah that the aura of the place changed in some indefinable way. Everyone from the housekeeper to the boot boy moved with more alacrity, showing a greater sense of purpose. Conversations between Lady MacKenna and Lady Turley grew more animated. At dinner, Harry regaled them with the latest scandals from the *ton*. Sarah had to admit that the infuriating man's vibrant personality had a disturbing effect upon her, just as it did on every one else.

Soon after she arrived at Ashingby, she discovered with delight that it had a well-stocked library. 'Use it to your heart's content, my dear,' Corinne had said. 'They're not my sort of books, but I dare say you'll find something to your taste.'

Since then Sarah had browsed with interest and pleasure. About two days after Wrenningham's arrival, she made her way there in the late afternoon, and believing the room to be empty, as usual, moved quietly to the section where books on the flora and fauna of Norfolk were shelved. Her father was an amateur naturalist and had taught her the names of plants and animals that grew and lived wild around Cassie's Rock.

At Ashingby she had noticed birds and flowers and shrubs which were unfamiliar. Absorbed in a beautifully illustrated volume she had removed from the shelf, she was startled by a sound behind her. She swung around and realized with dismay that she was not alone. Wrenningham had been sitting in a leather-covered wing chair, whose high back had concealed him from her view. He, too, held a book in his hand, which he must have been reading.

'My lord,' she exclaimed. 'Pray forgive me for disturbing you.' She dropped a curtsy and would have sped from the room, but he moved to stand between her and the door.

'May I ask what it is you are so engrossed in?'

His words gave her the impression that he had been watching her for some time 'The Flora and Fauna of Norfolk.' she told him. 'I've noticed many species here that I've not seen before.'

'Every country has its differences.' As he spoke, he stepped forward, and automatically she moved back, conscious that the morning gown her grandmama insisted on her wearing, gave her breasts a fashionable lift. Wrenningham's eyes swept over her, but he moved past and opened a glass-covered bookcase. 'This may interest you. It's a collection of studies painted by my aunt. She was an accomplished watercolourist, and a keen observer of nature.'

His cool manner enabled Sarah to recover from what she considered the folly of her over-active imagination.

He opened the cover carefully. It was a collection of original work, professionally bound, with sheets of tissue protecting the pages. Sarah was enchanted by the delicate watercolours, executed with exquisite detail. The written words, explaining the subjects, were entered in a bold yet elegant hand.

Wrenningham moved closer to her and, as he turned a page, his hand brushed against her arm, making her uncomfortably aware of him.

'Your aunt was a very talented lady,' she said.

'In this family all the female members have been educated and accomplished.'

Not trusting him, Sarah wondered if that meant he found her lacking in some respect — even though her short sojourn in society had shown her that most of the ladies were poorly educated. Even some of the richest and most powerful could write little more than their own names.

'Papa had the same idea,' she said with pride. 'He insisted that his daughters should be educated to the same degree as his sons. That then they would pass on their knowledge to their own children.'

'As well as making more interesting companions for their husbands,' he observed, drily. 'But I cannot linger here any longer. I have to inspect some of the farms on the estate. Please use the library whenever you wish.'

He strode from the room, closing the door quietly behind him. Sarah turned back to the book she had been reading but it was some time before she could regain her concentration.

★   ★   ★

Two days later, Sarah noticed Corinne's depressed spirits had lifted. The weather was grey, slightly chilly, but Corinne actually suggested to Sarah that they should take a turn about the garden. Most certainly it was not the arrival of the earl that had brought about such a miraculous change.

Arm in arm, they strolled along the newly

raked gravel path beside the immaculate lawn, where in a far corner the gardener was scything the grass to within an inch of its roots.

'Sarah! I've been so longing to tell you. Polly, my maid, brought a note for me yesterday afternoon. Forbes has made all the arrangements.' She stopped and looked carefully all round, even though they had walked some distance from the house and no one, not even the gardener, was within hearing. Then she announced with a note of triumph, her words tumbling out in an excited rush, 'We're going to elope! We're setting out for Gretna Green! Tomorrow!'

Sarah drew in a deep breath. 'Oh, Corinne — are you really, really sure?'

'I was never more sure of anything in my life.' She clasped her hands together in a gesture of tremulous joy. 'Forbes has planned it all. He'll be waiting for me at the turnpike crossroads with a post-chaise harnessed and ready. We shall be beyond King's Lynn by nightfall — on our way to be married.'

'It's such a big step, Corinne. Have you thought of the future?'

Corinne gave a bright little laugh. 'I think of nothing but the future. I see heaven on earth stretching before me.'

'It's everyday life I'm thinking of, my dear.'

Sarah tried to urge caution, suddenly scared for her friend's future. 'The pay of an army officer is not great — '

Corinne brushed any such objection aside. 'I am not entirely ignorant in the matter of finance, Sarah. I know we will have to wait until I am twenty-one before I come into my full inheritance, but once I am a married lady I shall be able to request an advance.'

Sarah was somewhat disconcerted by Corinne's attitude, for she was generally the most impractical of people. She recalled Wrenningham's words — 'Thackstone is nothing but a fortune-hunter.'

'Is that what Forbes wishes you to do?' she asked.

'Not at all. You don't know him as I do. He says he wants nothing of mine, that my inheritance is for me only but, of course, it will be my joy to share everything I have with him.'

'Dear Corinne,' Sarah was about to express her doubts but her friend gave her no chance.

'Forbes is a man of honour. I won't listen to a word against him.'

'I'm only thinking of your happiness.'

'I know what I'm doing, Sarah. And I'll be free! I'll no longer have to endure the strictures that Harry puts upon me. He wants me to marry that old widower, the Marquis of

Heigham, You've seen him, haven't you?'

'He's old enough to be your father!' Sarah was aghast.

'He squeezes himself into corsets — and even then looks like a barrel. They say when he takes off his wig he hasn't a hair on his head.' Corinne wrinkled her pretty nose in disgust.

'Surely Wrenningham wouldn't expect you to marry such a man!' Sarah was shocked.

'You don't know Harry! He's obsessed with lineage. He thinks blood is more important than anything else on earth. And the marquis is descended from William the Conqueror, or one of those silly old kings — I care not which.'

'Most certainly you cannot marry the Marquis of Heigham,' Sarah agreed, very positively.

'Nor shall I. I have given my heart to Forbes — and he is the only man in the world for me. You will help me, won't you?'

Sarah was torn between doubts over the integrity of Forbes, and the pleading sincerity of her friend. 'I'm not sure — '

'It's not much I'm asking you to do, Sarah,' Corinne interrupted. 'Just be my dear, dear friend — as you always are — and set out with me tomorrow afternoon for a drive in

49

the country. Only that. Just as you have been suggesting almost every day since we arrived here. It's not much to ask, is it? My entire future happiness depends upon it Say you will, please?'

Corinne's sparkling eyes were alive with love. Sarah thought of her parents, who had taken this same step twenty years previously.

'Of course, I'll help you.' What else could she do in response to such heartfelt pleading?

'I knew I could depend upon you.' Corinne was almost dancing with delight. 'I shall send Polly, my maid to the meeting place in the morning, with a few things I need for the journey. We'll say we are going to call upon a friend of mine, Ellen Warboys, a girl I was at finishing school with. Last year she married a parson so now she lives at the Rectory at Gilton. You must instruct the groom to drive to their house. It will seem perfectly natural for me to visit Ellen.'

'And then?'

Corinne glanced over her shoulder. 'Lady Turley is watching from the window' she said anxiously. 'I think we should turn back to the house, I'll explain the rest of the plan when we are on our way.'

* * *

The following day the weather was even more grey and chilly. Rainclouds threatened, which would make it difficult to explain the desire of the two young ladies to set out to pay a purely social call. Sarah glanced anxiously out of the window all through the morning, then by some miracle, at about one o'clock, the clouds parted. She felt horribly guilty as she ordered the carriage to be harnessed and just before two o'clock she and Corinne were driven away from Ashingby Hall.

Forty minutes later, they arrived at the lonely spot where the turnpike crossed the country road. The White Hart Inn was long and low, white walled and thatched. The coach trade formed a large part of the innkeeper's income. He prided himself on being able to supply some of the best horses in the county, and his ostlers could change a team of four within three minutes. Accommodation for horses was even more spacious than for people, up to fifty could be stabled with ease. A farrier had set up his smithy immediately alongside.

As their carriage approached, Corinne leaned out of the window and ordered the groom to stop at the inn. As soon as the man let down the steps, she alighted, picked up her skirts and sped round the side of the building, disappearing through a large archway.

Sarah followed, walking quickly. In the yard a post-chaise was ready. Polly stood beside it waiting for her mistress. The horses, fresh and restive, were held by a boy whilst the postillion relaxed, leaning against the stable wall. Forbes Thackstone was pacing up and down the yard. Impatience showed in his movements. His handsome face was drawn into taut lines, but instantly warmed into a wide smile of pleasure and relief as he saw Corinne. He strode towards her and clasped her in his arms.

'Dearest one! You're here! I was so afraid that tyrant would find some way to prevent your escape.' Passionately they threw their arms around each other, then Forbes set Corinne aside and turned to Sarah. 'Miss Dunthorne. How good of you to assist my sweet girl!' He clasped Sarah's hands with such a display of joy and gratitude that she could not help responding.

'I love her too,' she said. 'Take care of her.'

'Have no fear of that!' He seemed sincere, yet she could not entirely still her doubts. Fervently she hoped she had been right to assist in this elopement.

'I trust no one has followed you?' Forbes asked anxiously.

'We have seen no one,' Corinne assured him.

'Then let us be on our way.' Forbes beckoned the postillion to mount in readiness.

Corinne turned and threw her arms around Sarah, who hugged and kissed her and wished her well. It was too late now to ask her to think again. Forbes was ushering Polly into the chaise.

'You'll do as I asked?' Corinne whispered to Sarah.

'I will. Exactly as you've suggested.'

The happiness that glowed on both Corinne and Forbes's faces soothed away Sarah's doubts. Her parents must have looked just that way when they set out on their big adventure.

'The longer you can keep our secret the better our chance of evading pursuit and reaching Gretna Green safely,' Forbes said to Sarah, in a low voice. Then he took Corinne's hand and led her to the open door of the chaise. 'Take your seat, my dearest.'

He climbed in after her and the door had scarcely shut before the horses sprang forward and the chaise hurtled away out of the yard. Sarah followed the vehicle out and waved her daintily gloved hand as the chaise dashed away up the road and disappeared round a bend. A journey of over 300 miles lay ahead of them. Travelling day and night, it would take about two and a half days to cross the border into Scotland.

Sarah stood for a moment, saying a silent prayer for their safety on the long journey. The sky, which had been overcast, had darkened, heavy black clouds rolled in from the west. A gust of wind tugged at her cloak, she pulled it closer around her and moved towards the carriage.

Wrenningham's coachman held open the door, his features studiously blank but she had no doubt that he relished the stir he would make when he recounted the scene he had just witnessed, that evening in the servant's hall.

'Pray continue on to Gilton,' she instructed the man.

He glanced up at the stormclouds chasing across the sky. 'Very good, miss. To the Rectory, wasn't it, miss?'

'I do not now wish to call at the Rectory,' she told him. 'You will continue along the road towards Norwich.'

'Storm's a-comin, miss,' he said.

'Travel at your best possible speed,' she said firmly.

'Yes, miss.'

Sarah looked at her gold enamel watch, a

pretty piece of French jewellery which she wore pinned to the bodice of her gown. Five minutes to three. So much time must pass before she heard from Corinne again! She sat back in the carriage, but she was in no mood to relax and enjoy the drive. Excitement had kept her spirits high but now began to subside. The enormity of what she had been a party to began to engrave itself on her conscience. She did not regret the assistance she had given Corinne, but that did not prevent her from worrying about the consequences. What would Lady Turley and Lady MacKenna say? She had been reprimanded already for assisting Corinne and Lieutenant Thackstone to meet. That which she had now done, was much, much more serious. Wrenningham would be furious. She told herself she had no reason to care about his reaction and tried to convince herself his opinion was of no concern to her — yet, strangely, infuriatingly, she knew that was not so.

More relevant, was the effect her action would have upon Lady MacKenna. For herself Sarah was prepared to take the consequences, and make a full and frank admission of her part in Corinne's elopement, but repercussions would spill over and affect her family. She tried to push Monica's accusing face from her mind, telling herself she had done only what her conscience dictated, but her heart was heavy.

The coachman was obeying her instructions and driving the team at a gallop. The carriage swayed as they passed Gilton Church, with its fine Norman tower of knapped flint. Beside it was a large comfortable house, where Corinne's friend lived, but the place was of no interest to Sarah. She was trying desperately to convince herself that she would be able to make her grandmama understand. Even if Lady MacKenna decided to send her back in disgrace, she must somehow convince her that the rest of the family must not be blamed because of her misdeeds.

In the short time she had known Lady MacKenna, Sarah had come to love her dearly, so it wasn't only for the sake of her family back in America, that she wanted to make a good impression. She and Lady MacKenna had liked each other from their first meeting, and over the many hours they had spent together, affection had sprung strongly and naturally between them. Sarah really cared for her good opinion, and was deeply troubled that today's escapade would change all that.

Yet Sarah remained convinced that she had

been right in assisting Corinne and Forbes to elope. It was abominable to think of her delightful young friend being forced into marriage with that positively awful old marquis! Thank goodness there had been no sign of pursuit. And if any enquiries had been made at the White Hart after they had left the inn, she knew that the staff had been well paid by Thackstone to make no mention of the post-chaise. They were only to say that the carriage had taken the Norwich road.

So deep in thought was Sarah, that she did not notice the change in the weather until the sound of lashing rain and crashing thunder became so fierce that it was impossible to ignore it. The carriage came to a standstill. The groom knocked on the door and opened it slightly.

'Begging your pardon, miss, but I think we should turn back. The road ahead is always bad; if this rain keeps up it may become impassable.'

Sarah's heart sank. Would the storm prevent Corinne and Lieutenant Thackstone continuing with their journey? How awful it would be if they were unable to proceed! She was reassured when she reflected that the turnpike would be in better condition than this country road. Undoubtedly, the weather was now absolutely abominable. She was sorry for the coachman having to sit out on the open box, yet she was reluctant to turn back.

'I hoped to go further than this.' She leaned forward and put her head out of the window so that she might assess for herself just how bad it was. Her bonnet was soaked within seconds. What was even more terrible she saw a horseman riding fast along the tree-lined road towards them. His head was down against the driving rain and he was some distance behind, but she had no doubt that it was Wrenningham.

The coachman confirmed her apprehension. 'Looks like the master's a-comin', miss.'

The relief in his voice was in direct opposition to the apprehension that gripped her. She drew back into the carriage, sat upright and waited, bracing herself for the onslaught.

She heard his horse slither to a sudden stop. The earl's voice rang out, cutting through wind and rain, instructing the man to hold his horse. The carriage door was flung wide and Wrenningham's soaked and dripping figure filled the opening. One glance at his glowering expression confirmed Sarah's worst fears.

'Where's my ward?' he demanded.

Sarah tilted up her chin and faced him. 'At

this moment I fear I do not know exactly.'

'Don't prevaricate with me, mistress,' he snapped. 'I called at Gilton Rectory. They've received no visitors all afternoon.'

His words were uttered so furiously that Sarah trembled. She clenched her hands into tight fists refusing to be cowed — yet what could she say?

'I have no need of your answer. You've connived with her in a meeting with that scoundrel, haven't you?'

Helplessly, Sarah nodded. His expression was thunderous.

'So! Where have they gone? To Gretna Green, I'll warrant?'

Again Sarah nodded. Though silent, her chin jutted in stubborn defiance.

'With your misguided assistance, and in defiance of my rightful authority! You've set yourself up as a decoy to lure me here in the wrong direction, haven't you?'

Another nod.

'No doubt they think to have sufficient lead to get away. But I shall pursue them — all the way to Scotland if need be. Have no doubt that I shall prevent this misalliance if it is humanly possible.'

'Can you not find it in your heart to give them your consent?' she pleaded. She might have saved her breath.

'You will wait at the White Hart until I return. If I am successful in catching up with them, I shall bring my ward back with me. You will then be able to return to Ashingby together, and perhaps scandal will be avoided.'

He withdrew and she heard him barking orders to the coachman. 'Drive back to the White Hart. Miss Dunthorne is to remain there and await my return.' In a moment he was gone. Hooves pounded away into the distance.

Never had Sarah seen anyone in such a cold fury. She was angry and resentful. Wrenningham acted as if he owned the whole earth — and with that thought her doubts vanished. She was glad she had helped Corinne to thwart his wicked and selfish plans.

Again she looked at her watch. It would be at least four o'clock before he reached the inn and, even if he carried on without stopping for an instant, he would be more than an hour behind the runaways. Would that give them sufficient advantage? She twisted her hands together in an agony of doubt, very conscious that Wrenningham on horseback would be able to cover the ground a good deal faster than the chaise.

The carriage was turned with difficulty, for

the road was narrow and the verges had been softened by the wet. It rocked so greatly she feared it might overturn, but the coachman was skilled and soon they were driving back the way they had come. Sarah stared disconsolately out of the rain-swept window. She had no illusions about the hours ahead, she knew they would be the worst in her whole life!

On they trundled until they reached the White Hart Inn. She toyed with the idea of countermanding the earl's instructions and ordering the coachman to return to Ashingby. But when the man opened the carriage door, she couldn't do it. He was soaked; it would be cruel to ask him to drive on. A great gust of wind almost blew her off her feet. It was a relief to step down into the inn, where the pamment floor was several inches lower than the ground outside, a log fire blazed cheerfully, its glow flickering over the smoke-yellowed walls and the low dark-beamed ceiling. The landlord and his wife both hurried forward to greet Sarah.

'Good day to you, mistress. His lordship said as how you'd be stopping by and resting here awhile. The inn is full, with the weather being so bad, but I've had a private room made ready upstairs.'

Sarah was surprised that Wrenningham had

troubled to make the arrangement, for she had imagined him to be in such headlong pursuit, that he would be deflected by nothing.

'This way, miss,' said the woman. 'You must be chilled to the bone.'

Sarah followed her upstairs to a spacious room, at one end of which was a large four-poster bed. The atmosphere was warmly welcoming, a blazing fire in the narrow grate, and no sooner had she entered than a maid bustled in bearing a pitcher of hot water.

'Give me your wet cloak and bonnet and I'll see that they get properly dried.' The landlady lifted the garments from Sarah's head and shoulders and handed them to the maid to carry downstairs. 'Come straight back up here, Milly, so that you can see to anything the lady needs.'

'I shall be glad to wash my hands and warm myself at the fire.' Sarah said.

'Very well, miss. Would you like any refreshment now, or would you prefer to wait until the gentleman returns?'

Sarah began to wonder, with considerable embarrassment, just what instructions Wrenningham had given, but feared to make matters worse by asking questions, to which the landlady would probably not know the answers anyway.

'I'd like tea if you have it.'

'Very good, miss.' The landlady paused in the doorway and added, 'Anything else, you have only to ask and we'll do our best. The gentleman was most particular that I was to see you had anything you might require.'

'Thank you,' Sarah repeated firmly. 'But that will be all.'

The door shut behind the landlady's bulky form leaving Sarah with the disconcerting conviction that she was suspected of being a lady of loose morals. Whatever could he have said to give that impression? He had been in a great hurry, but that was not sufficient excuse in her eyes. He should have taken greater care with her reputation. She had been pleasantly surprised when she first realized that he had stopped at the White Hart to instruct the innkeeper and his wife to expect her; now, with a resurgence of resentment, she decided that it was simply his autocratic way of keeping her under his control.

Since there was nothing she could do but wait, she shrugged her shoulders and decided to take advantage of the comforts available. After attending to her toilette she sat beside the fire in a big Windsor armchair, well supplied with feather-stuffed cushions.

Milly brought up a tray covered by a snowy cloth on which was a pot of tea, two cups and saucers, milk, sugar and a toasted bunloaf, sliced to reveal juicy raisins, buttered and spicy. 'Is there anything else you'll be requiring, miss?'

'Nothing at all, thank you, Milly.'

Relieved to be left alone, Sarah poured herself a cup of tea and picked up a slice of the delicious-smelling bun-loaf. She tried to relax, but that was impossible, for her mind was imagining what might be happening on the turnpike. Now warm and physically comfortable, she remained distraught; wringing her hands, she stood gazing out of the window. It was raining so hard that twilight came early. Where were Corinne and Forbes? Had they been held up by the storm? Would the earl, riding his thoroughbred at breakneck speed, catch up with them?

She felt cold at the thought. He would have the law on his side, for Corinne was under twenty-one and could not marry without her guardian's consent. Over the border, Scottish law would prevail and she would be free to marry whomsoever she pleased. But Scotland was such a very, very long way off and Wrenningham was so furiously determined. Sarah thought of that other suitor of whom Corinne had spoken, the elderly Marquis of Heigham. She shivered and moved back to the fire.

Time dragged by and all she could do was wait, alone and helpless, her mind filled with doubts and fears. About an hour later, Milly returned for the tea tray. Tasty though the bun-loaf was Sarah had managed to eat only a small piece of it.

As she turned to leave, Milly said, 'Mistress says do you know what time the gentleman will be back, and would he like roast beef for his dinner tonight?' Sarah shrugged, but Milly waited with such an expectant expression that she felt obliged to be positive. 'I am sure roast beef will do very well, Milly. As for when his lordship will return, I do not know.'

'Very good, miss.' Milly bobbed a curtsy and hurried away.

Another hour passed by tediously. Then Sarah's attention was drawn to a commotion rising from the forecourt below her window. She looked out and saw a carriage, from which stepped two elderly gentlemen. The stouter one reminded her of Mr Rawlingson, Lady Turley's friend, the one with whom that lady loved to share the gossip of the *ton*. But he was swathed in coats and had his hat pulled low over his forehead so Sarah could not be sure if it actually was he.

The two men minced their way carefully around the huge puddles to enter the inn. Their carriage was taken to the back yard for the horses to be unharnessed. The worst of the storm seemed to have passed. For the umpteenth time Sarah looked at her watch. A quarter to eight and all she could do was wait and worry. She moved back to the fire, poked it, put on another log, gazed at the flickering flames, and wished she had the power to read a message in them. An elderly neighbour back in Cassie's Rock had been able to make up wonderful stories from what she saw in the embers and ashes.

Suddenly the sound of booted feet came to her ears. The door crashed open. She started to her feet as Wrenningham entered. Her heart was beating so fast it hurt. His clothes were soaked, dripping on the floor, he was bareheaded and his rain-damped hair clung darkly around his tense face. He flung his cloak aside, slapped his booted leg angrily with his riding whip. His lips made a straight tight line and there was a steely glint in his eyes. His mood was so obviously one of controlled fury that, although it made her flesh quiver, she took heart. He had not brought Corinne back with him.

'Did — did you see Corinne?' she asked breathlessly.

He did not reply immediately, but deliberately closed the door behind him and strode further into the room towards her. Instinctively she stepped back, her hands flying up protectively as if to hold him off. Her movement halted him, but the icy expression on his thin features altered not one iota.

'Corinne is on her way to Gretna Green — thanks to you, Miss Dunthorne,' he thundered.

She breathed a sigh of relief. It took all her self-control to remain calm, but she refused to quail before the expression of cold anger that gleamed from his wild, storm-grey eyes. Dropping her arms to her sides and clenching her hands into tight fists she asked, 'My lord did you catch up with them?'

'I was within sight of the chaise — I'd have drawn alongside in a matter of minutes — then a loose stone on the road rolled under my horse's hoof. He took a bad fall. There was no way I could continue. The creature was sorely lamed and I had to walk him back a couple of miles to an inn. I hired another animal, but it wasn't of the same quality as my own. I was forced to abandon the pursuit.'

Her eyes remained fixed on him and she trembled. She was glad — so very glad — that Corinne had got away — but what now would be her own fate?

4

The taut silence between Sarah and Wrenningham was broken by a muffled knock. He swung round and wrenched open the door. The landlady stood on the threshold, holding before her a covered dish from which wafted steam and a succulent smell of roast beef. Immediately behind her was Milly bearing a tray so heavily laden that she could scarcely hold it, her plump face redder than ever.

'The roast beef as you ordered,' beamed the landlady. 'It's been ready this half-hour past. I hope I've done right to bring it straight up?'

The earl flung the door wide and stepped back to allow the women into the room. Placing their burdens on the top of a chest of drawers, they immediately set about flinging a white linen cloth over a table. In a few moments two places were set, covers lifted from the meat and vegetable dishes, filling the room with a mouth-watering aroma.

Sarah glanced anxiously at Wrenningham. He was pacing back and forth across the room. She had not anticipated that they would be expected to dine together in such intimacy. But he appeared to accept it and even looked on with interest and anticipation. Her anxiety increased when the landlord appeared in the doorway, one large hand grasping a frothing jug of ale and the other holding by their necks a couple of wine bottles. Then she noticed the earl was standing more calmly with his back to the fire, the glowering expression had disappeared from his face and he watched with obvious approval and pleasure. She was reminded of days when her papa had returned from attending to some particularly long and difficult case.

Good-tempered though he was normally, hunger and weariness would render him irascible until he had rested and eaten — she hoped it would prove to be the same with her present companion.

'I trust you'll find all to your liking, my lord,' said the innkeeper, drawing the cork from one of the bottles.

'If it tickles my taste-buds as it does my eyes and nose, then it is bound to be excellent.' Wrenningham flung off his wet outer garments revealing a delicately embroidered silk waistcoat above a lace-trimmed shirt, with wide sleeves. Though he was of a rather slim build, his shoulders had a breadth that was unmistakably masculine. In a business-like manner, he picked up the carving knife and fork and prepared to attack the joint that was roasted to perfection, crisp and brown outside and pinkly moist in the middle.

Milly picked up the discarded clothes and carried them away. The landlord watched his aristocratic guest with approval for a moment, then nodded. 'We'll leave you to enjoy your repast, sir. If there is anything else you require you have only to ring the bell over there.' He indicated a small handbell, and shooed his wife out of the room ahead of him. In the doorway he paused. 'I shall give instructions you are not to be disturbed.' He bowed low, turned smartly and left.

The significance of his final remark embarrassed Sarah to such an extent that she could only stare in dismay as the door closed behind his portly frame. Surreptitiously, she glanced at the earl who, having carved a couple of large slices of beef, paused, looked up and momentarily caught her eye.

'How very thoughtful of you to order this excellent supper to be brought up here,' he said.

She lowered her eyelids and hot colour flooded her cheeks.

'I was asked whether you would care for such a meal,' she protested. 'I had no idea it was to be served here — in — in such privacy.'

'It seems to me the arrangement is excellent,' he interrupted. 'I thoroughly approve.'

'But I do not!' She tossed her head with mounting anger. 'I have my reputation to consider — '

'I did not think you cared for reputations,' he said coldly. 'You certainly displayed no concern for that of my ward, even though you profess to be her friend.'

'I am her friend. What I did was to ensure her happiness.'

He gave a weary sigh. 'Since that is a matter upon which we disagree entirely, I do not propose to enter into further discussion, especially when this excellent fare lies before us.'

'You know it would be most unseemly for us to dine here alone,' she protested.

'Nevertheless here we are, my dear young lady, and it would cause considerable extra work for the landlord, not to mention that it would undoubtedly stir up a commotion throughout the whole establishment, if we now ask to have all this moved elsewhere.' With the carving knife and fork in his obviously capable hands he indicated the well-spread table.

Sarah began to weaken, the appearance of the food had changed his mood and it might be unwise to keep him away from the table. Besides, she too felt gnawing pangs in her stomach, for she had eaten only a light lunch and that many hours ago. As if to emphasize her thought, Wrenningham looked at her, one eyebrow quirked upwards with almost boyish appeal. He heaved a sigh, shook his head sadly and added, 'I am as hungry as a hunter.'

A twinkle came into her eyes. 'The food would most certainly not benefit from being moved — '

'It would in all probability be stone cold by the time we could tackle it,' he agreed immediately. 'How very practical you are, Miss Dunthorne — ' She lifted her head sharply, uncertain whether he meant that remark in a defamatory way, but he continued smoothly, 'that is a virtue all too seldom found among ladies, in my experience. So let us eat. Some wine?'

He set down the carving tools, lifted a bottle and without waiting for her consent filled her glass with the rich red liquid. As she still hesitated, he walked to her side of the table and held out her chair. 'Be so good as to be seated, Miss Dunthorne.'

His words were gentle but the tone was commanding. It reminded her that she had little option but to obey. To do anything else would certainly cause an unfortunate scene. No sooner had she taken her seat than he placed before her a plate with some delicately carved slices of beef.

'Pray serve yourself with vegetables,' he said, turning his attention back to the joint to carve another generous helping. They both added crisply roasted potatoes and good country grown carrot, onions and spring greens.

'Have you tried a little of the freshly made horseradish sauce?' he enquired, holding a small pot towards her. The prospect of a good meal had certainly improved his mood.

'What is it?' she asked.

'The grated root of a wild plant, covered in vinegar, strong but an excellent accompaniment to beef. The country folk here in Norfolk use a particularly good recipe in the making of it.'

She lifted the jar to her nose and drew back sharply as the tang assailed her nostrils. Her reaction brought a smile to his lips, and at once he looked so much nicer, more human. Undoubtedly he was one of the most handsome gentlemen she had ever set eyes upon. To please him she took a very small spoonful.

'It is — interesting,' she admitted.

She took a rather large sip of wine to cool her mouth. Wrenningham refilled both their glasses and the thought struck her that she must be careful not to take too much so that her mind became fuzzy. Yet she felt like celebrating as she relished the thought that for Corinne and Forbes the first step of their plan to elope had been taken successfully. Where were they now, she wondered? She silently prayed for their safety as they continued on the long journey. To keep a semblance of normality she tried to make polite conversation, but although Wrenningham seemed more relaxed, his responses were short. They ate in silence for a while. The edge taken from his hunger, Wrenningham began to assess Sarah with what he imagined to be dispassionate appraisal. She was obviously enjoying the excellent food and he approved of that, it probably accounted for her healthy and radiant good looks. Her rich, dark-brown hair caught tawny highlights from the flickering candlelight. Perhaps her face was a little too round for aesthetic classical beauty, but her complexion was flawless, her colouring as delicate as that of a Dresden shepherdess.

Seven years ago he had sworn that he would never again be so foolish as to give his love and trust to a woman. The psychological scars in some ways caused him greater anguish than the physical cuts and thrusts he had endured in battle. Lady Rosalind Smythe had captured his heart when he was a young lieutenant, about to set off to France for the first time. He had adored her with the ardour of youth, and when she had accepted his proposal of marriage, shown every sign of returning his affection, and agreed to become engaged to him, his joy had known no bounds. His father had been alive then, a middle-aged man, likely to live for many years. Harry had no thoughts of succeeding to all the responsibilities as well as the wealth that went with the estate. He had a private income, enough with which to support a wife, and his beloved Rosalind had agreed to marry him as soon as he returned from the war.

Whilst he was abroad however, Rosalind was courted by an elderly widower, Lord Cathay. His wealth was temptingly available to her immediately, and her family exerted pressure on her to accept an offer of marriage that would be advantageous to them all.

The blow had been devastating. The intensity of love he felt for Rosalind had withered, died long ago. He felt only dislike for her on those rare occasions when their paths had crossed since then. Her infidelity, however, had left him distrustful of all her sex. He had vowed never to repeat the mistake. He would never marry, never tie his life permanently to that of any woman and he had never wavered from that decision.

It did not still the strong sexual desire that frequently flared in his vigorous loins, but he took such pleasures dispassionately. He was able, quite easily, to distance himself from any emotional involvement, and always made it clear to those women who had shared his bed that their liaison with him would never be more than that.

He had been content that the estate would pass to Corinne and her offspring. Now that had been turned on its head. He was sure that was the reason Thackstone had been so eager to marry Corinne. He'd be damned if he'd let that fortune-hunter get his hands on Ashingby and all that he had come to hold so dear. For the first time ever he felt the urge to beget an heir. Even if it meant that he must take a wife.

Soon he would be returning to his unit. It never occurred to him to leave the army; that had been his life and his love for too long, and being a soldier he did not expect to live to a ripe old age and die peacefully in his bed.

It had seemed likely that his end had come in Spain, in the last of many battles in which

he'd fought under the command of Wellington. The pain in his body had been intense
and his arm seemed shattered. He'd tried to
staunch the blood that gushed through his
slashed sleeve, warm, thick and scarlet. He'd
wrapped a cloth around his upper arm, above
the wound, tried to make a tourniquet, using
only his left hand and his teeth.

'Let me do that, sir,' said one of his men.
He seized the makeshift bandage and pulled
it tight. The flow was reduced. The battle was
over. It had been a last stray bullet that had
gone through his arm and entered his body.
Fortunately it was not so deep as it had at
first appeared. He'd been lucky again.

The scene of carnage on the battlefield was
all too familiar. The dead and dying lay all
about; the sight and stench was sickening.
Some writhed in pain, and called to him to
shoot them, to put them out of their pain and
misery. He had on occasion complied with
the request, when a man was evidently
wounded beyond mortal help, just as he
hoped another soldier would give him blessed
relief should he ever be in such a state. The
men of his battalion, who, so short a time
ago, had fought fiercely and well, were now
tendering assistance to all the fallen. There
was little enough they could do other than
share their canteen, or give a slug of gin. The

throbbing of his wound, the loss of blood, had taken away his strength. Wrenningham had scarcely been able to keep on his feet as he stumbled towards the field-dressing station. He was not yet thirty years old, and he had served king and country honourably and constantly for the past ten years. He was wearied of war and all the horrors it brought and yet he knew no other life.

Whilst those recollections had chased through his mind, Wrenningham continued with his supper. He finished the last mouthful from his plate and glanced across at Sarah.

'Another slice of beef, Miss Dunthorne?' he enquired.

Sarah started. Wrenningham had been quiet for so long she had begun to wonder if he had forgotten her existence.

'No, thank you, my lord.'

'I trust the food has been to your liking?' he asked.

'Excellent,' she agreed.

He carved another slice of beef for himself. There was apple pie for dessert — 'As light as a maiden's kiss,' he described it.

No doubt he knew all about such things, she thought, and, looking at his firm mouth, softly lipped, wondered what it would feel like to be kissed by him. Hastily she dismissed such an unladylike thought.

She was amazed at how calm he had become. Although he had been quiet for some time, it seemed to her that as the meal had progressed he had grown more affable. As they lingered on, they began to talk quite freely and she could almost have believed that he wished to charm her. The occasional small silences were by no means oppressive and his manners so charming that her defenses were lowered. He was less arrogant, no longer seeming to be an adversary.

By the time they finished eating he appeared to be completely relaxed. What was more, he gave every appearance of enjoying her company — but could that really be so? Was it simply a façade — a false civility? Undoubtedly his anger had faded, for he was leaning back in his chair, totally calm, twiddling the stem of a glass of claret in his long fingers and her natural optimism reawakened. Impulsively she voiced the thought that had been in her mind all evening. 'Will you forgive them?'

The moment the words were out she wished she had stayed silent. His face hardened. The friendliness that had developed was wiped away immediately. The air between them became charged with an unknown, uncontrolled force. Wrenningham jumped to his feet, strode across the room and back, then halted beside her glowering down from his vast height.

'My forgiveness has no bearing on the matter.' His voice was harsh and sharp, his words measured, deliberate. 'Corinne has made her decision. The action she has taken was ill-advised and foolish. More to the point, there is, I believe, no undoing it. A Gretna marriage is just as binding as any other.'

Sarah stood up and faced him, refusing to allow herself to be intimidated. 'But you will receive her again?' she pleaded, deliberately keeping her voice soft and gentle.

He appeared to consider this seriously, taking his time before he replied. 'I think that is unlikely. Corinne has rejected my advice and placed herself under the protection of Thackstone. As I understand it, I therefore have no further responsibility for her.'

'But she is your cousin — I am sure she will need and will wish to keep your friendship.'

'I doubt if you are correct in that, Miss Dunthorne. Corinne has made her position abundantly clear: she will be only too pleased never to set eyes on me again.'

'No. I cannot believe that!'

She was about to reiterate her plea, but he interrupted her, sharply. He was so close to her, and so overpoweringly large, tall and broad-shouldered that she felt herself tremble a little.

'As far as I am concerned, that is an end to the matter,' he said, coldly.

She backed away. Only a couple of steps and she could go no further, for her legs came into contact with the side of the bed.

'At least she cannot now be forced into marriage with that dreadful old Marquis of Heigham,' she said.

He reached out and grabbed her shoulders. 'Who told you that?'

She did not feel his question was worth answering. 'It doesn't matter. I shall always be glad I was able to save her from such an unspeakable fate.'

'Did Corinne tell you that?' For a breathless moment Sarah thought he was going to shake her, but he just held her there, in an iron grip. 'That is yet another reason why I need never again trouble myself over her or her affairs.' He leaned forward so that his face was only inches away from hers. 'I do not wish to hear her name mentioned ever again,' he said.

Her mouth opened in fear, a small cry escaped her lips. She gazed at him with wide-open eyes, at once scared and fascinated. Still holding her shoulders, he moved closer and she felt the pressure of his body against hers.

'Do I make myself quite clear, Miss Dunthorne?' he said.

His fingers were digging into her shoulders with a grip that was painful. His masculinity threatened her, the musky smell of his body enveloped her, his breath was warm on her face, yet she was not repulsed. His nearness awakened a mad excitement such as she had never before experienced. She felt as if her knees would give way beneath her. She was acutely aware of the bed immediately behind her, afraid she would fall back on to it.

'Well?' he demanded.

Her senses began to return to her, and in that moment anger flared.

'Yes.' She shouted the word, making it a challenge. Then, again, her voice rising louder, 'Yes. Yes. Yes.' She struggled to get away from his hold.

'Good.'

He snapped the word sharply and relaxed the grip of his hands on her shoulders. Sarah, leaning back, pulling away from him, staggered and lost her balance. She knew she was about to fall and instinctively grabbed hold of Wrenningham's shoulders.

Immediately his arms closed around her. He pulled her towards him and held her there, encircled in his arms. She had a momentary sensation of being safe, cossetted, comforted, as if she was a child again. She looked up at him, opened her lips slightly, ready to say a polite 'thank you', but the words were never uttered. She had a fleeting vision of his face bearing down upon her and then he kissed her.

Surprise — and his lips — took her breath away. The sensations that were coursing through her body were unfamiliar to her; she knew nothing of the emotional effect a man could awaken in a woman. Though she had helped her father with his medical work he had shielded her from the full anatomical knowledge of a man's physique. Her heart was beating so fast she felt it must escape from the confines of her chest.

She sensed that a change had taken place in Wrenningham as well as in herself. A sound like a groan came from deep in his throat — for a moment she thought that he was hurt. Her mind flashed to those wounds not yet fully healed, but he didn't draw away from her and when the sound came again she realized it had more to do with pleasure and relief than pain.

'Sarah.' He murmured her name and all the aggression had gone from his voice. Then his lips claimed hers again and in that same moment she heard the door open.

'Did you call, my lady?'

Sarah froze. Wrenningham lifted his head, swung around, took a step away from her. The maid was standing in the open doorway, her eyes wide open, amazement reddening her face even more than normal. Then she covered her mouth with her hand and, quite definitely, Sarah heard her chuckle.

Behind Milly, in the passageway, were the faces of the two elderly gentlemen who had arrived by carriage earlier. Their mouths open in blatant curiosity, they stood as if rooted to the spot. This time, quite unmistakably, she recognized the stouter man as Mr Rawlingson, the gentleman with whom Lady Turley was so fond of exchanging society gossip. What was even worse, she knew for certain that he recognized both Wrenningham and herself. Her heart sank. Sarah had found the elderly caricaturist unpleasant when she first met him, the salacious expression on his face at that moment confirmed her opinion.

Milly bobbed a quick curtsy. 'Beg your pardon, my lady. I thought I heard you call.' With another barely suppressed giggle, she withdrew, shutting the door behind her.

Sarah was aghast. Unceremoniously she pushed past Wrenningham, instinctively hurrying to the other side of the room, putting as much distance as possible between them. She had never been so ashamed and embarrassed in her whole life! She swung round to face him and was astonished to find him with his face creased in laughter.

'Did you see those faces?' he chuckled, 'I truly thought their bottom jaws might have dropped off!'

She shivered, suddenly so cold her skin came up in goose bumps. 'I do not think the matter one for fun,' Sarah objected. 'You know who one of those gentlemen is, do you not?'

'I have no recollection of ever seeing them before, and I doubt whether either of them knows me, I've been out of the country so much in recent years.'

'That was Mr Rawlingson,' she informed him.

'Rawlingson? The cartoonist?'

Sarah nodded. 'He's a close friend of Lady Turley's. I've been introduced to him. I'm sure he recognized both of us. My reputation will be utterly destroyed. Goodness knows what my grandmama will say.'

The earl's face sobered, though a disturbing twinkle remained in his eyes.

'If he dares to print a word against you, Miss Dunthorne, I will challenge him to a duel.'

'Pray stop acting as if this is a laughing matter. I suppose for you it is some sort of revenge for my helping Corinne to elope. But I'm glad I did it. I'd do the same again and again if need be. Now, please have the decency to leave this room, and allow me to retain some shred of respectability.'

As he did not move, she ran to the door and flung it open sharply. Her fury was increased as she heard the sound of footsteps retreating hurriedly along the dimly lit passage. Someone had stayed outside, obviously eavesdropping.

Wrenningham had heard too. He strode to the door and looked up and down the passage. There was no one in sight. He stepped back into the room.

'Go,' she hissed, keeping her voice low.

'Certainly, Miss Dunthorne.' His resumption of the formal use of her name distanced him from her. 'I'll go, but before I leave, I must assure you that I shall protect your good name should any false imputation besmirch it.'

'I fear it's too late. There's nothing you can do,' she said gloomily. She could see no way in which he could protect her. It was always the woman whose name was dragged through the mire; the man was more likely to be thought a devil of a fellow and become more popular than ever.

'I promise you, you have nothing to fear. You have my word upon it,' he declared.

She found no comfort in that, even though he evidently thought such an assurance was all that was needed. 'Leave me, sir!'

'In one moment,' he continued smoothly, as if he had already put so insignificant a matter as her reputation behind him. 'First I must advise you about arrangements for tomorrow. You will return to Ashingby in the carriage.'

She shrugged indifferently, still waiting in the doorway for him to depart. 'Will you not be returning with me?'

'No. I shall be off at daybreak in order to make arrangements for my horse to be doctored.'

He strolled towards the door. His unhurried movements somehow made her sensitively aware of his lithe vitality, his self-contained masculine strength. She stepped aside quickly, avoiding any contact. Outside the room, in the passageway, he paused and regarded her steadily. He inclined his head in a brief nod, as if something in her face pleased him. He was serious now and she wondered what he was thinking. In the dim light it was impossible to read anything from his face. He lifted one hand and gently lifted a stray lock of her hair, held it in his hand as if weighing it. She started back, for such an intimate gesture unnerved her. He was calm and cool, but her emotions were in turmoil.

'I'll send the maid to clear the table and help you to prepare for the night,' he said.

'Thank you.'

'In all probability I shall have left before you rise in the morning so I'll give instructions that you will take breakfast here in your room.'

She nodded, feeling too subdued to argue over any of his arrangements and what would be the use? He was accustomed to giving orders and having them obeyed. Probably that was one of the reasons why it hurt him so much that Corinne had flouted his authority.

'Good night, Miss Dunthorne.'

Later that evening, in the wide, soft, feather bed Sarah tossed restlessly, her mind and her emotions in turmoil. Milly had cleared away the dinner things, damped down the fire for the night and brought up hot water. She made no reference to the scene she had witnessed earlier, nor did Sarah attempt to give any explanation. They both acted as if such an incident had never occurred.

Sarah thumped the down-filled pillow and wished the last few hours had never happened, but the touch of Wrenningham's lips seemed to remain imprinted upon her mouth. Even as she lay alone between the lavender-scented sheets it was as if she could still feel the strength of his arms holding her, crushing her so possessively close that the hard frame of his torso had pressed against the soft curves of her breasts.

Never before had she experienced such disturbing sensations and it was all the more humiliating when she forced herself to face reality — to acknowledge that no such thoughts troubled him. He had shrugged off the incident as unimportant — and so it was to him! That was evident by the way he had made those precise and coolly practical arrangements for the following morning. She had certainly landed herself in a most unenviable position.

She dismissed his claim that he would protect her good name. What could he do for her? And how different it was for him! With his fortune, breeding and good looks no rumour would diminish his place in society. His position as one of the most eligible bachelors in England would not be harmed one iota. For her it was totally different. When she thought of facing her grandmama it was as if an icy hand clutched at her stomach. Punishment was certain, but what form would it take? Only Corinne seemed to have gained from today's events. Sarah consoled herself with that thought and at last fell asleep.

★ ★ ★

'Well, miss, what have you to say about this disgraceful episode?'

Lady MacKenna looked her most formidable. She was sitting up in her bed, even there contriving to look impressively tall, straight and delicately thin. She wore a soft, pale-pink woollen shawl over her shoulders and a lacy cap in a similar shade covered her snowy hair. Her face showed her displeasure and her sharp eyes regarded Sarah so penetratingly that she would not have dared to speak anything but the truth, even if she had had a mind to.

The morning's arrangements had taken place exactly as the earl had stipulated. Sarah had breakfasted in her room. When questioned, Milly had told her that his lordship had left an hour earlier and that the other gentlemen had also departed to continue their journey to London. That last piece of information had been something of a relief, for she had no wish to encounter them again. Now here she was at eleven o'clock, back at

Ashingby Hall. The moment she entered the house she had been instructed by the butler (who had quietly expressed pleasure at her safe return) that her ladyship was still in her room. She always rose late, and Sarah was to go to her immediately.

Sarah's heart fluttered as she advanced across the large room towards the four-poster bed, bracing herself to take whatever retribution should be meted out to her. It would be worse than useless she knew, to prevaricate — and in any case she was not ashamed of the part she had played in Corinne's elopement. As for those unfortunate events that had followed, they had all been out of her control, and she had resolved that the least said about them the better.

She launched into the little speech she had rehearsed in the carriage on her way here. 'Dear Grandmama, first of all, I must beg your forgiveness, I am indeed sorry for I am aware that my actions must have caused you distress — '

'They most certainly have,' Grandmama interrupted. Her voice was steady, controlled, but its tone caused Sarah to tremble. 'All night long Beatrix and I have been worrying over your safety. It was wicked of you to go off like that and leave no message.'

'I know — I would never willingly have

caused you so much concern. I most certainly never intended to stay away for so long.'

'I should hope not.'

'It was all due to the storm.'

'You should never have set out in the first place.'

'I just had to help Corinne,' Sarah pleaded. 'She was determined to go — '

'That is no excuse for your folly in assisting her.'

'Oh, dear Grandmama — you have no idea how determined she was! Truly she was so desperate that I just had to help her. She and Forbes Thackstone are so very much in love — and that damned Wrenningham — '

'You mind your language, young lady.'

'I'm sorry, but he is so highhanded. He absolutely refused even to consider allowing them to marry.'

'We have been over that before. It was wrong for you to get involved, Sarah. You knew I would disapprove.'

That was true and Sarah hung her head, but only momentarily. She had nothing to be ashamed of. 'But you know how happy my mama and papa have been in their marriage,' pleaded Sarah.

'That's been your trouble. You've grown up with your head filled with romantic ideas about runaway marriages. Let me assure you that for most people such liaisons turn out to be disastrous. I could quote you a dozen cases where young people have married entirely for love, with absolutely nothing upon which to live, and ended up in misery. Your parents were fortunate.' With a sweep of her hand Lady MacKenna waved that matter aside.

'I believe it will turn out the same for Corinne,' Sarah said softly.

'Hmph! Time alone will tell,' Lady MacKenna snorted. 'Now I want to know what happened yesterday. I gather from your rather self-satisfied expression that Harry was unable to prevent them from setting out on this escapade?'

Sarah nodded. She felt considerably disconcerted that her grandmama was able to read her face so accurately, but kept her gaze firmly on the old lady's face, refusing to be cowed by her.

'They were too far ahead for him to catch up with them,' she said.

'Were they indeed!' snapped Lady MacKenna. 'Harry's suspicions were aroused very soon after you two gals set out. He sent for Corinne's maid, and when it was discovered that the gal was nowhere in the house, and that a few of Corinne's most treasured things were also missing, he guessed what was afoot.

He had his fastest horse saddled immediately and it was no more than half an hour after you left that he set out in pursuit. I am surprised that riding that throughbred of his, he was not able to catch up.' She raked Sarah with her keen, black-button eyes. 'There was something else that held him up, I imagine? What was it? Tell me, Sarah, truthfully now! What was your part in this affair?'

Sarah shifted her feet. 'I suppose you could say I acted as a decoy,' she admitted.

'Go on.'

'Forbes was waiting at a little country inn. He had a post-chaise harnessed and ready and within a few minutes they were away towards King's Lynn.'

'And you, Sarah?'

'I instructed my driver to proceed towards Norwich.'

'And Harry followed you instead of them? Now I understand.'

Lady MacKenna probed for more detail, and Sarah told her of the storm, of being stopped by Wrenningham, how he had turned back to continue his pursuit and had given instructions that she should wait for him at the inn.

'The weather was too inclement for us to proceed,' she ended. 'I waited and waited. I

94

thought Wrenningham would never return. I thought he must have caught up with them, but his horse had been lamed and he'd had to give up the chase.'

Lady MacKenna looked quite shocked. 'So he also passed the night at the inn? And you completely without a chaperon!'

'It was not my wish that it should be so,' Sarah said. 'But there was no alternative. There was no harm done — '

'How little you know of English society!' declared Lady MacKenna. 'We can only hope that you were not recognized.'

Sarah swallowed. 'I fear that we were. Mr Rawlingson and another gentleman also stayed at the inn overnight.'

'Good gracious me! And did Mr Rawlingson recognize you?'

'Yes, Grandmama. Lady Turley had introduced him to me only a few evenings previously.'

Lady MacKenna's face turned a sickly, yellowish-white colour. She looked so shaken that Sarah began to feel quite alarmed.

'Dear Grandmama — ' she began, soothingly.

'Don't you dear Grandmama me! I'm appalled that you can stand there and tell me all this so brazenly. It's probably being talked about in every bedroom in Town already.'

'I am truly sorry, Grandmama. Please believe me — I had no wish to cause you distress. You do not deserve that, for you have been so good to me.'

'It has become quite apparent to me you have inherited that same rebellious streak which caused your parents to bring so much unhappiness to your grandpapa and myself. No doubt it is the same with all of you.'

'No — no. You must not think that. The others are quite different from me. I was the wrong one to be chosen. If only they had sent my sister Monica rather than me, it would have been very different I am sure. And she does so long to be allowed to visit you, to see London.'

Tears filled Sarah's eyes at the thought of how she had failed her family, knowing what high hopes they had placed in her. Yet, even as she was saddened that it should be so, she could not regret the help she had given to her friend. That was her one consolation and she was sure that her papa would understand when she explained it to him, when, as seemed inevitable, she was sent home in disgrace. She took comfort from that thought, but she had little hope that the rest of her family would take such a patient and forgiving attitude.

'I shall not make an instant decision about

exactly what course to follow,' said Lady MacKenna. 'That can wait until I have spoken to Harry — and I understand he may not return for a day or two. When I have heard his account of events, I shall decide how to deal with you.'

'Yes, Grandmama,' Sarah replied meekly.

'One thing is certain,' continued the old lady, 'before we leave here I shall expect you to make a full and sincere apology to Wrenningham. You may go now, and think over what you will say.'

5

It would not be easy to apologize to Wrenningham. In Sarah's opinion he was the one who was at fault. If he had been more caring, more understanding, less obsessed with his pedigree and inheritance, he would have given permission at least for Corinne and Forbes Thackstone to become engaged. By forbidding them ever to meet he had left them no alternative but to take matters into their own hands or be miserable for the rest of their lives. What had happened was entirely Wrenningham's fault.

She worried about it all that day and into the next. It was Friday afternoon before the earl returned. Soon now she would have to stand before him and, despite his forwardness in clasping her in his arms and kissing her, *she* was expected to apologize to him. Truly the role of a woman was a difficult one.

Wandering aimlessly around the garden, seeing little of its beauty, Sarah's thoughts rampaged through her troubled mind and the more she pondered upon it, the more difficult and the more unfair it seemed. How could she be expected to express regret for something she was pleased to have done? Especially when his conduct that evening had certainly not been above reproach! The awful thing was, however, that if she did not apologize — and abjectly at that — her entire family would suffer.

She pictured them as she had last seen them, gathered on the quayside to wave goodbye as the ship moved slowly away. She loved them all so much — Mama and Papa, and her lovely sister Monica, whom she knew was dreaming of the day she would be permitted to visit her grandmama in London. The boys, Freddie and Thomas, both tall for their ages, strong and noisy, clattering about in their hobnailed boots and little Ben who was ill so often that he could not go to school. Sarah had given him lessons at home, making sure that he could read and write as well as any other child of nine. How could she go back home and face them, having to confess that she had let them down so badly? Somehow she must square her shoulders and find some words that would ameliorate Wrenningham.

Thursday came and went, Friday dawned, midday passed and he had not returned. Lady MacKenna remained in her room. Lady Turley had gone on a prearranged visit to friends some miles distant and was expected to stay there for a few days.

Sarah ate a light meal in the big dining-room, alone with her thoughts, picking at the food. She wandered outside again and normally would have delighted in the warm sunshine, but she was too uneasy over the dreaded encounter with Wrenningham to feel any joy. She made her way to the walled garden, redolent with twenty different scents from herbs and roses. The soft air hummed with insects, and magic was added by bright fluttering butterflies, whilst doves courted and cooed and made love on the roof of the octagonal dovecote. She sat in an arbour and whiled the time away, holding a book in her hands but seldom even glancing into its pages. Previously she had found the delights of the walled garden induced a feeling of peace and wellbeing, but that day it failed to lift her spirits. She tried to put together sentences, which would be adequate as an apology, but her pride made it so very, very difficult.

The sound of footsteps caused her to turn her head and, with a gasp of surprise, she saw Wrenningham — and realized that he was striding purposefully towards her. She was struck again by the elegance of his bearing, by his broad-shouldered, straight-backed military look, even though he was now in civilian dress of the very acme of elegance too. His handsome head was uncovered and held high, his left arm tucked into the front of his jacket, reminding her that perhaps his assertion that it was no longer any trouble to him was not entirely true.

She stood up to greet him and gazed unswervingly in his direction, noting how his eyes were riveted upon her in a manner that was quite disconcerting. Worst of all, she remembered, with a trembling sensation of unreality, exactly how he had kissed her. Shamefully that moment had remained impressed upon her mind with total vivid recall — and it did nothing to assist her to gather her thoughts and begin this apology she had been instructed to make.

She gained time by making a slow, low curtsy. When she rose, he was only a few feet away from her, her face level with the top of his magnificently embroidered waistcoat. Desperately she tried to form those words of her apology which she had been preparing, but before she could speak, he reached out, took her hand, lifted it, bowed and kissed her fingers.

'Pray be seated, Miss Dunthorne.' His voice was stiff, very formal and, as ever, commanding.

'I had rather stand, sir, There is something I wish to — '

He interrupted her. 'Miss Dunthorne, before you speak, be so good as to hear what I have to say.'

She would have preferred to launch into her expression of regret but she had no wish to anger him in advance. She bowed her head. 'As you wish,' she concurred.

Again he indicated that she should be seated and this time she obeyed. She sat well to one side of the long bench in the arbour so as to leave space for him to join her without being too close, He, however, remained standing. She looked up at him expectantly. There was a moment of portentous silence. Then he cleared his throat and said her name yet again. 'Miss Dunthorne, you appreciate that this imprudent escapade upon which my cousin has embarked has caused me great concern — '

'I do indeed and I am so sorry.' She would have seized the opportunity to launch into her prepared expressions of remorse, but he stopped her with an imperious wave of his hand and continued as if she had not spoken.

'I have thought over my position at great length — I have also spoken to Lady MacKenna. I left her but a few moments since, having put my proposition to her — you know that she is greatly concerned for your reputation — '

'I do know, and I — '

'Hear me out, then you may speak.'

Sarah closed her mouth abruptly. He appeared to be watching her intensely to ensure that she was listening carefully. She began to feel somewhat intimidated, and that roused her mettle. If only he had allowed her to voice those words of contrition this scene could have been over and done with by now! She held her hands together in her lap and, with her face as composed as she could make it, regarded him steadily.

'Before we parted yesterday I gave you my word that I would protect your good name and what I have to say will enable me to keep that promise. As I mentioned, I have discussed the matter with Lady MacKenna and we are agreed that there is only one way in which this can be done.' He paused significantly.

Sarah felt restive. She wished he would say whatever it was he had to say, and allow her to try and make her peace with him. When that was done she would be free to return to her family as soon as a passage could be arranged, for she had no doubt that she would have to leave.

'There is only one way in which this can be done,' he repeated, so evenly, so matter-of-factly, that she was completely unprepared for the words that followed, 'and that is — for you to become my wife.'

Sarah gasped. Her hands flew to her face, then down, clasping and entwining themselves, as restless as those butterflies she had disturbed earlier. She felt numbed, convinced that her ears had deceived her. Her eyes widened in disbelief, raked his face and saw he was totally calm, serious and unemotional.

'I can see that I have surprised you, Miss Dunthorne.'

'Why, yes, my lord. Yes, indeed. You have surprised me beyond measure.' She was beginning to regain her equilibrium. What he said was carrying gallantry to excess; his proposition not only unnecessary but quite out of the question!

He nodded. He even smiled faintly, but there seemed to be a touch of irony in it. 'I can see that you find it strange that I who have lived a bachelor life for so long should be willing to change that. However, present circumstances call for an alteration to my status.'

She could make little sense out of his words. 'My lord, I appreciate your concern, but I assure you there is no need for you to make such a sacrifice on my behalf. Truly you have no need to marry me to save my good name. I shall very soon be returning to

America and no one there will know anything about the matter.'

He looked somewhat shocked. 'You misunderstand the position, Miss Dunthorne.'

'No, no — please believe me, there will be no problem for me when I go home to my family in Cassie's Rock. I shall easily be able to explain to my papa the circumstances which led to my being in that bedroom at the inn and why you were there also. I know that he will not doubt me. Indeed, I am convinced he will commend me for assisting Corinne and Forbes —' She stopped short, realizing that she had allowed her tongue to run away with her. 'Forgive me — I should not have said that! It is my duty to apologize to you.'

'Not now, Sarah —'

'Yes. I must. My lord, please listen to me, for if I do not express my deep regrets my grandmama will never again invite any members of my family to visit her here in England and they do so want to come, especially my sister Monica.'

'It is very commendable of you to think of your family, even at a time like this —'

'I think of them all the time. My visit to England has been quite, quite wonderful, I shall never forget it, but it will be no hardship to me to return.'

'Sarah, please sit quietly and listen to me.'

It was the second time he had dispensed with formality and used her given name, but there was a growing note of exasperation in his voice.

She closed her mouth firmly and sank back on the seat, looking up at him appealingly. She had expected him to be relieved that he did not have to marry her and noticed with considerable surprise that his face had lost its expression of cool calm. Indeed, his features looked strangely contorted, as if he was fighting against some strong emotion. She wondered what was disturbing him so greatly, and judging by her knowledge of him, and by the way in which he had proposed, knew it was certainly not love. More likely it was anger, or at least irritation. She clasped her hands tightly together, rested them in the lap of her delicately sprigged muslin gown and made a real effort to compose herself.

'Now, please be so good as to allow me to continue without further interruption.' He paused.

As she remained still and silent he continued, 'Thank you. I have given a great deal of thought to this matter, and the conclusion I have reached has led me to make this offer of marriage to you. I know you are surprised, so I will explain clearly the circumstances which have led me to do so. It has all arisen because my cousin Corinne has seen fit to enter into this unholy and ill-advised state of matrimony with Thackstone. I have no doubt they will reach Scotland within the next twenty-four hours or so and then she and that blackguard will become man and wife.'

Sarah nodded. It pleased her to hear him say that, though she hoped he was wrong in his description of Forbes. The assistance she had given, coupled with the storm and the accidental but fortuitous laming of Wrenningham's horse made it more than likely that they would reach Gretna Green safely. It seemed to her that her friend's troubles were over, it was her own predicament now which was of concern. She fixed her eyes on Wrenningham's proud and handsome face, and wondered distractedly what more he could have to say. She had already told him that he was under no obligation to propose marriage to her but as he continued to state his case it became obvious that her opinion on the matter was of no importance to him.

'This has caused me to think long and hard about the provision of an heir for the Ashingby estate. I would have been content to leave that to my cousin Corinne. Indeed, I always assumed that in due course she would contract an alliance with a gentleman of equal standing with herself and with my own family. The duty to provide an heir therefore now devolves back upon me. I am a soldier. Before long, in all probability, I shall be posted to some theatre of war, and I would go more happily if I knew I had done my duty to my family name as well as to my king and country.'

Colour flamed in her cheeks, and she found it increasingly difficult to remain silent. He seemed not to notice her discomfort. Assured of his eligibility he had no doubt she would be proud and pleased.

'Miss Dunthorne, you have all the qualities I look for in a wife,' he continued. 'You come of good blood, and from families with a proven record of fecundity. For my part I am able to support you in what is probably a higher state of comfort than that to which you have previously been accustomed — Lady MacKenna can reassure you on that point, and I may add she is completely agreeable to my proposal.'

Sarah could bear to listen no longer. 'Grandmama may indeed be agreeable, but I, my lord, am not!'

The words exploded from her with all the the force she could muster. How dared he approach her in this way! He and Grandmama had talked over her possibilities as a wife as if she was an animal on the farm, a breeding mare or heifer, rather than a human being.

Wrenningham stepped back. His head jerked up. It was quite clear the possibility of rejection had never entered his mind. There was a moment of stunned silence, whilst they stared at each other, eyes locked in anger.

At last he spoke, his tone cold. 'May I ask on what grounds you reject my proposal?'

Sarah had no hesitation in answering. 'You may have a duty to provide an heir for Ashingby, sir, but I most certainly do not. What is more, you show not the least understanding about love or marriage. I am sure you will find plenty of other young women who will be only too delighted to oblige you as a breeding partner, but I consider the very concept distasteful in the extreme.'

'Perhaps I spoke too freely about that rather delicate matter — '

'Not at all.' Although she was sure her face was flushed bright red she remained very calm. 'Indeed, had I felt even the slightest temptation to accept your offer, it would have been to my advantage to know the exact terms. However, it was not that alone which guided me.'

'May I ask what else you hold against me?'

'You are a soldier and you spoke of the possibility of being sent to some other theatre of war. We both know that unless Britain mends her ways it is possible that America may resort to war and if that were indeed so you might then be fighting against my people.'

'War is not yet declared and it will not break out if America relinquishes its territorial ambitions to annex Canada.'

'I am sure you know perfectly well that the main cause of discontent among my countrymen is on the high seas. It is abominable for the British Navy to insist that they have a right to stop and search our American ships — and then to press our men as well as your own into acting as crews in the most dreadful conditions. It is nothing short of brutal kidnapping. We are enemies, sir, I see no reason why we should not stay that way.'

Her breasts heaved with the intensity of her emotions. It infuriated her to see a wry smile twist a corner of his mouth.

'Do you not have a Christian duty to love your enemy?' he enquired, quite softly.

Her lips tightened. Could he really not believe that she was serious? 'It may be unChristian, my lord, but in your case I should find that exceedingly difficult.'

He flinched. His eyes narrowed. He drew

himself up to his full height and in doing so seemed to recover his equanimity. She had never seen him look more proud, more self-assured. 'If that is the case,' he said, 'there is no point in continuing this conversation, interesting though it is. Allow me to escort you back to the house.' He offered his arm as if nothing untoward had taken place between them.

She ignored it, picked up her skirts and ran, her only thought to get away from him. She sped along the raked gravel path until she was breathless, her chest heaving and that was not only from the physical exertion.

As she neared the wide sweep of steps that led to the main entrance of the huge, gracious mansion she slowed her headlong rush to a more decorous pace. Her eyes roved over the magnificent pile, a house in the grandest style, pale-coloured stone, perfectly propor-tioned. It was a sobering thought that Wrenningham had offered to make her mistress of Ashingby, one of the most beautiful houses in the whole of England, set in hundreds of acres of gardens, parkland and farms. She could have been a countess. She, plain Sarah Dunthorne, from Cassie's Rock in the State of New York, America.

It was ridiculous! It almost made her laugh to think about it. Just because his lordship was in need of an heir! How right she had been to refuse. How terrible would such a position be, when there was no love to accompany it! The sooner she got away from that arrogant man's company the better pleased she would be.

She made her way to the double glass doors on the south side of the house which overlooked the formal lawns and colourful borders, with huge old cedar and beech trees in the background. Hurrying inside she would have passed straight through the drawing-room to seek solace in the peace and privacy of her own room but a voice stopped her.

'Sarah.'

She spun round. Grandmama sat in a high-backed wing chair, her tapestry frame with its half-finished picture was beside her, skeins of wool spread colourfully over a tiny octagonal table, With precise, careful movements of her long-fingered, thin, pale hands Lady MacKenna put aside her needle and removed her thimble.

'Yes, Grandmama?'

The old lady lifted her head and fastened her eyes speculatively upon her granddaughter's face.

Sarah waited a moment and bit her lip, shrinking from the inevitable questioning.

'Harry went into the garden to look for you.' There was no mistaking the delighted expectancy that glowed from her lined and elderly, but still lovely face.

'Yes, Grandmama.' There was no point in prevaricating. Sarah took a deep breath. 'He has just made me an offer of marriage.'

'My dear gal.' Grandmama smiled with abundant delight. She held open her arms. 'I couldn't be more pleased.'

Sarah did not move. She felt like an executioner, knowing she was about to kill that very dear old lady's hopes of what to her was an absolutely excellent match.

She swallowed, then took a deep breath. 'I'm sorry, Grandmama, I could not accept.'

Lady MacKenna's face clouded, a puzzled, disbelieving expression wiped all pleasure from her expression.

'What do you mean? What nonsense is this?' Her voice was hoarse with anxiety.

'Dear Grandmama — I knew you would be disappointed — '

'Disappointed! Have you taken leave of your senses, Sarah? You receive an offer of marriage from the richest, most sought after and eligible bachelor in the whole country and you refuse!' There was heavy sarcasm in her voice as she ended, 'Do you not consider him good enough for you, miss?'

'I appreciate he is a very fine gentleman and all that you say, Grandmama, but when I marry it will be to someone I can honour and love, and I do not feel so towards the Earl of Wrenningham.'

'Stuff and nonsense. All that can come after you've stood with him at the altar. It's all this romantic rubbish that's given you the wrong ideas, and I dare say your father has had something to do with it.'

'I should like to think that when I marry it will be to someone as good and kind as my papa,' Sarah said quietly.

'Fiddlededee! My daughter would never have been dragged off to the wilds of America but for him and his romantic notions. I don't call that kind. It certainly wasn't kind to me. Purely selfish I should call it!'

'I'm sure he didn't mean to hurt you, Grandmama.'

'That's as may be! Things would have been different if you'd been brought up here in England. Then I might have been able to instil a bit more sense into you, Sarah.' She paused, obviously considering. Her shrewd little black eyes gleamed. 'Tell me, have you definitely turned Wrenningham down?'

'Yes, Grandmama. Quite positively.'

'I will talk to him.'

'Truly that would make no difference.'

'You realize you will never receive another offer as good as this? To me it seemed absolutely heaven sent.'

'Not at all,' replied Sarah. 'There was nothing heaven sent about it. It was only because he wished to produce an heir.'

'And what is wrong with that, may I ask? Is that not what marriage is all about?'

'No. At least not entirely,' protested Sarah. 'It is about loving and companionship.'

Grandmama was not listening. 'I would never have believed you would be such a simpleton, Sarah. Heaven knows you really don't deserve to have received such a proposal. For goodness sake, do think again. I will tell Harry that you were taken by surprise — that it was just youthful bashfulness and you did not really mean what you said — '

'No!' Sarah was aghast at the suggestion. 'It is true I was surprised, but that did not affect my answer. I am truly sorry to cause you so much displeasure, Grandmama, but I cannot — and I most definitely will not — marry Wrenningham.'

Lady MacKenna's expression darkened. 'Very well, my girl. Then you will leave my care at the very earliest opportunity.'

'Yes, Grandmama. I realized it would have to be so and although I regret — '

'Do not waste your breath on regrets that

you obviously do not mean.' The old lady shook her head in anger and sorrow and Sarah felt desperately unhappy at causing her so much distress. She stood with her head bowed submissively as she continued to berate her.

'I cannot tell you how displeased I am with your conduct, Sarah. I shall make arrangements for you to return to America as soon as possible.'

'Yes, Grandmama.'

'Meanwhile I shall write a letter explaining what has happened and send it to your parents. I shall, of course, tell them exactly how you have transgressed.'

'Grandmama,' Sarah said softly. 'I — I realize what a disappointment I have been to you, and I do not plead forgiveness for myself — I have not been a good ambassador for my family, but they are not all like me — '

'I am pleased to hear it.'

In desperation, Sarah took a bold line. 'Indeed, Grandmama, I am sure that had my sister Monica, received the proposal instead of me, she would have been only too happy to accept — '

'Would she indeed!' The voice was masculine, deep-toned and authoritative. Sarah recognized it immediately. She swung round in dismay to face the earl, who stood framed by the open french doors. He advanced into the room.

'Miss Dunthorne, it is one thing for you to reject my offer of marriage, it is quite another for you to select a substitute. Should I ever be of a mind to do that, it shall be a lady of my own choosing.'

'I — I — ' Sarah stammered helplessly.

Wrenningham shot her a scathing glance, then turned away to address her grandmama. 'Lady MacKenna, pray do not feel that you are under any obligation to depart. I should not wish you and Miss Dunthorne to undertake the long and tedious journey at such short notice and unaccompanied — indeed I absolutely forbid it.'

'That is exceedingly obliging of you, Harry.'

'I shall myself be travelling to London in three days' time. May I suggest that we make the journey together, then I shall be able to see to your safety and comfort? Indeed, I shall be offended if you do not stay, for what has happened is but a trivial affair.'

'Most civil of you to say so, Harry, especially after my granddaughter's ingratitude for the sacrifice you were prepared to make to protect her good name.'

'Think nothing of it, dear lady.' He lifted her pale, thin hand and kissed her fingers with the utmost gallantry, and seemed so light-hearted that Sarah formed the opinion that he was quite relieved that she had rejected his offer.

'Now, however,' he continued, smoothly, 'I must make my excuses, for I have matters concerning the estate to attend to.' He bowed to Sarah, then strode from the room with a dismissive air and the door closed behind him.

Sarah was left contemplating his words — 'it was but a trivial affair!' To her mind it was insult piled upon injury!

'You're a fool!' declared Lady MacKenna. 'There goes the greatest catch in the whole country! And you just let him slip out of your fingers as if he was worthless.' She shook her head. 'Young people are not the same as they were in my day! He'll never ask you again, you know.'

'Yes, Grandmama,' Sarah murmured sub-missively. Suddenly her eyes filled with tears — which was ridiculous because she most certainly did not want Wrenningham to ask her again — ever — did she? Without even pausing to take proper leave of her grandmama, she turned and fled to her room and flung herself down on the bed, more upset and angry than she ever remembered being in her whole life.

6

Sarah was not one to lie still wallowing in her misery. She jumped off the bed and began to pace restlessly up and down the room, her feet soundless on the thick carpet. The room was spacious and elegantly furnished. The four-poster bed was draped with rose-pink satin, matching curtains hung at the two wide windows that overlooked the front lawns and formal beds. She had delighted both in the room and the view when she first saw it — now it seemed more like a prison.

She sat down on one of the white and gold, deep-buttoned chairs by the window and tried to divert herself with a book. It was a novel that she had previously found engrossing, now it seemed quite meaningless. Her emotions were in turmoil. How could Grandmama expect her to agree to Wrenningham's outrageous proposal! What he sought was nothing but a marriage of convenience. It was doubly galling to recall the dismissive tone of Wrenningham's voice as he remarked that it 'was but a trivial affair'.

She was sad that her visit should end in disgrace — and distraught to think that she might have ruined the chances of similar visits for Monica and her brothers. She had never wanted to come to England and now she was to be sent back to America several weeks early — and the sooner the better as far as she was concerned. She would be glad when she was separated from Wrenningham by the width of the mighty Atlantic Ocean!

Yet the delicious memory of that persuasive kiss with which he had beguiled her, remained. It took an effort of will to thrust that aside. She must be guided by her mind, not by her emotions. Thank goodness she had heard about Wrenningham from Corinne long before she met him! But for that she might have believed that he cared for her. She wished Lady MacKenna had not accepted Wrenningham's offer to stay on at Ashingby.

A knock on her door broke into her disturbed thoughts. She glanced at her watch. It was time to start preparations for the evening. Her maid, Lucy Motts, had brought up a can of hot water, which she proceeded to pour into the basin on the washstand.

Lucy was about the same age as Sarah; the daughter of a farm-worker on the Ashingby estate, she had been sent into service when she was twelve years old. First she had worked in the farm dairy, from five o'clock in the morning till evening time. No wonder she'd dreamed of leaving the country and had applied for work in one of the fine houses in London. Soon a position was offered to her.

At first all had gone well; naturally hard-working, willing, and intelligent, she had quickly made herself useful in the household. She developed into a very attractive young woman with a rosy complexion and curly blonde hair.

'It was the master's son that was the problem, miss,' she had confided to Sarah, soon after she became her personal maid. 'He tried to get into my bedroom, more than once, an' my door didn't have no lock, so all I could do was wedge a chair up against the door-handle. I daren't tell the mistress — she'd have sacked me, even if she'd believed me.'

'You were quite right to leave,' Sarah said.

Lucy never ceased telling Sarah how fortunate she was to have become her maid. Listening to the girl's chatter helped to calm Sarah. Her life had been so easy in comparison to that of her maid. 'You said your family live in this area, Lucy?' Sarah prompted.

'Less than an hour's walk away. I went to see them yesterday, on my afternoon off. It was such fun — there was so much to say — an' you'd never believe how the little ones have grown.'

'How many brothers and sisters do you have, Lucy?'

'Five brothers and three sisters, miss. They weren't all there. Eliza's away in service now, and Jemmy's a stable-boy.'

'Nine of you,' exclaimed Sarah.

'An' there was two that died. I didn't have time to go to the churchyard to see them, but I will before I go back to London. Little Emily's had the whoopin' cough. The worst of it's past, but it's left her so weak an' pale.'

'I'll send something to help to build her up.'

'Cook let me take some beef-tea an' some rice pudding. She managed to eat a little of it, an' Ma said she was a bit stronger than she had been the day before.'

'Could I come with you to visit your family, Lucy?' Sarah asked.

'Course you can, miss — if you'd really like to. We'm only poor folk — '

'I don't mind that. There are lots of poor folk where I live in Cassie's Rock, and I used to visit with my father sometimes. Papa always said an outing in the fresh air was good for children who were recovering from whooping cough.'

'I took her out in the sunshine yesterday, miss, but she can't walk far.'

'We'll take little Emily out for a carriage

drive,' declared Sarah.

'I don't know as you should do that, miss!'

'Why not? I couldn't ask for one of his lordship's vehicles, but if I hire one from the village, there can be no objection to that, can there?'

'I suppose not, miss. If you're sure — '

'Of course I'm sure.' Sarah was excited at the prospect. 'I'll hire a wagonette — we can take all your family. Cook can pack a picnic lunch. We'll spend the day on the beach. How about that, Lucy?'

'Oh, miss! That would be really wonderful! You're so kind, miss.'

'Nonsense. I'll enjoy it. How many will we be? You, me, your mother, seven children. I'll see cook this evening. Is there anything Emily particularly likes?'

'She's got a sweet-tooth, miss. She'd love some sweetmeats.'

'We'll go tomorrow. Can you let your family know, so they'll be ready?'

'I'll walk over and tell them, miss, soon as I've done your hair.'

'There's no need to hurry back. I can get myself ready for bed.'

'Oh, no, miss. That'd be neglecting my duties. I couldn't allow that, specially when you're so kind to me. I'll hurry an' be back here in a couple of hours.'

Sarah smiled. 'I shall so look forward to meeting your family tomorrow.' She meant it. She felt happier than she had done for several days.

★　★　★

The mood stayed with Sarah as she descended the stairs, crossed the spacious entrance hall, and entered the drawing-room. She had delayed leaving her room, having no wish to be alone with Wrenningham. She expected Grandmama would already be there. Wrenningham, however was alone, resplendent in a fashionable cut-away coat of plain black material, unbuttoned to reveal a white satin waistcoat embroidered with gold thread. His powerful legs were encased in sage-green breeches and silk stockings, black pumps on his feet. The collar of his shirt was upright, and held in place by a cravat of white silk. The elegant cut of his clothes emphasized rather than diminished the manliness of his bearing.

He fixed his deep-set eyes upon Sarah and a slight smile lightened his features, as if they had never had that altercation. He was evidently at peace with himself and with her too; confirmation, it seemed to her, that he did not care one jot about her rejection of his proposal.

'We dine alone,' he said. 'Lady MacKenna sent word that she is tired and has elected to dine in her room.'

'Perhaps I should go and see — '

'I think not. She particularly asked not to be disturbed.'

She remained close to the door, on the opposite side of the beautifully proportioned room; Wrenningham stood by the open casement windows. 'Come,' he said. 'See how lovely the garden looks in this soft evening light.' Sarah felt obliged to take some steps across the large room, yet halted a few paces short of him. Rosebeds filled the air with their delicate scent, full blooms, pink, white, crimson and cream stretched from the terrace to a large circular pool in the middle of which a fountain played. Lawns made a rich green carpet. In the distance, cattle grazed beneath sturdy old trees.

'It is very lovely,' she agreed! 'I hope it will not be too long before you return to see it again.'

'Who can tell what the future holds, Miss Dunthorne?'

Her heart softened, was gripped with fear, remembering that he was going away to war. A vivid picture flashed into her imagination, and in her mind's eye she saw his fine, strong figure lying on a distant battlefield in a pool of blood. She shuddered.

'I shall pray for your safety, my lord,' she said impulsively.

One of his dark eyebrows twitched upwards. 'When such a short time ago you told me how impossible it would be for you to love an enemy?'

'Love is a very different matter,' she said solemnly.

'And will you pray for all your enemies?' he asked.

'I wish no ill to anyone. I wish there would be no wars.'

'Amen to that. But we live in a very imperfect world,' he agreed.

A moment of silence followed. Then Sarah cleared her throat, remembering her manners. 'My lord, I must thank you for your kind hospitality whilst I have stayed here, and Grandmama insists that I apologize for the disagreement I had with you regarding Corinne's elopement and — '

He stilled the flow of her words with a sweep of his hand and a shrug of his shoulders. 'That was one battle I fought and lost,' he said. 'Corinne was determined to do as she pleased. I only hope Thackstone will take his responsibilities seriously.'

'Why should he not?'

'Gambling is a trait that runs in the Thackstone family. His father and grandfather before him lost a fortune at cards — that's why he was so anxious to get his hands on Corinne's money.'

Sarah stared at him aghast. 'Are you sure? Does Corinne know of this?'

'Do you imagine I didn't tell her?' The autocratic note was back in his voice. 'She simply she refused to listen. I hoped she would outgrow her infatuation — '

'She loves him,' Sarah protested.

'Rubbish! I've no time for this emotional tangle you call love. That's where I made my mistake. I did not foresee that you would be so willing an accomplice for my wilful cousin.'

'You are wrong when you say love does not exist,' Sarah persisted. 'I have the example of my own dear parents to prove it.'

'What rash decisions that misguided emotion has led otherwise intelligent people to take!' he observed.

Sarah considered that statement, and decided Wrenningham was referring to his offer for her hand, rather than to Corinne's elopement. It was added proof that she had been right to reject his proposal. His statement did not merit an answer, it did however remind her that she had to continue with her apology.

'My lord, there is one more thing I have to say to you.'

Again that eyebrow quirked up quizzically.

She continued. 'It is — that I am very conscious of the honour you did me, in asking me to become your wife.'

'Are you, indeed! Your speeches grow prettier and prettier, Sarah. The question is — do you regret your refusal?'

'No, sir, that I cannot say,' she replied.

'Think what you are missing, Sarah.'

His voice was a lazy drawl, as if it was a matter for amusement rather than one of any consequence. He was, however, looking directly into her eyes. She held his gaze and answered him seriously. 'Grandmama has been at pains to point that out to me. But I have never yearned for great worldly wealth.'

'It was not merely of material things I was thinking.'

It was a relief that at that moment the butler entered the room to announce that dinner was served.

Wrenningham offered his arm and escorted her through to the dining-room. Two places only had been set, one at the head of the table and the other on its immediate right. The earl himself held her chair whilst Sarah seated herself, then moved to take his own place. Lady Turley had not yet returned from visiting her friends. The footman appeared almost immediately with a steaming tureen of French onion soup, to which a liberal dash of sherry had been added.

Sarah had feared that the tone of the evening might have been constrained since she was dining alone with Wrenningham, but he seemed determined to keep the atmosphere pleasantly sociable. He enquired whether she had been into the library again, and which books she had looked at, a shared interest she was happy to discuss with him. From there the conversation turned to their schooldays, Wrenningham telling her quite freely that he had not been at all happy when he was first sent away to boarding-school, though later when he was at Eton, and then at Cambridge University he had enjoyed his studies.

For Sarah, schooling had been a happier experience. In her early years she had been educated at home, at first by her parents, then sharing a tutor with her sister and brothers. She had not been sent to finishing school until she was fourteen, and although Miss Rybrough's establishment was some distance from home, and she could visit her parents but once a year, she had been happy there. There had been a constant flow of letters, so that she had always felt herself to be part of the family. As well as the basic subjects she had learned French and dancing, geometry and geography, embroidery and music.

She had also been taught to make her own clothes. One winter her mother had sent her the material to make a coat, and although it had taken her a great deal of time, she had thought herself very smart in it when finished, especially as she had made it fashionably loose, and with a belt. It had been a pretty rust colour, and the material of such fine quality that it had been as good as new when she grew out of it, and passed it down to Monica.

She did not tell Wrenningham of some of her more daring escapades, for she had had the reputation of being something of a tomboy. Nor did she disclose how she had been reprimanded as being improper, when she wrote to a girlfriend, agog to hear if it was true that the friend had received attentions from Stanley Davison. Also, was it true that Mr Peabody, the music teacher, was paying attention to a young lady in Niagara? It had seemed to her only natural that she should be interested in the affairs of her dearest friends

— and they had not minded in the least.

The meal was, as always, tasty and extremely satisfying. Sarah took a little wine, but Wrenningham refilled his glass several times. He did not linger at the table and together they repaired to the drawing-room where the butler served coffee.

'May I prevail upon you to entertain me on the pianoforte?' suggested the earl.

Sarah wished with all her heart that she had not mentioned that she had studied music at school.

'Unfortunately, I have not brought any music with me,' she excused herself. Then added frankly, 'Even if I had, I fear my talent would disappoint you — besides I am unfamiliar with the piano. At home we have only a harpsichord.'

'Then I will play and you shall sing,' Wrenningham said.

He proceeded to take his place at the handsome modern Broadwood grand. The candles had already been lit and by the soft light he flicked through a pile of sheet music.

'Do you know this delightful old English song 'Greensleeves'?'

He ran his fingers over the keys, strong hands, square-tipped, fluid of movement, their touch surprisingly delicate.

'Oh, yes, my mama plays that quite often.'

131

Sarah had no hesitation in singing to his accompaniment. She had been told many times that she had a pretty voice; it blended easily with Wrenningham's rich baritone, when he encouraged her to join in a duet with him. The musical interlude that followed was exceedingly enjoyable. He moved easily on from one piece to another.

She joined in with him in the jolly tune of 'The Raggle-Taggle Gypsies'. She was laughing as they finished. She had no wish to stay up late, however, and just before ten o'clock declared her intention to retire.

'As you wish,' Wrenningham said easily. 'But just one more — it's by Henry Purcell. 'Ah! how sweet — Ah! how sweet — how sweet it is to love'.' His eyes were dancing with wicked mischief as he sang.

Sarah pursed her lips. She knew better than to be deceived into thinking that he understood what real love was! She moved away from the piano and he stood up and closed the lid.

'Tomorrow,' he said, 'I shall be making a tour of the estate would you care to join me?'

'My lord, I fear I must decline. I have already made arrangements, with Lucy, my maid, for tomorrow.'

His expression hardened. 'With your maid?

Is it so urgent? I could show you much that is of interest.'

'I have no doubt that I should enjoy it very much, but really I must ask you to excuse me.'

'I can scarcely expect to take precedence over whatever women's matters you have to see to,' he said, with more than a tinge of sarcasm. 'I bid you good night, Miss Dunthorne.'

He held open the door for her, and, as she ascended the stair, she saw him make his way to the study. She wondered what he would say if he knew the real reason why she could not accompany him. Not for the world would she break her word, and if he liked to think she was the sort of female who could be so set about what he described as women's matters, so be it.

She paused outside Lady MacKenna's room. She would have liked to assure herself that the old lady was comfortable, yet hesitated to disturb her. If she was asleep, even the lightest of knocks might waken her, and Sarah doubted if she would be welcome. That troublesome granddaughter — in whom she was definitely not best pleased.

7

Sarah slept well, but awoke soon after day-break. The sun streamed into her room and, delighted that the weather promised to be fine for the outing she had planned, she scrambled out of bed. As she approached the window she heard the sound of horse's hooves outside and a man's voice. She stayed far enough back to remain out of sight of those below. Evidently the earl had not left quite as early as he had anticipated. The groom held his horse in readiness. The big black animal pawed the ground, tossed its head, and the man talked to it firmly but calmly.

Then Wrenningham strode out of the house, smart in bottle-green riding coat, buckskin breeches and polished leather boots. He was bare-headed, and she was struck by the thickness of his dark-brown hair, making him look almost youthful. Her heart beat a little faster — why it should be so she could not fully comprehend — except that he was by far the finest-looking man she had ever seen.

With a brief nod of thanks to the groom,

Wrenningham took the reins and swung himself up into the saddle. Scarcely waiting for the touch of its master's boots, the spirited animal sprang forward, horse and rider were away, gravel scattering from the flying hooves. In seconds they were out of sight, hidden by the luscious growth of the rhododendron bushes that bordered the drive.

Sarah felt a pang of regret — it was a brilliant morning, it would have been wonderful to ride out with the earl, to see the full extent of his vast estate — she smothered the thought before it could worm its way further into her mind. That would have meant being in his company for a whole day, and almost certainly would only end in anger and confrontation. She was glad she'd had a valid reason not to accompany him. In a slightly peevish way, it pleased her that he had not expected her to refuse. It would have been interesting, but the outing with Lucy and her family should be fun. She had missed the rough and tumble company of her brothers — strange to think that as the day started here, they would still be asleep.

It would be an hour before Lucy came with the hot water for her ablutions. Sarah picked up the book that she had put down in despair the previous evening, and began to read.

'My ma said to tell you it's ever so good of you to take us to the sea, miss.' Lucy was beaming all over her pretty face as she came into Sarah's room. 'An' you should've seen little Em'ly's face! It was a picture!'

'How was little Emily?' Sarah asked with concern.

'Better, I think. She took the beef-tea Cook sent, and some of the rice pudding, so that's a good sign, in't it, miss?'

Sarah nodded. 'It's always a relief when children start to pick up an appetite. Let's hope a nice day out will help her too.'

'We've never had a day out like this before, not with so many of us goin' together,' Lucy exclaimed.

'It's a lovely morning, let's not waste a minute of it. What time will they be ready?'

'Miss, the childers'll probably be ready now. Ephraim wanted to get ready last night.'

Lucy poured hot water into the pretty flower-patterned bowl as she chatted and Sarah soaped her flannel and began to wash.

'What dress shall I put out for you, miss?' Lucy asked.

'My checked gingham,' Sarah said.

Lucy looked slightly disapproving. She opened the doors of the press and then held up the dress. It was checked in brown, green and a thin line of crimson on a cream background.

'You mean this one, miss?'

'Yes, that one,' Sarah said firmly. 'I made it myself.'

Lucy sniffed as if to say she wasn't surprised to hear that.

'The children are expecting a grand lady, miss.'

'I don't want to wear any of the fine clothes Lady MacKenna bought for me; I'd have to be careful not to damage them. I want to be completely carefree. I'm going to the beach to play with the children.'

At that Lucy relented. 'I reckon you won't look much older than the children when you get this on.'

★　★　★

Lady MacKenna never rose from her bed before about eleven o'clock, so Sarah knew she would eat breakfast alone. In the entrance hall she noticed a copy of the previous day's *Times*. She carried it into the breakfast-room. A footman served her with coffee, ham and bread rolls, and brought in butter and honey.

She had read the newspaper on several

occasions whilst she had been in England. The front page carried advertisements and personal announcements, after a cursory glance through them, she opened the paper and at once a headline caught her eye.

ELOPEMENT IN HIGH LIFE

Suspicion has surrounded the whereabouts of The Honourable Miss Corinne de Vere since she quitted Ashingby Hall, the home of her guardian, the tenth Earl of Wrenningham, on the early afternoon of Wednesday. Miss de Vere set out in the company of her friend, Miss Sarah Dunthorne, who was staying with her maternal grandmother, Lady Primrose MacKenna, as guests of the noble earl. It was believed that the two young ladies had the intention of calling upon Mrs Ellen Warboys, who has recently been married to the Reverend Robert Warboys of Gilton, and resides in the Rectory House there. However, neither of the young ladies arrived at that destination.

As far as can be ascertained, Miss de Vere ordered the coachman to turn into the yard of the White Hart Inn, which is well known to travellers in this remote part of Norfolk. There, a gentleman was awaiting with a post-chaise, ready to depart at speed. The young lady was soon ensconced in the chaise, where her maid was already in attendance. It is believed that the gallant gentleman to whom the young lady has resigned herself is Captain Forbes Thackstone of the King's Regiment. Their present whereabouts is not known, but it is understood that they were travelling northwards.

The Honourable Miss de Vere, is the daughter of the late Lord Edmund de Vere, who was mortally wounded when bravely leading his troops during the English expedition to the Dardanelles, against Turkey in 1807. Lord de Vere was the younger brother of the ninth Earl of Wrenningham, who was killed in a hunting accident only a year later. Miss de Vere is heiress to a considerable fortune from the estates of her late mother, when she comes of age. She is next in line to the Wrenningham estates in Norfolk and in London.

Miss Sarah Dunthorne, daughter of Doctor Dunthorne, was born and educated in a small town known as Cassie's Rock, in New York State, America. She is the granddaughter of

Lady Primrose MacKenna. It is believed that Miss Dunthorne returned to Ash-ingby after the elopement where it is understood that she remains as a close friend of the earl.

Sarah gasped with annoyance as she read that final sentence. How dared they print such a thing! How had the paper acquired so much information? She supposed it had been from the servants, and also from those at the inn. Had Wrenningham seen it? And her grandmother? Sarah had an urge to hide the paper, but knew that would be useless. Lady MacKenna was an avid reader of *The Times* but no doubt she had already read it. Also, Lady Turley was due to return from her friends' today, and she would certainly have seen the account.

Although there had been no actual news, she was sure Corinne and Forbes must be in Scotland and safely married. She turned a page over — and again her attention was riveted, this time by a headline in the section Parliamentary Intelligence'.

BRITISH SHIPS ATTACKED ON THE
GREAT LAKES
The matter of British boats being stopped on the lakes had been reserved

for subsequent negotiation. It was known that certain States were averse to the coming war.

Sarah felt a shiver run over her. It was all very well for the British Parliament to discuss such matters so coolly and dispassionately. They wouldn't be involved or in danger. Her home was a short drive from Lake Ontario. What was really happening over there?

It took so long for news to arrive, weeks, sometimes months. A few days ago the newspaper had reported that the *Mary Ann* packet had arrived from New York, and among the despatches it brought was information that Congress had voted 50,000 volunteers, and the object of their attack was undeniably against British territory.

She took comfort from a more reassuring speech in the next pararagraph: 'There is no need for apprehension of an immediate attack upon British possessions in North America.'

She took another cup of coffee, then pulled herself together. Leaving the breakfast-room she went through the door that led to a long passageway at the end of which was the huge kitchen. Maids were washing dishes or cleaning vegetables in the big stone sinks. Around the walls were shelves and hooks on which hung gleaming pots and pans, a

141

testament to hard work. The fire glowed in the big black stove, roasting jacks were still in place, though a wall oven had also been installed. Two assistant cooks stood by the central table, but what they were so energetically pounding and whisking, Sarah could not see.

Cook was leaning into a large hamper, showing only a well-rounded rump, clothed in ample skirts. Sarah waited until the good lady had straightened herself before greeting her.

'Good morning, Mrs Nockolds.'

Cook was breathless from her efforts, her white mob-cap had been knocked askew, and her plump face looked even redder than usual.

'Mornin', miss. I'm nearly ready. Just a few more things to go in.'

'Thank you.' Sarah peered down at the array of parcels mysteriously wrapped in linen cloths. 'What are you putting up for us?'

'I reckon as how the sea air'll give you all an appetite.' Cook nodded her head as she spoke. 'There's a couple of roast chickens, all cut up, plenty of bread, ready buttered. Some watercress sandwiches and there's cheese and onions, a dozen hard-boiled eggs and in this here cloth is a cold fruity dumpling. The little 'uns'll be specially partial to that.'

'That's wonderful, Mrs Nockolds Thank you, very much.'

'You'll find plenty for everyone, I reckon. They're a big family, the Mottses. Oh, and I've put in some more beef-tea and sweet-meats for Emily. Lucy say she's still poorly from the whooping-cough. It'll do her good, I reckon.'

The hamper was strongly woven from willow, its lid thrown back as Mrs Nockolds leaned over again, to put in yet more items. 'These are raspberry tarts — Hodges picked the fruit fresh this morning — I made them myself, so I know they're good. They're still warm, but I've wrapped them carefully.'

'I'm sure they're absolutely delicious.'

'There's three bottles of my special lemon barley water, too. And a big jug — Lucy will be able to get water, so it can be diluted. Mugs are in that bag.'

'You are good, Mrs Nockolds. You've thought of everything!'

Cook beamed. 'I've enjoyed doing it. Haven't packed up for a children's picnic for years.'

'The waggonette should be here soon — I've asked for it to be brought to the kitchen door.' Sarah felt almost as excited as a child herself as she hurried away upstairs. She had not yet had an opportunity to speak to her grandmama about this outing, but she felt quite sure that Lady MacKenna would approve. Her mama had often spoken about the picnics they'd had when she was young. As she hurried up the great staircase, Sarah encountered Lady MacKenna's maid. 'Good morning, Smithie,' Sarah greeted her with a smile. 'Is my grandmama awake?'

'No, miss. I've just been in to see her, and she's still sleeping soundly.'

'I trust there's nothing wrong?'

'Nothing at all,' Smithie assured her. 'She keeps very late hours; she was playing patience in her room until almost two o'clock this morning. It's perfectly normal for her ladyship.'

Sarah knew Lady MacKenna was what her papa called a 'night-person', at her best late in the day, just when most were settling down to sleep, whereas Sarah liked to be up and about early.

'I wished to apprise her of my plans for today,' Sarah said.

'Yes, miss.' Something in the maid's voice suggested *she* already knew — not surprising, with the bustle going on in the kitchen — but Sarah had the feeling that Smithie did not approve.

'I'll write a little note for grandmama and I'll leave it on the landing table. Perhaps you would see she gets it when she wakens?'

'Yes, miss.'

The letter written, Sarah picked up a light shawl and a wide-brimmed straw hat — which she had decorated with a cluster of roses and daisies from the garden — and was ready for the day.

The wagonette was a high vehicle, drawn by two sturdy horses. It had upholstered seats along each side, so that the passengers all faced inwards. A footman struggled out of the kitchen with the heavy hamper. The coach-man opened up a well beneath the floor-boards in which it could be stored for the journey.

'Ready, miss?' asked the coachman.

Sarah and Lucy climbed in and sat side by side. Cook and the kitchen staff waved them off.

The Hall, that impressively grand building, was soon left behind and they went steadily on through the home woods. At the lodge cottages, a lad of no more than seven or eight had opened the gate. He bowed respectfully as they passed through.

Out on the dusty road, the coachman set the horses off at a smart trot. The countryside was enchanting, high, bushy hedges, wild roses showing delicate pink faces, and yellow-hammers, dunnocks and wrens flitted about. The trundling wheels on the road and the clip-clop of the horses' feet were the only sounds. Presently they came to a group of white-walled cottages, with sloping thatched roofs. A cluster of children were dancing up and down with excitement as they caught sight of the wagonette. All were fair-haired and bore a remarkable resemblance to Lucy. Their mother stood by the wicket gate that led into their cottage garden. She beckoned to the children, then to Sarah's amusement, they formed a line with their backs to their garden fence. Shoulder to shoulder they stood, almost still and strictly in order of height.

'I told them to line up in order of age, so's I can introduce them to you.' Lucy said. 'An that's my ma.'

Mrs Motts must have been a pretty woman when she was younger, but the ravages of child-bearing, hard work and an insufficient income had taken its toll.

'Ma, this is Miss Dunthorne, from America,' Lucy said, with obvious pride.

Mrs Motts bobbed a curtsy, and managed it very neatly, despite holding a small girl on her hip. 'It's very kind of you to do this for us, Miss Dunthorne,' she said.

'I'm enjoying it just as much as any of you,' said Sarah.

'Now, I'll introduce you to my brothers and sisters.' Lucy waved her hand in the direction of the line of children. The older boys had clean shirts, and the girls and smaller boys wore spotless white pinafores.

'Jemmy and Eliza aren't here, of course, but this is Ephraim.' Self-consciously, stiffly, he bowed.

'Hello, Ephraim,' Sarah said.

'The next one's Mary.' Lucy continued along the line. The little girl bobbed down prettily even before her name was mentioned.

There was also John, Charlie, Amy, Ann and little Emily, the baby who was held in Mrs Motts's arms.

'How is she today?' Sarah asked.

'She seem a little brighter, thank you, miss.'

Eagerly they clambered into the wagonette — or were lifted or pushed and pulled. A group of women and children and a very old man also gathered around to watch — Sarah wished she could have taken them all. The coachman flipped the reins over the horses' back, willingly they leaned into their collars and the wagonette rolled on.

'How about a song?' Lucy suggested, after they'd covered a couple of miles or so. 'Come on, children, let's have one of your nursery rhymes.'

Ephraim struck up a merry little jingle

— Sarah hadn't heard it before, but it was simple enough and she was soon able to join in the chorus. 'One Man Went to Mow, Went to Mow a Meadow'.

Alongside the road they caught glimpses of a stream, overhung with alder trees and edged with rushes and bright yellow irises, with fine oak trees. What a joy to be out in the warm sunshine, beneath the wide open Norfolk sky.

Then Lucy, in her sweet, clear voice, started up another song. Sarah recognized it at once as one of the melodies Wrenningham had played on the pianoforte the previous evening, 'The Raggle-Taggle Gypsies O!'

Her thoughts immediately switched to Wrenningham with his offer of a ride around the estate; again she felt a slight pang of regret, but hastily pushed it aside. It was much better for her to be here, with Lucy and her family.

★ ★ ★

Wrenningham, mounted on his powerful black stallion, was riding through an ancient patch of coppiced woodland. He employed a reliable and conscientious manager, Robert Williams, who came from a landed family, but being a younger son, had no hopes of any inheritance. Wrenningham paid him well and accommodated him and his family in a large house, overlooking a lake. Mr Williams, who had sole charge whilst the earl was absent, was well satisfied with his situation, and repaid his lordship's trust by giving loyal and unstinted service.

Nevertheless, the earl felt it his duty to survey as much as possible when he was at home, checking that all was in as good order as could be expected. He also spoke to tenant farmers and was pleased with what he had seen and heard.

Emerging from the wood he reined in to survey the scene that stretched before him. Small fields rolled away, down to the shallow valley of a meandering stream. A narrow road wound alongside the slow-flowing water. Over the still air the sound of voices came to him — women and children — singing.

He could just see the tops of the heads of the people being carried along the road below, for it was partly shielded from his view by a high hedge and some oak trees. He envied them their happiness and wondered who they were, what joyous expedition were they undertaking? He was sufficiently curious to turn his horse back into the wood where he followed a wide track, knowing that a short distance further on the road would turn to hug the edge of the trees. There he waited. Merry laughter preceded the wagonette. It was driven by a nondescript coachman, and in it, singing merrily, were a group of children and three women, whose dress showed them to be country folk. One was middle aged, the other two younger, one of whom caught his eye. She wore a simple gingham gown, but sat proudly upright. Her face was hidden by a large straw hat, decorated with fresh flowers that were wilting slightly in the heat of the sun. She turned to stare directly into the woods and he drew in a sharp breath. It was Sarah! What the devil was she doing there? So this was why she had refused to accompany him! He felt deeply offended, stared at the two other women and thought he might have seen the younger one somewhere. A quick assessment confirmed his original opinion — they were not ladies of his class of society.

The wagonette continued on its merry way, rounded a bend, turning towards the coast. What was Sarah was up to? but he hesitated to ride after them. They were heading towards the fishing village of Winterton. His curiosity was aroused. Later on, he decided, he also would go there. Meantime, there were two more farms he must visit and also the watermill. Williams had mentioned some rather expensive repairs were needed and had asked for his opinion. He dug his heels into the horse's flanks and set off at as fast a pace as the terrain allowed.

8

'I can see the sea — I can see the sea,' chanted the children.

Suddenly the wide expanse of the North Sea was spread before them — grey-green, streaked with deep sapphire. On its wide expanse were barques and schooners carrying a press of white canvas, fishing boats and barges too, with ruddy coloured sails.

The wagonette passed little houses built of cobblestones from the beach. In the centre was a church, with a tall, solid tower of grey stone. The coachman took them to a point where a slope used by fishing boats made an easy descent to the beach, golden in the brilliant sunshine.

Out they all scrambled. The coachman backed the wagon on to the marram grass, unhitched his horses and led them to a nearby hostelry where they could be fed, watered and rested. Away went the children, tossing off their boots and socks, eager to paddle in the sea, to dig and build sandcastles, search for pretty stones, and shells. Sarah flung aside her hat, kicked off her shoes, rolled down her stockings, lifted her skirts and paddled with the children at the edge of the sea.

Lucy joined her there and the two of them laughed and splashed about, picked up long streamers of shiny brown bladder-wrack and ran with it along the edge. Ephraim had brought his father's garden spade with him, his ambition to build a magnificent sand-castle.

'It'll be the biggest one ever made in Winterton,' he boasted.

They all swung into action, took turns with the spade or used their hands, with a great deal of flinging about of sand.

'Have a care,' exclaimed Lucy. 'You'll bury Miss Dunthorne if you keep on like that.'

'Sorry, miss,' they called out. But they were too excited to stop. Sarah moved aside rather than spoil their fun. The castle grew quite tall — a cone shape, the boys patted it, flattened the top, made battlements, all so busy and happy until Sarah asked — 'Anyone hungry?'

The castle builders stopped at once. The girls, who had been searching for objects to decorate the castle walls, dropped the precious items.

There was no need to repeat the question. They all scrambled back up the beach to where the hamper had been left in shady spot. Sandy hands were wiped on pinafores that were already crumpled and grubby. Lucy took the jug and went to fetch cold water to mix up the barley-water drink. Sarah handed out the contents of the hamper and was delighted when Emily reached up eagerly for her share.

Mrs Motts watched with a smile. 'I do believe the sea air has done her good already,' she said. 'I can never thank you enough, miss, doin' all this fer us.'

Sarah brushed her thanks aside. 'You must sit down and have something to eat, too. And here comes Lucy — who's for a mug of lemon barley?'

'Me — me — ' was the chorus.

There was scarcely a crumb left to be packed back into the hamper when they'd finished and then it was back down to the beach, to the digging and paddling. They watched the fishermen bringing in their boats, rowing as close to the shore as possible, then leaping off and manhandling them up on to the sand. Ephraim, John and Charlie wanted to help, pushed and pulled with all their might, convinced that their efforts were essential to beach the boats safely. The fishermen unloaded baskets of silvery fish. The sleeves of hand-knitted navy jerseys were rolled up, revealing brawny arms. They lifted the baskets on to horse-drawn carts, to be taken to shops or sold around the houses.

All the children were playing happily. Sarah wandered a short distance along the beach, away from the family. She liked them, but now she preferred to be on her own. Her thoughts were far away as she paddled across a short stretch of water — it wasn't deep, barely reached her calves — and out on to a sandbank. She strolled along, happy in the tranquillity of the scene. It reminded her of childhood days, not so long ago, when Papa had piled his young family into his buggy and driven over to Lone Pine Beach on the southern shore of Lake Ontario.

Yet it was totally different here, a village whose history went back for centuries; the ancient church with the high tower served as a beacon on stormy nights. On Lone Pine Beach there was virtually no sign of civilization, it was an uninhabited bay, backed by a great dark forest. Only the vast expanse of water, the fact that Lake Ontario stretched away to the horizon, just as the North Sea did, made them seem similar.

The soft sand oozed through her toes; she made patterns with it, young enough to amuse herself with such inconsequential idiocy. She twizzled around, wishing she could recapture the carefree spirit of youth

— but reality intruded. Those days had gone for ever. Those reports in *The Times* were proof of that. She wandered on, trying to see into the future — imagined Grandmama reading of Corinne's elopement. Was there really going to be war? Thank goodness she would soon be leaving England and on her way back to America —

'Miss. Oh, Miss!' A shrill voice pierced her thoughts.

It was Lucy, running towards her — waving wildly — shouting at the top of her voice.

'Miss — come back. Tide's coming in — '

Sarah looked around her. The sandbank was barely half the size it had been and the sea was swirling in fast. A wide stretch of water lay between her and the beach. Her sandbank had become an island, and was getting smaller with every passing minute. She must waste no more time.

She gathered her skirts up high and began to wade for the shore. The sand sloped down, each step brought the swirling water higher up her legs, over her knees, up to her thighs. An incoming wave splashed up higher, wetting her gown.

'Keep a-coming, miss,' Lucy called. 'I'll meet you.'

Lucy had thrown aside her overskirt and bundling her petticoat up high began to walk into the water. Her hand outstretched.

'Keep a comin', miss.'

Sarah trudged steadily on — her skirts hampered her, the water was now up to her waist. Waves buffeted her. She feared they would knock her over. If it became any deeper, the waves would break over her head.

'Give me your hand,' Lucy shrieked.

She tried. 'I can't reach — '

'You can — you must. Come on!'

The sand slipped under her feet, but just then Lucy's hand caught hold of hers. It steadied her. Together they fought their way back to the beach.

She sank down on the blessed safety of the sand.

'Thank goodness you came along when you did.'

'I nearly had a fit when I saw you out there on the sandbank! I should have told you about the tides here, but I just never thought as how you'd go wandering away like that.'

Lucy was crying. She'd been more frightened than Sarah. She hastily pulled on her skirt, and stepped out of her wet petticoat. 'We must get you home and changed straight away, miss.'

'Don't worry, Lucy. No harm done. I don't want to cut the outing short.'

She was interrupted by a strong, masculine voice. Wrenningham was striding along the beach. 'What the hell's going on?' he demanded.

'It's all right,' Sarah assured him. She scrambled to her feet.

'You're soaked!'

That was so obvious she did not answer him.

She said, 'Lucy, will you find the coachman, please?'

'Yes, miss.' Lucy bobbed a quick curtsy to her and another even quicker one to Wrenningham and hurried away along the beach, her wet petticoat in her hand.

'You're not going anywhere in a public conveyance in that state,' the earl said.

His eyes swept over her. Sarah was conscious that her dress was soaked right up to her armpits. The thin cotton material clung to her, rendered almost transparent by the wet. She tried to brush away the sand that stuck to the material, but every movement only served to make her look even more messed up.

'You look like a pot-girl at a country inn,' he growled.

'Would you rather I had drowned?' she snapped.

'I had rather you'd had the sense not to go

out there in the first place when the tide is coming in.'

'How was I to know? I've never been here before.'

'Precisely. When you are in a strange place, it is all the more necessary to move with caution. In particular, never trifle with something as powerful as the sea.'

'I shall certainly not do so again.' She began to walk back to where she had left the Motts family, but was hampered by her wet garments, skirts clinging to her legs. A gust of wind whipped her hair loose. She struggled between trying to pin it back, and shaking out her clinging skirts. Wrenningham offered his arm, but she chose to ignore it.

'Do not add to your foolishness by rejecting my assistance,' he said. 'Or I shall put my arm around your waist to steady you.'

That left her no alternative. She rested her hand lightly on his, but he grasped it and tucked it closer, so that she was indeed supported by his strength.

With every step her skirt clung wetly around her legs, outlining the lines of her long slender thighs. She would have been able to compose herself, had she not noticed Wrenningham's eyes constantly swept down in that direction.

It made her tone rather sharp, as she asked,

'What brings you here, my lord? I understood you were to make a tour of inspection of your estate.'

'And so I did, Sarah. But when I saw you in the hired wagonette, I felt it my duty to see that you came to no harm. It's just as well I turned back.'

'There was no need for you to trouble yourself.'

'I disagree. And, apart from this — er — misadventure' — another undisguised examination of the outline of her nether limbs — 'you owe me an explanation.'

'On what point, may I ask?'

'Simply this — I am troubled that a guest of mine should have such a low opinion of me as to prefer the company of any rag, tag and bobtail, rather than accompany me.'

'It is not my habit to cancel engagements seriously entered into just because another offer has been made to me,' she replied stiffly.

'Nor would I expect you to. However, it would have been more honest if you had told me the reason for my rejection. And as if that was not insult enough, why hire a stranger to drive you?'

'I did not feel I had any right to impose further upon your generosity.'

'Humph!' he interrupted angrily. 'Do you think me so mean-spirited as to refuse the loan of my wagonette? Did it not occur to you that I would have been much less concerned had I known you were in the care of my own servants?'

'I did not intend to annoy you, sir — '

'I'm glad to hear it.' His voice remained stiff.

Sarah felt out of her depth, as she did so often with this enigmatic man. Was it his pride that was wounded? Or was it because she had preferred the company of Lucy and her family to his? She did not really believe that could be true. Perhaps she had inadvertently broken some protocol. Sometimes life in high society was a mystery to her.

They walked back along the beach to where Mrs Motts and the children were huddled in a little knot, drawn close together, the youngest ones clinging to Mrs Motts's skirts. They had seen what had happened and were upset. Lucy was making her way up to the road, John at her side, following instructions to call the coachman ready for the return journey.

Sarah waved her hand to reassure them and, as soon as she was close enough, called out, 'I'm perfectly all right. Please don't concern yourselves about me.'

'Oh, miss — it might have been so terrible.'

'But it wasn't,' Sarah laughed. 'I'm

perfectly all right — apart from being soaked to the skin.'

'I blame myself — '

'For mercy's sake, you mustn't do that, Mrs Motts. It wasn't anybody's fault, and anyway there's no harm done. Just another lesson I've learned.'

'I hope you take it to heart,' said Wrenningham. 'Come, Sarah. One of the lads is holding my horse, just up there by the sea wall.'

She pulled her hand from his arm. 'The wagonette will be here presently.'

'Sarah, you cannot be allowed to travel in a public conveyance.'

'It is not a public conveyance,' she said. 'I hired it privately.'

'That makes no difference. I will not permit you to make an exhibition of yourself by riding along the public highway looking like a half-drowned stray cat.'

'At least that is slightly less objectionable than your previous description of me.' Her tone was icy.

He laughed — and that infuriated her.

'You will ride with me, Sarah.'

'I shall be observed even more closely if I ride with you, sir.'

'I shall take you by back lanes and through the woods — we can travel all but about half a mile of the journey on my private land. Come.'

It was not a prospect that comforted Sarah — in fact, it caused her heart to quicken quite alarmingly. He was exerting strong pressure to impel her to move in the direction he wished. Short of struggling, there was no escape with Mrs Motts and her children watching and listening!

'You should go with his lordship,' counselled Mrs Motts. 'You could catch your death of cold in those wet clothes.'

Sarah gave up. 'Perhaps you are right, Mrs Motts. But please don't feel you have to hurry away. The wagonette is hired for the whole day.'

'Very kind of you, but it's high time we set off for home,' Mrs Motts spoke with quiet dignity. 'And I'd just like to say how greatly the children have enjoyed themselves — and Lucy and I have too. We've never had a day like it in our lives.'

'It's given me real pleasure to have your company, Mrs Motts — and that of all your children.'

She glanced at Wrenningham, and noticed his right eyebrow shoot up superciliously.

'Ready?' he asked languidly.

'Not quite.'

'If you don't move soon,' threatened

Wrenningham, 'I shall carry you.'

Sarah had no intention of allowing him to do that.

'Goodbye, Mrs Motts — goodbye, children.'

'Three cheers for Miss Dunthorne,' shouted Ephraim. 'Hip-hip — ' The hooray that went up from the Mottses scattered the seagulls wheeling overhead.

Holding tightly to Sarah's hand, Wrenningham strode up the wooden ramp from the beach to the track by the sea wall. Charlie was holding Sabre, and tipped up his fingers respectfully to his forehead as the earl approached. Wrenningham wasted no more time on words; he caught hold of Sarah and tossed her up on to the mighty animal's withers with as little ceremony as if she had been a sack of corn. He took the reins from the lad, threw down a coin, then sprang into the saddle behind Sarah.

One word from his master and Sabre sprang forward, hooves clattering on the cobbled way, powerful haunches driving him up the slope, making light of the weight upon his back. Sarah grasped the thick mane, and held on, her body moving with the animal — and coming into contact with Wrenningham in a way that she would have preferred to avoid.

She was riding side-saddle in front of him. His arms were around her as he held the reins — did they need to be so close? She dared not turn her head to look at him — his face would be too near, his eyes too directly in line with hers.

Even more discomforting was her awareness of the sensuality and sinewy strength of his thighs, accentuated by the rhythmic canter of the horse. She shifted her position.

'Keep still,' he ordered. 'You're perfectly safe in that position.'

She froze. Did he really imagine it had been the fear of falling that had caused her to move? Nevertheless she obeyed his instruction.

9

The big, black stallion carried both Wrenningham and Sarah, effortlessly, along the
village street. People stared as they passed by,
women and girls curtsied and men and boys
bowed or lifted their hats. The earl was
known to all. Their appearance would arouse
speculation and gossip. Wrenningham, she
guessed, would not give a damn — he set
himself far above any criticism. Presently they
left the public road and entered a private
bridle-way that was part of the Ashingby
estate. It was narrow and rutted, bordered by
high hedges. The perfume of May blossom
enveloped them, dainty stitchworts and other
wild flowers lifted their heads. Presently the
track entered a wood, the ground carpeted
by years of fallen leaves, clumps of
primroses beneath the coppiced hazel
bushes. In other circumstances Sarah would
have been enchanted.

The track narrowed. Wrenningham reined
in, slowed the horse until it was merely
ambling along. The trees closed around them.
It was late afternoon and quite deserted, even
the wood-cutters and foresters had returned

to their homes. Only the soughing of the light wind in the trees and the swish of dead leaves beneath Sabre's feet, disturbed the silence.

In the loneliness and the beauty of the place Sarah held herself very still. She was acutely conscious of the earl, who sat so proud and straight in the saddle behind her. The peace of the ancient woodland increased her awareness of how closely her body was in contact with his. She had not ridden in this manner since she'd been a child, taken out by her Papa — and then the physical nearness had been an innocent, loving joy. She had never before felt such disturbing sensations as were coursing through her, awakening a vivid memory of how he had kissed her. In this situation — could she trust him? Intuition — that primitive, feminine part of her — told her that his mood had changed. Initially, he had seemed to be anxious to get her back to the Hall with the greatest possible speed. Since they had entered the wood, that urgency had diminished.

Slowly they progressed. His arm tightened, pulling her pliant young body closer. She felt his breath warm on the nape of her neck. She'd left her hat lying on the sand and was bare-headed, her hair untidy — it had to be, for she had not combed it since she left that morning.

'Sarah.' His voice was soft, the word whispered in her ear, seductive as a caress. She froze. She did not trust him — or herself.

'Sarah.' Again, just her name.

'Yes?'

'Do you realize how enchanting you are?'

She tossed her head. 'And I look like a — a' — she sought to remember what he had called her — 'like a pot-girl at a country inn.'

'Such wenches can be bewitching.' His voice held a chuckle.

He was enjoying himself. She was at his mercy, to tease or toy with. The horse came to a standstill in a leafy glade, a clearing among the trees where grass grew thick and luscious, and was intertwined by the plant they called lady's bedstraw. The animal lowered its head; she heard its teeth tear at the grass. Wrenningham allowed it to graze, gathering both reins loosely into one hand. To her consternation, whilst his right arm still supported her back, his free hand dropped to rest on her knee. She stiffened, drew in a sharp breath.

Then again he kissed her. He had only to lean forward fractionally and his lips brushed her neck, just below the hairline. She felt a sense of panic at the excitement that swept over her. His mouth nuzzled in behind her ear — she must not permit him to behave so.

What would he do next! Whatever he had in mind — she must stop him. She moved her head sharply — tossing it away from him, but seated as she was, side-saddle on the horse, her movements were restricted. Whether by design or accident she could not be sure, but when she attempted to wrench herself free from those beguilingly nibbling lips, Wrenningham moved his arm. Now it was no longer encircling her supportively and to her dismay, far from moving away from him, as she had intended, Sarah found herself leaning backwards — gazing up at him.

It was a moment before she could realize how she had arrived in such a vulnerable, almost wanton position. Fury took hold of her as she noticed his eyes dancing with wicked mischief, mocking her surprise. Then, with slow deliberation, he leaned over, drew her closer into his arms again. Like a rabbit mesmerized by a stoat she lay still, watching as his face came nearer to hers, his eyes holding her gaze and she read in them a strength of desire such as she had never known existed. Then his lips descended on hers — and her own emotions played havoc with her senses.

What was she doing? How could she lie there so wantonly, allowing him to make use of her in this way? Such behaviour would be indecorous even if she had consented to become his wife. Surely no real gentleman would subject a young lady to such treatment. His conduct was totally reprehensible.

Then she became aware that his hand which rested with such intimate impertinence upon her knee — was moving, that it was making a slow, caressing movement. She felt a sense of panic. She would not be used lightly in this manner. She struggled to get away from him.

Her wriggling, twisting movements disturbed Sabre. The spirited horse was immediately restive, threw up its head, pranced around. Fearful of being tossed off, Sarah was clinging to the very man from whom she had been trying to escape. She need not have worried. Almost immediately, Wrenningham had the animal under control. Collecting the reins together in his hands, thrusting Sarah into an upright position as he did so, he set the animal ambling on again, at a gentle pace.

Sarah, recovering from her fright, remained angry. 'My lord, it was unforgivable of you to use me so.'

He did not reply immediately. 'Then I would be wasting my breath if I apologized.' It was a statement rather than a question.

'Most definitely!' she snapped.

'I am relieved to hear it, because I had no intention of doing so.' His voice was low and beguilingly gentle. 'You are deucedly provocative at times.'

His calm manner increased her exasperation. 'Sir, you are intolerable. The sooner I am rid of your company, the better pleased I shall be.'

'That wish will soon be granted. I depart for London tomorrow. I shall be recalled to my regiment in the near future.'

A shiver ran over Sarah. The mention of war made her blood run cold. She felt inadequate to say anything. Ridiculously she wanted to wish him well, yet could not bring herself to say the words. A short time thereafter, they were within sight of the Hall.

He rode into the stable-yard, a lad came forward to hold the horse, and the earl sprang off its back. He raised his arms to assist Sarah to dismount.

He held her but briefly, looking quite seriously into her eyes as he did so.

'I shall remember this day, Sarah,' he said. 'And especially I shall cherish the vision of you with your gown dampened and near transparent.'

Her temper flared again. 'If you were a

gentleman, sir, you would not mention such a thing!'

'Ah, but I am a soldier. It helps me to keep my sanity if I carry with me memories of beauty.'

'Sir, do not heap shame upon me!' she murmured.

'That was not my intention,' he answered, evenly. 'But how shall I be able to banish such a picture, especially should it spring into my mind on the eve of battle?'

Whatever she said he seemed determined to twist to his advantage. She could stand no more of it. She picked up her skirts, ran through the nearest door and found herself in a long, dark passage where she had never been before.

'Wait. I'll show you the way.' Wrenningham had followed her. 'I'll tell the staff to send up a bath and hot water.'

He was back almost immediately. 'These back stairs will take us up to the servants' landing.'

Sarah followed along a maze of uncarpeted ill-lit passages — up a wide stair. At the top, a figure seemed to glide towards them, ghost-like in the gloom. Then Sarah recognized the quite substantial figure of Smithie, Lady MacKenna's maid.

Smithie looked startled — indeed scandalized, as she drew aside to allow them to pass, bobbing the regulation curtsy, her gaze lingering on Sarah. Wrenningham nodded curtly, as he strode on. 'Through that door and we shall be in the family rooms,' he said.

Then Sarah recognized where she was. He opened the door of her bedroom and ushered her through.

'Your bath should be up presently,' he said, as he closed the door.

In her room she caught sight of herself in the full-length, giltframed mirror. Smithie's expression had betrayed just what she had thought — and who could blame her! This, too, was how Wrenningham had seen her, how he had said he would remember her. His words burned in her mind — provocative, he had called her. Her hair was wind-blown, twisting in unruly chestnut curls around her face, falling from its pins. She had made the gingham gown eighteen months previously, before her figure had fully developed and it was now rather tight over the bust. She had never imagined that such a simple gown might actually be rather revealing. She tore it off, and threw it on the floor. Yet she was thankful she had not worn any of the beautiful gowns Grandmama had insisted on having made for her, for they would have been ruined.

A discreet knock on the door heralded the

arrival of the bath. Two girls spread a mat on the floor, placing on it a large circular bath tub. Footmen carried in cans of water and withdrew. One of the maids poured water into the bath, whilst the other assisted Sarah to remove the remainder of her clothes, and step into the warm water. She sat down with her knees almost up to her chest, whilst the girls soaped and rinsed her. It was more of an ordeal than a pleasure, but nice to feel clean and fresh as she was vigorously towelled dry. They were both shy and had little to say, even though Sarah tried to put them at their ease as they handed her a clean petticoat and laid out the gown of her choice. Then there was the business of scooping the water from the bath into buckets, and carrying all away. Sarah thought of the long trek downstairs and along passages to the yard where the buckets could be emptied. As they left she handed the gingham gown to the smaller of the two.

'You may keep this; it should fit you — just needs a wash.'

'Thank you very much, my lady.'

Feeling clean and tidy again, Sarah seated herself by the window and picked up a book. She read for about half an hour, then, following a light tap on the door Lucy hurried in.

'Oh, miss, I'm ever so sorry, I came as

quick as I could — that old wagonette seemed as slow as a snail.'

Sarah seated herself at the dressing-table, and Lucy set to work with brush and comb and pins, but she looked anxious — almost nervous — quite unlike her usual cheery self. Sarah couldn't understand it.

'Did you have any trouble on the way back, Lucy?'

'No, miss. It was a wonderful day! I can't thank you enough — '

'I've been thanked quite enough already, Lucy,' Sarah said drily. 'We've all had a good day, and I hope we're all the better for it. So what's the matter, Lucy?'

'It was his lordship, miss. He looked so cross — and I thought you were upset too.'

'Perhaps I was, but certainly not with you, Lucy.'

'Thank you, miss. But then they say as how you'll be leavin' — '

Sarah had a sharp stab of conscience. She hadn't given a thought to what would happen to Lucy when she was sent back to America. She had assumed that the maid would remain in the household, but in truth Grandmama would have no further use for her.

'That's true, Lucy.' She sighed. 'I'm afraid Lady MacKenna is most displeased with me.

You must have heard about Miss Corinne's elopement?'

'Well, yes. We all know about that.' Lucy nodded her head emphatically. 'Beavers, the coachman, was full of it. Is that why Lady MacKenna is cross with you?'

'That — and other things! I'm to be sent back to America on the next available boat.'

Lucy paused in the act of trying to fix an errant curl over her mistress's ear. Sarah looked up, her maid's reflection stared wild-eyed from the mirror, consternation written all over the pretty young countenance that gazed back.

'That's what I heard, miss. That's what upset me — and I was sure that taking us out today made things worse — for me as well as for you.'

'No,' Sarah said. 'Having this lovely outing today with you and your family did me a great deal of good. It's helped me to get things into perspective. Although I'm deeply sorry that I've upset my dear grandmama, I shall now return home earlier than planned and I really do not mind that at all.'

'Haven't you been happy here, miss?' Lucy asked.

'Oh, yes. It's been wonderful. I shall never forget London and Ashingby, and in spite of everything I love my grandmama very dearly, and I shall be sorry to leave her.'

She sat quietly for a moment. Lucy put the finishing touches to Sarah's coiffeur. When it was done Sarah turned to her.

'Lucy, will you come with me to America?'

'Me, miss? Oh, I don't know as I'd like that.'

'It's a wonderful country — and you'd be with me.'

'Do you mean that, miss? Could I really stay with you?'

'Yes, of course. For ever, if you wanted to.'

'Promise? 'Course if I go, I wouldn't know no one else there, would I?'

'I understand how you feel, Lucy. It is a big step to take, and you must talk it over with your parents. Please tell them also that I should very much like to have your company and I give my word that you shall stay with me, and under my protection, for as long as you wish,' Sarah vowed solemnly.

'All right then, miss. I'll come. For I really wouldn't want to start all over again with a new mistress. I'm sure my ma and pa will look on it as a good opportunity.'

'You'll like it in Cassie's Rock — and you'll just love my mama and papa. If you want to come to England, you just say so, and I'll pay your fare and see you on to the next boat.'

'Then I'll give it a try, miss,' Lucy said with a smile.

A knock on the door interrupted them.

It was Smithie. 'Lady MacKenna's compliments, miss, and would you step along to her room?'

The maid's expression left Sarah in no doubt that she had informed her grandmama of the meeting on the back stairs. Nothing could make matters worse however, so she felt perfectly calm as she stood up.

'Thank you, Smithie.'

She looked at herself in the long mirror — how different she looked now, compared to the scarecrow state she'd been in when she arrived home in the wet and dirty gingham dress!

Rich chestnut curls framed her forehead with ringlets held back by blue ribbons in the Greek style. Her gown, of white satin, with short puffed sleeves, was cut in the Empire line, high-waisted, and threaded with ribbons to match those in her hair. Satisfied that she was immaculate from top to toe, Sarah made her way along the wide corridor. The door of her grandmama's room was opened before she had time to knock. Smithie had obviously been listening for her approach, quiet though it had been. The maid announced her and left the room, closing the door behind her.

Lady MacKenna was seated in a high-backed chair by the window. She was also in full evening attire, though the style she adhered to was that of ten years earlier. Her hair was piled high and decorated with ostrich feathers, her gown richly embroidered, full skirt, supported on wide side-hoops, carefully spread out around her. She surveyed Sarah with displeasure.

'Good evening, Grandmama.' Sarah executed her most elegant curtsy.

Grandmama's expression did not soften. 'What's this you've been up to, now, gel?'

Since she had left a note for her grandmama to apprise her of the outing, Sarah assumed she had no need to explain that.

'I had a small mishap, Grandmama, at the seaside — there was no harm done.'

'I was shocked to read the note you left for me — gallivanting around the countryside in a hired wagonette! That is not the way I expect a granddaughter of mine to behave.'

'But Grandmama, Lucy's little sister has been so ill, and I thought an outing would be beneficial to her. It never occurred to me that you would disapprove.'

'Visiting the poor to bestow largesse is one thing; riding about in a wagon with a load of noisy children is quite another.'

'My mama often told me how greatly she enjoyed picnics when she was a child — and truly we were not really noisy.'

'I would have forbidden it, had I known in advance. However, there is one point which I do not understand. What part did Harry play in this escapade?'

A flash of interest lit those bright black eyes — Sarah read a tinge of hope — did she think even yet that a marriage might be arranged?

'Wrenningham came upon us purely by chance. I'd walked out on to a sandbank, not realizing that the tide was coming in.'

'Oh, my dear, you might have been drowned!'

Sarah was heartened to hear the involuntary endearment.

'Lucy came to my aid, but I had to wade back to the beach. My gown was quite wet and Wrenningham insisted that I ride back with him.'

'Is that all?' Her disappointment showed.

'Yes, Grandmama.'

'You were alone with him, Sarah. Did it not occur to you that you might have made use of such an opportunity to make amends for your previous behaviour?'

Sarah lifted her head proudly. 'If you are referring to the earl's previous proposal, Grandmama, you must know that nothing will change my mind — nor, I believe, would that gentleman ever wish that I should.'

'As stubborn as your mama. What I've done to deserve such dolts as offspring, I shall never understand. You'll never have such an opportunity again — you know that, don't you?'

'As you say, Grandmama,' Sarah said meekly.

'Well, it's too late now. I've done my best for you — and it's all been thrown back in my face. Harry's leaving at dawn tomorrow, driving his curricle. We shall travel at a more sedate pace, in my carriage,' Lady MacKenna continued. 'Now, help me to my feet, Sarah. Let us go down and join Harry for dinner. And for goodness sake, make it a sociable, civilized evening.'

'Yes, Grandmama.'

It was easy to keep that promise, for it might well be the last time she would ever see him.

10

' 'Pon my soul — I don't know which of you two gals is the more addlebrained!' expostulated Lady MacKenna.

It was two days since they had returned to Lady MacKenna's London house, and the Honourable Mrs Corinne Thackstone had been announced by the butler. Sarah was feeling desperately unhappy. The journey had been tedious in the extreme; she had lost all joy in routs and balls, and knew a loneliness more intense than she had ever experienced before.

Corinne sauntered languidly into the withdrawing-room, her ungloved hand ostentatiously displaying both wedding and engagement rings. Sarah leapt to her feet and rushed over to her with outstretched arms. 'Corinne! I've been thinking about you so much! Did you meet any trouble on the way to Gretna?'

'None whatsoever — except the journey took us four days, because the weather was appalling. I do not think I could have borne it but for the constant attention and support my dear Forbes gave me.'

'I just hope he maintains such consideration,' Lady Turley's voice was laden with doubt.

'Oh, but he does. I know you think our marriage will end in disaster, but we are determined to prove you wrong.'

'And I'm sure you will,' said Sarah.

'It was nearly midnight when we arrived at the Marriage Inn,' Corinne continued.

'Whatever did you do at that time of night?' Sarah asked.

'The postillion managed to wake up the innkeeper and he came downstairs and let us in. He was still wearing his night cap and he looked so funny.' She chuckled at the memory. 'He rushed off to find someone who knew how to marry us and a big country gentleman came in, and he wasn't properly dressed at all and he had such a strong Scottish accent I hardly knew what he was saying.'

'Disgraceful!' Interjected Lady Turley.

'Forbes has rented a charming little house for us, not far from here. He is the most attentive of husbands.' Corinne tossed her golden ringlets and pouted her comely lips in the direction of Lady Turley.

'Hmmph!' said Lady Turley. 'The honeymoon period! It will be a different matter when the bills start arriving!'

'You made considerable bother for everyone,' Lady MacKenna told Corinne. 'Not to mention compromising Sarah.'

'Sarah? Compromised?' Corinne was aghast.

'Sarah had to remain at the inn. Harry was there also, and they were seen, late at night!'

'How terrible! Can he not do something to make amends?'

'The earl did the honourable thing,' said Lady Turley. 'He asked for her hand in marriage.'

Corinne's face broke into a delighted smile. 'That's wonderful!'

Sarah was shocked at her friend's attitude. Was this the same young lady who had denounced her cousin so often? Corinne — who had called Wrenningham monstrously hard, impossible to please! She was about to remind Corinne of this when another voice rang out, loud and clear.

'What is so wonderful?' Wrenningham advanced into the room. He was clad in full regimentals, his black gold-trimmed hat under his arm. Corinne sped towards him, threw herself into his arms exclaiming, 'Why that you are to marry Sarah!'

Her headlong rush obliged him to catch her, but he took hold of her shoulders, and moved her aside. 'I think you must have heard only part of the story,' he told her coldly. 'There is no truth whatsoever in that assertion. As for you, madam, your life is now entirely your own. I have done my best for you. You must now look to your husband for advice and support.'

'I was about to explain — ' Sarah began.

'There is no need to go over the sordid details,' said the earl. He waved one shapely hand, brushing the matter aside as of no consequence, making her feel demeaned by his attitude.

Turning away from both Corinne and Sarah, Wrenningham advanced across the room towards the sofa where Lady MacKenna and Lady Turley were seated, Primrose so upright, thin almost to the point of emaciation, Beatrix slumped, plumply shapeless. Different not only in appearance, but in many characteristics also, they had remained close friends for decades.

He kissed their hands, then said, 'I fear this must be a brief visit. I shall shortly be leaving, to rejoin my regiment.'

'You are returning to Spain — to the Peninsular?' asked Lady MacKenna.

'No. That is what I expected, but I have orders to take up my duties in the Canadian Colonies of North America.'

Sarah gasped. 'Then I must return home as soon as possible.'

'But the war with the American colonies was over long ago, was it not?' queried Lady Turley.

An indulgent smile lightened Wrenningham's face. 'You are quite right, dear lady. It is almost twenty years since we granted independence to the American states, but they are not content.'

Both ladies murmured regret. Then Lady MacKenna said, 'I have hesitated to make arrangements for Sarah's return passage only because she has no chaperon for the voyage. I wonder, Harry, would it be possible for Sarah to travel on the same ship as you? It would be most improper for her to travel alone.'

'My maid, Lucy Motts, has agreed to accompany me,' Sarah said.

'Naturally. But that is no protection for a young lady. I should feel much happier if Sarah could travel under your protection, Harry.'

'Oh, no, Grandmama!' Sarah breathed the exclamation of horror.

'Be quiet, miss. It's for your own good.' Lady MacKenna waved Sarah's objections aside.

He turned deliberately and looked at her. She knew her displeasure at the prospect must show on her features. It infuriated her when a smile lifted one corner of his mouth.

'Grandmama, you mustn't trouble Lord Wrenningham.' She might just as well have stayed silent.

His eyes flashed a message that did nothing to reassure her. To Lady MacKenna, he said, 'I shall make the arrangements immediately — the ship sails in four days. Now I must take my leave of you.' He kissed the hands of each of the ladies, and of Corinne also, as if she was a mere acquaintance.

As he raised Sarah's hand to his lips, he said, 'I believe the voyage takes six or seven weeks — time to get to know each other considerably better.'

A shiver ran over her. He was accustomed to having his own way, and he would have considerable power over her on the ship. But since she wanted to return home, she had no alternative but to travel on the same ship as Wrenningham.

★ ★ ★

The Expeditious sailed out of Portsmouth harbour on a fine sunny morning in late June in that fateful year of 1812. Sarah stood by the bulwark looking back as the green landscape of southern England grew steadily more and more distant. Her feelings were mixed. She would never forget those past five months — though in many ways she wished that she could.

She had arrived with a warm, open heart and, at her first meeting with her indomitable grandmama, a wonderful rapport had sprung up between them. She would always cherish the happy, loving relationship that had existed in those early months, and profoundly regretted that her visit had ended with so much bitterness.

Her refusal to become betrothed to Wrenningham had angered the old lady beyond forgiveness. Equally, nothing would make Sarah change her mind. Perhaps both grandmother and granddaughter were too much alike, both strong and wilful.

Grandmama had written a letter to Sarah's parents, explaining the circumstances of her disgrace and hasty return. She had read it out to Sarah before sealing it, but had entrusted her to deliver the missive in person. Grandmama had stated her opinions strongly and Sarah knew her parents would be distressed to read it. Undoubtedly her unexpected homecoming would be difficult, not least because she would have to admit that in all probability neither Monica nor any of the boys would be invited to London.

The sound of a sob jerked Sarah's thoughts away from herself, reminding her she was not alone. Lucy Motts stood beside her with tears streaming down her face.

'Please don't cry, Lucy,' Sarah appealed. 'I promise you shall not come to any harm, indeed there are better prospects for many people in America than there are in England.'

'So I've been told, miss,' Lucy muttered, miserably. 'But now it's time to go, I can't help feeling it a bit. I've never been so far from my home and my family before.'

'I know, Lucy, dear. You're bound to be homesick at first. I was, when I first came to stay with Lady MacKenna.'

'You was, miss?' Lucy looked at Sarah with damp, disbelieving eyes.

'It's true. It made no difference that I was in such luxury as I had never believed existed. I was miserable because everything was so strange — and I missed my family so much. I felt quite sick for a short time.'

'Well I never!' exclaimed Lucy, so intrigued by this information that, momentarily, she forgot her own sorrow.

'It's true. Then I really got to like living in England. Now I believe I could live just as happily in either country.'

The words came out without thought, but it was true, there had been much that she'd liked both in London and the countryside. She smiled encouragingly.

'I'm sure you'll come to feel the same way, Lucy, and if you're not happy in America you shall return quite soon. I promise you that.'

'Thank you, miss. I'll do my best.' Lucy blew her nose and dried her eyes. She seemed comforted.

Sarah glanced around the ship, watching the sailors, shinning up the masts, heaving on ropes, springing to obey the orders that were barked out, one after the other. Whistles blew. The ship creaked and shuddered, as if it was reluctant to take another battering from the Atlantic waves. But it had been the same when she had made the voyage to England and they had arrived safely.

Most of the passengers were travelling below decks, closepacked into the steerage accommodation, which on the voyage from America had been filled with forest timber. Now temporary partitions had been installed in which soldiers and civilian immigrants mingled together, making little units of families or friends.

Sarah and Lucy had journeyed together by coach from London, and had been met by Wrenningham when they arrived in Portsmouth. He had brought with him three soldiers who had shouldered their boxes and carried them away below somewhere, whilst the earl had escorted her aboard *The*

Expeditious. He had left Sarah and Lucy on the deck, hurriedly excusing himself to oversee the embarkation of his troops.

The sails filled and the ship began to plough along the English Channel towards the Atlantic Ocean, on the start of its long voyage. The wind tugged roughly at Sarah's hair. She clutched her light cape and, as she struggled, looked up to see Wrenningham striding along the heaving deck towards her. He appeared to be every bit as much at home on the ship as he was in the grounds of Ashingby.

'Allow me to conduct you to your cabin, Sarah,' he said, offering his arm.

Lucy followed as he led her to a low door, which he opened to reveal a short flight of steps. Holding tightly to the rail she descended, unsure where she was going for it seemed dark below after the brilliance of the sunlight. Soon her eyes became accustomed however, and almost immediately he ushered her into a small cabin.

'Your quarters,' Wrenningham said. 'A trifle cramped, but I trust you will find it sufficient for your needs. It is the best available on this ship.'

The cabin appeared to be comfortable enough, with bulkheads of dark oak and two square windows through which the sun shone, gleaming on the trunks containing their luggage which had been placed in the centre of the floor. There were two roundbacked chairs, a small table and a bunk, a spare mattress and piles of blankets.

'I shall leave so that you may settle in. I'll return later to escort you to the captain's table for dinner.'

He left, ducking as he passed through the low doorway. Sarah gazed after him for a moment. What would those coming weeks be like? He was supposed to be her protector. From experience, however, she had found that whenever she was at close quarters with him, his very presence seemed to pose a threat.

'Which gown will you wear this evening, miss?'

Sarah shrugged. What did it matter? She had no wish to dress up for the sake of Wrenningham, but in deference to the captain and the other passengers she decided to wear one of her newest and most becoming gowns. It was of palest apple green, in a soft satin material, with a low, wide neckline and clung from a band immediately beneath her bosom, outlining her graceful figure.

Lucy dressed her hair in a mass of curls at the front, neatly coiled on the crown, and artfully twisted tiny tendrils of ringlets around her face.

She had been ready only a few minutes before there was a light tap on the door. The earl stooped to enter, then looked up, their eyes met and the old challenge crackled in the air between them. The cabin was filled immediately with the vibrancy of his personality. His thin features remained unsmiling.

'Dinner is about to be served,' he said. He ushered her through the door ahead of him. As she passed he said softly, 'My fellow officers will be enchanted to meet you. And the lady passengers will turn green with envy.'

'Am I overdressed?' she asked.

'Hardly that,' he said. His eyes were on the *décolletage* of her very revealing gown.

She was carrying a light shawl and covered her embarrassment by slipping it around her shoulders.

Several officers had already gathered in the wardroom. The scarlet of dress uniforms gave a festive air to the dark-panelled room. Wrenningham and Sarah were the last to arrive and their entrance caused a considerable stir.

There were four other cabin passengers — a middle-aged couple, the lady's gown lavishly decorated with frills and glittering jewellery, and two single ladies both of whom were in their early thirties. Their gowns, one of puce-coloured cotton and the other of a dull fawn, high-necked and long-sleeved, had obviously been chosen more for practicality than for fashion.

Sarah had the uncomfortable feeling that far from being green with envy, as Wrenningham had suggested, the ladies viewed her gown with scandalized eyes. Defiantly she allowed the shawl to slip from her shoulders.

The earl introduced her to the master of the ship, Mr Clibbert, a grey-haired, bearded man in his mid-fifties.

'Welcome aboard, Miss Dunthorne.' The warmth of his voice matched his words. His first and second mates were brothers, Richard and Edward Branley. Next she was introduced to Mr and Mrs Williams, who had been living in Canada for twenty years. Successful farmers, their eldest son was now able to take over their land, which had allowed them to return to their home county of Cornwall for a visit.

'Good to see the folks, but we'll be glad to get back,' Mr Williams said.

Miss Jones and Miss Reader, were lifelong friends and shared a cabin; they hoped to find employment as teachers or governesses.

Lastly, Wrenningham introduced Sarah to his officers, who bowed low, kissed her hand, and expressed delight at her presence on board.

At table, Sarah found herself between two of Wrenningham's officers, both of whom vied for the privilege of holding her chair. A cabin boy staggered in bearing a steaming tureen of ham and pea soup.

'It is a pleasure to meet any lady friend of the colonel,' Captain Smalley remarked, a trifle cheekily, holding her gaze with boldly admiring eyes. 'I always suspected he had a dark secret in his life.'

'I have no part in the earl's life,' Sarah said firmly. 'He was dragooned by my grandmama, into acting as my chaperon for the journey.'

'I would need no dragooning, if you cared to transfer the duty, my lord,' the captain quipped.

'Regretfully, responsibilities cannot be relinquished so lightly,' Wrenningham replied laconically.

'I have no wish to be a burden to either of you,' declared Sarah. 'I am an American citizen and have learned from my earliest years to take care of myself.'

'American, eh!' Mr Williams's voice was challenging. 'One of those damned Yankees who keep casting predatory eyes over Canada.'

His tone roused Sarah's defensive spirit. 'I believe all people should be permitted to live their own lives. And that goes for our sailors too — they should never be pressed into compulsory service by the British Navy.'

'It would not be necessary if your American ships were not manned by British sailors who have deserted.'

'But then again,' Sarah said, keeping her voice quietly modulated. 'Perhaps they would not desert in such great numbers if they had better conditions.'

'You can't run a good ship with an unwilling crew,' declared the master. 'Treat the men well, pay them fair and they'll serve you loyally — that's what I've found. Ah!' He rubbed his hands with anticipation. 'Here comes the roast.'

It was a welcome diversion, for Sarah had felt herself out on a limb, her views at variance with all around her. The earl had made no attempt to enter the discussion. He was seated opposite her between Mrs Williams and the master and as she glanced at him she found him regarding her thoughtfully. She thought she read a warning in his eyes, but she was in no mood to heed it. Contrarily it made her more determined than before to stand her ground, and defend her country's good name. There was a hiatus in the conversation whilst the beef was carved and the Yorkshire pudding and vegetables served. The matter was not ended however.

'My lord.' Mrs Williams demanded Wrenningham's attention. 'Are we to understand that war is now inevitable, since you are posted to Canada?'

'There is yet hope that it may be avoided,' he replied.

'Damned Yankees,' Mr Williams exploded again. 'Stabbing England in the back! As if we haven't enough to contend with, fighting the French.'

'Let's not cross bridges before we reach them,' Wrenningham said, in a firm, calm tone. 'War has not yet been declared. If it is, we shall be ready. Meantime, I suggest we turn our thoughts to more congenial conversation.'

To Sarah's relief, even Mr and Mrs Williams allowed themselves to be diverted from the subject, for she was horrified by their belligerent attitude.

The conversation continued, and time passed pleasantly enough, but the wardroom was small and ill-ventilated. Despite the lightness of her gown, Sarah found the heat oppressive. She tried to remain composed, but the stifled feeling increased. She pushed back her chair and stood up. 'Please excuse me. It's exceeding hot in here. I must go out and breathe some cool fresh air.'

She had moved only a few steps towards the door when Wrenningham appeared at her side. 'Allow me to escort you.'

The other officers stood up. He guided her from the room, up the companionway and out on to the deck. There was a sharp chill in the air. She drew her shawl close around her shoulders and walked over to the bulwark. Leaning on its reassuring solidity she gazed across the rolling water of the night-black sea. Stars, brilliant jewels, studded the sky; the moon cast a golden beam like a beacon. Lights of other ships gleamed far away in the darkness.

'Where are we?' she asked.

'Still in the Channel. In a day or two we'll be heading westwards across the Atlantic. It's good that the stars are so clear, they help the sailors to chart our course. See — there's that old favourite, the plough.'

She followed the direction of his pointing finger. There was magic in the night, she was conscious of being at one with primitive elements that were usually held in check. They were only a short distance from land, but already the falsity and sophistication of London society had faded. It was an effect of the sea, the wind and the stars, as if part of civilization itself had been left behind.

She turned from the stars and found

Wrenningham gazing down at her, but his eyes were shielded by the darkness and she could not read his mood.

'A word of warning, Sarah,' he said. The tone of his voice was not in accord with the romantic beauty of the night. 'Take care you do not make too many enemies.'

She turned her face away from him, looking towards the sea, but not actually seeing it. 'I cannot and I will not remain silent whilst my country is denigrated so shamefully.'

'I agree that Mr Williams is not the most tactful of gentlemen,' the earl murmured, 'but he is not ill-informed. You are on a British ship and you will have to live with these people for several weeks. War is not inevitable, but it would be foolish not to face the fact that it is certainly likely. Very likely indeed.'

He was one of the enemy. The joy of the lovely night drained away. Tears started into her eyes. She dashed them aside, and lifted her head. 'I'll go to my cabin now.'

She had no wish for him to accompany her, but he followed. He opened the door of the cabin, then stood in front of her, preventing her from entering.

'Take heed of what I have said. Guard your tongue in future. If you continue to antagonize these people I cannot foresee the consequences.' He stepped aside allowing her to enter her cabin. Lucy was waiting and she derived comfort from the open honesty of her maid's pleasant, smiling face.

★　★　★

As the voyage continued, a routine of sorts was established among the passengers. Despite her outburst on that first night, Sarah was sensible enough to realize the wisdom of the instructions that Wrenningham had impressed upon her. Try as she might, she could not feel friendly warmth towards either Mr or Mrs Williams. He, in particular, continued to make outrageously provoking statements and it was only by steely will-power that she managed to stay silent, though she sometimes seethed inside. The elder of the two single ladies had the same effect upon her, though she did have some amicable conversation with Miss Reader. The army officers were rather too willing to seek out her company, especially Captain Smalley, who fancied himself as a ladies' man. His entertaining company helped to while away the long hours, and she would have been quite lonely without his attention. She was in no danger of falling in love with him and, sure his attentions were merely flirtatious, saw no harm in enjoying and responding to his light and inconsequential conversation. He had no interest in anything controversial, never joined in discussions of a serious nature, but the pleasant familiarity that developed between them, helped to pass the days.

Sarah was occasionally aware that Wrenningham was watching her and routinely he escorted her to the wardroom for dinner in the evening. She placed her hand on his arm and they walked the short distance from her cabin, sometimes in near silence, more often making cool irrelevant small talk.

Thankfully the weather was fine, and with a moderate breeze the ship was making good progress. The days passed relatively uneventfully. Captain Smalley continued to pay attentions to Sarah. Often, with her hand tucked into the crook of his arm, they would stroll around the deck, watching the sailors at work, or listening to their songs as they pumped out the bilges.

And now my boys we're outward bound,
Young girls go a-weeping,
We're outward bound to Quebec town,
Across the Western Ocean.

From time to time other vessels were sighted, names would be exchanged by means of signals, and checks taken to confirm their position. They watched the sailors fishing with hook and line and were delighted when one caught a codfish weighing almost 18 lbs. Sometimes they saw porpoises, whales and once a grampus.

They had been about ten days at sea when they sighted a British frigate. The usual signals were exchanged — but this time a grim message was added. Sarah, standing beside Captain Smalley watched as the various flags were run up and down, giving and receiving messages.

'Do you know what they say?' Sarah asked.

'I could work it out, if I bothered to read them,' he replied, lazily. 'I get more pleasure from watching the expression on your lovely face.'

She laughed dismissively, adopting a simple accent. 'Fie, Captain, the things you do say to a poor country girl!'

'Ah, if only you were!' he sighed. 'Then I'd stand a better chance of persuading you how enchanted I am by you.'

'And the more fool I'd be if I believed you!' she retorted.

'But how very much more delightful this voyage would be if now and again you were to melt into my arms — like this — '

Matching his words with action he

encircled her waist with one arm. Suddenly she found herself held close, looking up into his face and with some anxiety knew that the badinage had gone too far. He was about to kiss her.

'Let me go,' she hissed.

She turned her head away, and was relieved to see that most people were concentrating on some new message being signalled from the other ship. Only Wrenningham was looking in her direction, and for some reason that was deeply embarrassing. He strode towards them and caught hold of Captain Smalley's shoulder, pulling him round to face him.

'This is no time for foolish dalliance, Smalley — did you not read that message?'

'I say, sir — that's a bit rough, isn't it?'

Captain Smalley shook the earl's hand from his shoulder and brushed the marks of its grip from the fine material.

'There'll be rougher times to come,' snapped Wrenningham. 'The Yankees have declared war.'

'Oh, no!' Sarah gasped.

It had been expected, of course, but the shock of its actuality was so devastating that it seemed to drain her of all strength. The ship gave a lurching roll, she staggered, and would have fallen but a strong pair of arms closed around her, holding her.

11

They made steady progress westwards and were only ten days or so away from the North American Continent. Sarah was on deck when the cry came.

'Deck there!' the man in the crow's nest yelled. 'Sail Ho!'

'Where away?' shouted the officer.

'Fine on the starboard quarter.'

The officer swung his telescope round, but the ship was below the horizon, too far away for him to see.

'What do you make of her?' the officer shouted.

After what seemed a long pause, the lookout shouted back, 'She's a Yankee, sir.'

'Clear for action,' ordered the officer. 'Beat to quarters.'

The men leapt to, clearing away the clutter, ready to manhandle the guns into position and load. Cabin boys became powder monkeys, bringing up linen powder cartridges. All lamps were extinguished, galley fires dowsed, buckets of water set beside each gun, gunners wrapped bandannas around their heads and ears to deaden the percussion.

'Ninth company — prepare for action,' Wrenningham barked as slowly the square sails of the approaching ship came into view — closer and closer.

Soldiers took up their prearranged positions, hidden from view, ready to spring a surprise on the enemy. Sailors ran across the deck, rigging rattled, sails made great flapping noises, the whole ship creaked as if strained to breaking point as she came about to face the enemy.

Sarah watched the square white sails of the approaching ship — tall masts, billowing sails, shapely hull set against the backdrop of rolling, white-capped sea and clear blue sky. A thing of beauty. But as it slowly came nearer to *The Expeditious* it brought menace and terror. The second mate hustled the passengers below. 'Stay down till you're told it's clear,' he instructed.

'I'll take charge below deck,' shouted Mr Williams. 'Everyone into their cabins. That goes for you too, Miss Dunthorne. And your maid.'

No sooner were they through the door than it was pulled shut behind her and she heard a loud scraping sound outside. She turned immediately and attempted to open the door, to see what was happening but try as she might it wouldn't budge. Something or someone was preventing it from opening.

'I can't open the door,' she called out.

'Just making sure you stay in there,' Mr Williams shouted back. 'We've pushed a trunk in front and tied it to the door. There's no way you'll be able to help your damned Yankee friends.'

Sarah felt the blood drain from her face in horror.

Lucy shrieked with fear. 'Oh, miss! Don't let them do it, miss. I want to get out. We'll be drowned like kittens in a sack if the ship goes down!' Lucy grabbed hold of the door and tried to wrench it open, but it was quite useless. Sarah put her arms around the girl, understanding her terror all too clearly, for she also was fighting against a mounting panic. Her sense of injustice was intensified by the fact that Lucy had been imprisoned with her.

'Mr Williams,' she shouted. 'Mr Williams — please — won't you allow my maid out? She is not American.'

'You won't get round me that way. On no account is this door to be opened, until the battle is over,' he shouted back.

'Lucy is British.'

'The girl's your servant, isn't she?' he sneered. 'How do we know what lies you've been telling her? Or whatever you've persuaded her to do.' He was gloating in their fear. They were his prisoners. There was no way they'd be able to get out, no matter what happened. The tiny window would not open. There would be no escape: if the ship sank they would go down with it.

'You speak to Mr Williams, Lucy. Ask him to let you go, tell him I promise to stay here.'

Lucy gave up wrestling with the door and shook her head. 'No, miss. I couldn't go and leave you locked in here all on your own.'

'Please, Lucy, ask him.'

'I wouldn't lower myself,' said Lucy. 'My place is with you.'

She was determined, and Sarah could not help but admit she would be glad of Lucy's company. For both their sakes she forced a calm she was far from feeling.

The sudden, crashing, deafening sound of gunfire drove away all rational thoughts. Battle had commenced. Sarah and Lucy threw their arms around each other and cowered into a corner of the bunk. Explosion followed explosion. Sounds of splintering timber. An enormous crash!

'God help us!' screamed Lucy. 'Why did I ever leave home!'

Momentarily, Sarah was sure that the ship was about to sink. She held her breath, listened to the shouts and creaks and bangs.

The lumbering sound of guns trundled across the deck. Men's feet, crack of rifles, screech of cannon-balls.

Never had Sarah believed that the air could be filled with so much terrifying noise! It might have been easier to bear if only she had some way of knowing what was happening. Sometimes there was a slight lull, but it was always followed by more, and louder, noise. The whole ship shuddered; she and Lucy were almost thrown off the bed. Was this the end? She could see nothing from the window for the fighting was all on the other side.

Then the ship steadied. She clasped Lucy's hands, held her breath. Each of them was both taking and giving comfort to the other. Was it over?

The lull was short-lived. It was followed by a great deal of shouting, running feet, clashing metal — somehow she realized that the two vessels were locked together. She tried to imagine what was going on! Were the Americans boarding *The Expeditious*? Were Wrenningham's men swarming over the side? Was the earl leading them? She knew him well enough to guess that he would be in the thick of the fighting. She agonized for him and did not trouble to analyse why she should care.

It seemed hours since Sarah had been

hustled down and thrust into her cabin. She felt she must go mad with terror and anguish. Tears streamed down Lucy's face. 'I wish I'd never come. I never wanted to leave England. I don't want to die.'

'We're not dead yet,' Sarah said sharply. 'Nor anywhere near it. The ship's still afloat — '

Her words were drowned in a great splintering thud, as if the whole ship had been struck by some tremendous force. Surely this must be the end!

'Oh, dear Lord protect us!' Lucy beseeched.

Sarah added her heartfelt prayer; she was thinking not only of herself, but of the men in the thick of the fighting — and in particular of Wrenningham. She tried to keep all of them in her mind, impartially, but his face seemed to blot out any others. It was as if an icy claw gripped her heart as all too easily she imagined his danger.

He would be an outstanding target, a big man in his scarlet, gold-braided uniform, for so he had been dressed, impeccably correctly, when she last saw him, addressing his troops, inspiring them, just before she'd been hurried below. The ordeal had been all the more terrifying, locked in, utterly helpless, not having the least idea how the battle was going. All she could see through her cabin window was the heaving sea. Sometimes waves splashed up with such ferocity that the water broke high up over the window. Then the whole cabin was plunged into darkness. Lucy screamed. 'Oh, miss — we're going down. The ship's sinking! Lord save us. Forgive me my sins.'

It seemed as if the vessel was being dragged under the waves. Sarah, too, held her breath, clung to Lucy — until the ship righted itself. Water ran down the window in rivulets, drained away and the blessed light of day again allowed them to see.

At last the roar of guns ceased. Sarah could scarcely believe it. The quiet that followed was almost uncanny. It was not total silence, there were shouts, footsteps, sounds of things being moved. Sarah and Lucy looked at each other, not knowing what to think.

'Oh, miss, do you think it's over?'

'Let us pray that it is.'

Another moment's silence. Eyes tight shut. Each with her own thoughts.

'I hope our men have won,' breathed Lucy.

Sarah spread her hands helplessly. *Our men* Lucy had said. The words had an ironic ring for Sarah. Anyway speculation was useless.

'At least they seem to have stopped fighting.'

'Perhaps they'll let us out,' Lucy said hopefully.

'It's certainly high time we reminded them we're here.' Sarah jumped to her feet and picking up her teak-backed hairbrush began to batter the door with it.

'Open up. What's happening?' she shouted. 'Is the fighting over? — for pity's sake, open the door.'

'I dare not.' Sarah recognized the voice of Miss Reeder. 'Mr Williams says you're to be kept locked up.'

'Nonsense! Tell him to let us out immediately.'

'I'll take no orders from you.' It was Mr Williams's voice 'Our men have won the day. They've taken the Yankee ship and they're clapping the prisoners in irons. They'll do the same to you!'

'What's this?'

Sarah knew that commanding tone.

'Help. We've been locked in!'

'Who's tied this trunk to the door?' Wrenningham roared. 'Stand back whilst I cut the rope and heave the thing away.'

A moment later the door was open and he was there. Sarah had her arms around Lucy, comforting her.

'Are you all right?' the earl asked sharply.

She was horrified to see that the sleeve of his scarlet jacket was slashed, a trickle of blood ran over his hand.

'We're unharmed, my lord. We've been very frightened, especially at being locked in. But you — '

He looked down at his arm. 'That's nothing. The old wound reopened, I think. Who shut you in there?'

'It was Mr Williams's idea — because I'm American.'

Wrenningham's jaw tightened with anger. 'The blustering fool! I'll have something to say to him.'

'Is the fighting really over?' She needed reassurance.

'Aye. The Americans have surrendered. There'll be no more fighting today — just the clearing up to be done.'

Sarah breathed a sigh of relief. 'I'm going up on deck.'

'No. I forbid it! It's not a pretty sight up there.'

'I may be able to help — I promised Mr Clibbert — '

Ignoring the earl's warning, she rushed out of her cabin and hurried up the companionway. Reaching the deck she gazed around horrified by the bloody chaos of the scene. Never in her life had she seen anything so terrible: destruction, carnage and death. She felt sick at the sight.

A shattered mast from the American ship lay across the stern of *The Expeditious* with sails and rigging entangled and enveloping. Both sides had taken a heavy toll, and those men who were still on their feet were already working at full stretch, attending to the wounded, clearing up the ship and assessing the damage.

Rolling up her sleeves, Sarah hurried to the side of a man lying on the deck, one arm half severed, in a pool of his own blood. He was alive but barely conscious. Without a thought to propriety she pulled off her under-skirt. Coolly and methodically she tore the fine linen into strips and applied a tourniquet above the horrific, gaping wound. The man stirred and she spoke reassuringly.

'Don't move. You'll be all right. I'm trying to stop the bleeding.'

'Thank you, miss.'

'Hush! Try and lie still.'

'Did — did we beat the buggers?' The strength of his voice raised her hope for his survival.

'You did. The fighting's over, thank God!' She increased the pressure on the vein. 'There!' The flow of blood had lessened. 'You'll have to see the surgeon.'

'I'll be all right, miss. There's worse injured than me.'

Lucy was standing just behind her, wringing her hands in horror. 'Oh, miss, it's terrible! Terrible!' She looked as if she was about to faint.

'Don't just stand there,' Sarah snapped mercilessly. 'Fetch clean linen. My underwear — anything you can find.'

Having an order to obey helped Lucy to pull herself together. 'Tell the cabin boy to bring water,' Sarah called as the maid began to thread her way through and over the tangled mess of human bodies.

Another man nearby moaned, Sarah moved across to him. She could see at once that he was dying. Sadly she could do little for him, other than clean up his bloodstained face, and moisten his lips.

She moved on — worked on. Thankfully Lucy had quickly recovered from her initial shock, and stayed staunchly by her side, assisting with that native common sense of the country born.

None of the cabin passengers ventured up on deck or offered assistance.

The worst cases were carried below to a makeshift operating theatre, where the surgeon performed his grisly task with alcohol for an anaesthetic. Screams of agony

214

rent the air, Sarah forced herself to close her ears and continue with her work. Other men, themselves bandaged and in pain, struggled to their feet and gave assistance. Gradually the mess and confusion was cleared away.

Sarah caught only brief glimpses of the earl. She knew that he had taken over command of the American ship, its name now revealed as *Dependable*. He was overseeing clearing-up operations. Both the British and the Americans were working together, enmity overlooked in the common purpose of keeping both vessels afloat. Her eyes rested on Wrenningham. He was making the best use of the various skills of the sailors and soldiers co-ordinating their efforts to effect the necessary repairs.

As she watched she felt relief that he was not seriously injured, for it suddenly came to her that she would have been sorely troubled had any ill befallen him.

Later on, the higher-ranking prisoners from the American ship were brought over. The captain first, followed by his mate, and they were immediately taken below to be kept in custody. Some of the British sailors were transferred to the American ship. The mate of *The Expeditious* was to take command of the navigational operation, with Wrenningham in overall charge. The two ships would sail in close convoy, the *Dependable* being booty. Among the wounded Americans Sarah noticed a fair-haired lad, no older than her own brother, carried in the arms of a burly British seaman. It wrung her heart to see how half his lower leg had been shot away.

'Lay him down here,' Sarah instructed. 'I'll apply a tourniquet.' She talked to the lad as she did so, asking his name and where he lived. He managed a wry smile when he realized she was also American and it seemed to give him confidence. She stroked his forehead, and held tight to his hand. She talked to him, trying to bolster his courage, whilst he waited to be taken down to the surgeon. At that moment Mr Williams ventured up on deck, and immediately his eyes fastened on Sarah. She ignored his presence, even though she was aware that he was listening to her conversation. A scowl settled on Mr Williams's face.

It was the hardest day Sarah had ever experienced. She and Lucy worked almost until they dropped. When at last they retired to the cabin, food was brought there for them, but they were too weary to eat it.

All the next day work went on apace to repair the damage and by the end of the day enough had been done to restore both vessels to a seaworthy state. Fortunately the weather was calm. The rain when it came was welcome; it was caught in canvas tilts and used to replenish both ships' diminished water supplies.

The way of life of the cabin passengers was totally disrupted. For the most part they all remained below. It was not until dinner on the evening of the third day that they gathered together again to dine in the wardroom.

By this time Sarah's nursing duties had become a little lighter, and it was a relief to realize that life was beginning to return to its normal pattern. She chose a fairly modest evening gown, and washed and changed, with Lucy's help as usual. Assuming that Wrenningham would be living on the *Dependable* she did not expect him to call and escort her to the wardroom, and simply walked there on her own. The other passengers had gathered ahead of her. Her appearance was greeted by a bellow of rage from Mr Williams. He barred her entry, 'Out, you Yankee!' he roared.

'Mr Williams!' protested Captain Clibbert. 'We have reason to thank Miss Dunthorne for the assistance she has given so selflessly.'

'I owe her no thanks,' bawled Mr Williams. 'I'm surprised she has the effrontery to enter this room. The trouble those accursed Americans have caused us! I saw her myself, passing messages to one of them. In my opinion she should be clapped in irons for the rest of the voyage.'

'Mr Williams — ' began Mr Clibbert.

'My husband is quite right,' Mrs Williams interrupted the captain. 'It was bad enough having her flaunting herself here, before we knew the Yankees declared war. We've all heard her rebellious views. You can't expect respectable ladies to sit at table with her now.'

'Quite right, my love,' said Mr Williams. 'What's more, I will not allow it!'

'Please, be calm,' pleaded the captain.

'I paid good money for this voyage. I shall make a formal complaint to the shipping agency if you harbour that woman — one of those who've attacked and nigh on killed us.'

The captain flinched. Apologetically he turned towards Sarah.

'Don't alarm yourself, Mr Clibbert,' Sarah said. 'I declare I could not eat a thing in company such as this.' She swept the assembly with furious eyes, and her lip curled as she noticed the shamefaced looks on one or two of the officers' faces. Miss Reader kept her gaze fastened on the floor. 'I shall retire immediately. Kindly arrange to have my dinner served in my cabin.'

A triumphant smile spread over Mr Williams's florid face, but he wouldn't let the matter rest. 'She should be locked up,' he declared.

'No!' cried Sarah. 'That I will not accept. You locked me in my cabin when the battle was on — '

'And a good thing I did, otherwise I dread to think what the outcome might have been.'

She began to feel afraid. The terrifying incarceration was still vivid.

'None of us can feel safe whilst you have free run of the ship, you Yankee spy!'

'What's this?' Wrenningham stood in the doorway, immediately behind Sarah. She had not heard his approach. 'Who is a Yankee spy, may I ask?' His voice was as incisive as an icicle.

'She's one of those accursed Americans,' yelled Mr Williams. 'What's to stop her releasing the prisoners, helping them to take over the ship? We could be murdered in our beds. I will not permit my wife and the other passengers to be open to such danger.'

' 'Pon my soul, I have never heard such an absurd suggestion. Miss Dunthorne will endanger no one,' declared Wrenningham. 'You have my word upon it. So let us put this matter behind us, and take our places at table.'

Sarah was grateful for his support, although his cavalier attitude did nothing to calm the situation.

'You can't watch her day and night,' sneered Mr Williams. 'I shall personally see she is handed over to the emigration authorities when we land in Quebec.'

'That, I really cannot allow,' Wrenningham said smoothly.

'My lord, I fear there is some truth in what Mr Williams is saying,' said Captain Clibbert.

'I've done no harm to anyone.' Sarah protested. 'I've done everything I could to help the wounded of both countries. None of these fine people set foot on deck until it was cleared!'

'I know, Miss Dunthorne. I am very grateful' Mr Clibbert said. 'I shall plead strongly on your behalf, but I fear that you will be in a difficult situation when we reach Canada. I've no idea how the authorities will react, but I shall have to report your presence as one of my passengers, and that you are an American citizen.'

'There! What did I tell you?' Mr Williams began triumphantly.

He would be eager to denounce her. In a situation of war, his lies might be believed. Sarah trembled. Wrenningham caught hold of her arm, steadying her.

'There is one way out of this difficulty,' he said.

All eyes were turned on him. Sarah experienced a momentary flash of hope. It died almost immediately. What could he do? There was silence in the room. His grip on her arm tightened.

'Do me the honour of stepping outside so that we may speak privately for a few moments.'

Mutely she nodded. He stood aside to allow her to pass, then paused to address the company. 'Pray do not keep dinner waiting. We may be a little time.'

12

Sarah allowed the earl to usher her out of the wardroom, then shrugged off his hand and hurried up the companionway ahead of him. A fresh breeze tugged at her hair and her clothes as she stepped out onto the deck. She was in a state of shock at the hostility that had been expressed against her. How could they be so cruel as to suggest she should be locked in her cabin! Claustrophobic terror returned at the very thought.

What could Harry do to counter Mr Williams's vile suggestions? The captain himself admitted he would have to hand her over to the authorities at Quebec. She wouldn't be able to return to Cassie's Rock until this dreadful war was over — and that might be years.

The earl caught hold of her arm, halted her when she would have walked on, blindly, uncaring. Gently he turned her to face him. 'I can see only one way to extricate you from this danger.' He paused, cleared his throat, as if embarrassed. 'It is a point we have discussed before.'

'What can I do?' Her voice was sharpened by desperation.

'Marry me.'

She was shocked.

He continued, quickly, 'I know you have no wish to.' His voice held a bitter note, as if it took controlled determination for him to continue. 'But I beg you to reconsider your decision.'

'No . . . I — ' She was shocked that he considered this a suitable time to propose to her again.

'Hear me out.' He spoke in a cool, level tone. 'As my wife, you will become a British subject, entitled to full protection under British law. You understand what I'm saying, don't you?'

She nodded, wordlessly. This was not the way she wanted to be married, out of necessity, with no thought or word of love!

'I promised your grandmama I would return you safely to your family. I would be failing in my duty if I had to leave you in Quebec and in custody.'

'I couldn't bear it,' she whispered.

'You must understand, I would not have repeated my offer of marriage, for you told me most definitely your views upon the subject.'

'Then — then — this marriage — ?'

She wanted his word that their union should be in name only, but she broke off, finding it difficult to put her confused thoughts into words when it was clearly no more welcome to him that it was to her.

'You must see the sense in what I am saying?' he said.

'It is indeed a — a most practical suggestion.'

'As Countess of Wrenningham you will be protected not only here on the ship but also whilst you are in Canada. I have no idea what we shall find when we arrive there. I hope we'll be able to cross the border to America, and return you to your family, but I can promise nothing.'

'Home!' she whispered. How she wished she was there now!

Wrenningham interrupted her thoughts. 'Be assured that I will do my best for you, Sarah, and the safest way will surely be for you to travel as my wife. You will be transferred with me to the *Dependable*.'

'There is a cabin available?' she asked tentatively.

'I shall vacate mine.'

'Lucy must come with me.'

'Naturally. I have instructed my man, Reynolds, to assist your maid to transfer your goods and chattels. He waits only for a word from me — as I wait for consent from you.'

'There is just one more thing-' Her voice was no more than a whisper.

'Yes?'

'Our marriage should be in name only — '

She wasn't sure if Wrenningham heard her, as a sound behind her made her swing round. Mr Williams's head was rising through the hatch, above the companion-way.

'Well? You've had long enough — when are we going to hear what this scheme of yours is, your lordship?' Mr Williams's voice was harsh, with the assurance of one who feels he holds the upper hand. 'It had better be a good one.'

The earl turned his back on the man, treating him with contempt.

'Well, Sarah?' He was not answering her question.

'Harry — I — ' She tried to repeat it, but the presence of her tormentor was unnerving her.

Mr Williams raised his voice. 'We are about to take ourselves off to our cabins for the night.'

'Pray do so,' invited the earl, with a dismissive wave of his hand.

'Not until I know what safeguards you're proposing, sir! We've been kept waiting too long already. That woman must be locked away.'

Harry clasped her hands firmly within his own. 'Be sensible, Sarah. Let me tell Mr Clibbert to fetch his Prayer Book.'

There was only one answer she could give. 'Very well.'

★ ★ ★

Shortly afterwards Wrenningham and Sarah stood before Captain Clibbert, in his cabin. He read the required passages from the Prayer Book. Lucy Motts and Captain Smalley, their witnesses, hovered behind them.

'I, Sarah — take thee Harry — to love and to cherish — to honour and obey.'

Would he hold her to that? Under the law she now belonged to him, as a personal possession. As she made the simple responses she also pondered on that little word — love. What a travesty of a wedding it was! Never had he spoken one word of love. Desire, yes! She had felt that when he had kissed her, but never any tenderness that suggested love!

Mr Clibbert closed the Prayer Book. 'I now pronounce you husband and wife,' he said. 'My lord, you may kiss the bride.'

Wrenningham's arms closed gently, protectively around her. She had to lift her face to his — for the sake of appearances they had to make it look as if it was a real marriage. His face hovered briefly above hers. Disturbingly she saw a devilish twinkle in his eyes. He kissed her, quite lightly yet unmistakably with an element of possessiveness.

The captain had written out a certificate in advance. They both signed, it was witnessed by Captain Smalley and Lucy, who simply marked a cross above her name. The marriage ceremony was over.

'Now a little celebration,' said Mr Clibbert. He produced two bottles of champagne from beneath his desk. 'Genuine stuff, this. I reckon the Yankee ship's recently had a rendezvous with the French.'

'However they came by it, I can't think of a better occasion on which to enjoy it,' declared Captain Smalley.

The captain filled five glasses. 'A toast — to the health and happiness of the bride and groom,' he said. 'May their lives together be long and blessed with fruitfulness.'

'Good luck to you, miss,' cried Lucy. Then she giggled a little. 'I haven't never had champagne before — it's all fizzy — just like the elderflower drink my mum makes.'

Dear Lucy, thought Sarah. That ingenuous

comment helped to lighten the atmosphere. Mr Clibbert refilled their glasses.

'If you are ready,' Wrenningham said to Sarah. 'I will take you now to your new quarters.' He tucked her hand within the crook of his arm and escorted her from *The Expeditious* to the *Dependable* and took her to the cabin which had previously been occupied by the American captain.

'I hope you'll find it sufficiently comfortable.'

'Thank you, it will do very nicely.'

Lucy, assisted by the earl's personal servant, Reynolds, was there also, busily attending to the removal of Sarah's few possessions. Sarah felt quite sorry for the man, who was trying to assist and mostly getting in the way, to judge by the criticisms Lucy constantly threw at him. The cabin was small but adequate, with bulkheads of dark oak.

'Lend a hand with these sheets, Mr Reynolds. *If* it won't be too much trouble to you,' Lucy said. 'Can't let my mistress take over this room in this state, it needs a woman's touch.'

'Then you won't be needing me,' Reynolds suggested.

'Don't you go — there's more to be fetched, yet.' In spite of her sharp tongue the young man seemed to be enjoying the maid's company and replied in kind. As they left the cabin Lucy burst into paroxysms of laughter.

'I fear the champagne has gone to Lucy's head,' Sarah remarked.

'She has just been to a wedding,' Wrenninghan said drily. 'Now I have duties to which I must attend. We plan to get under way as soon as possible. Until later,' he said. A smile lifted one corner of his mouth, teasing her. Then he was gone.

Soon the ship creaked and rolled and she was aware they were voyaging onward.

Reynolds brought dinner for her on a tray, but Sarah had no appetite.

'It's the excitement, miss,' said Lucy. 'I feel a bit that way myself.'

'That's the champagne effect,' Sarah said with an indulgent smile. She was pleased that Lucy was in such good spirits. The maid was too well trained ever to comment upon the sudden marriage.

She chatted on as she laid out Sarah's best night shift, assisted her to change, then unpinned and let down her hair. She made Sarah laugh by repeating some of the amusing comments of her new friend, Archie Reynolds. When all had been attended to, smilingly she bade her mistress goodnight and left the cabin.

This was her wedding night. She could still scarcely believe it! Her status had changed dramatically. There had been none of the normal preparations for a marriage, no time to become accustomed to the idea. She had made her vows — the law now bound her to Wrenningham.

Until later, my lady, he had said. Would he demand those rights to which a husband was entitled? He had not answered her whispered plea that theirs should be a marriage in name only — she was not even sure if he had heard her.

An hour passed since Lucy had left. The lamp swung, casting a flickering glow, the ship's timbers creaked, sailors' feet scuffed and thudded, the wind whistled in the rigging, the unremitting sounds of the ship under sail were all around. Sarah sat in the American captain's chair, clad in her night shift of finest white lawn, with elbow-length puffed sleeves and a neckline so wide she felt somewhat embarrassed, convinced that it was far too revealing. She hugged a large cashmere shawl close around her shoulders, its fringed ends hanging almost to the floor.

At last she heard the expected tap on the door and without waiting for an answer Harry entered. He strode over to where she was sitting, reached forward with both hands, evidently expecting her to place hers in their possessive grasp. She did not move.

'My lady,' he said — and he had that devilish look in his eyes that she had seen before. 'Will you not greet your husband with some show of friendliness?'

His words pricked her conscience. But for him she would be locked in her cabin on board *The Expeditious* at the mercy of the bullying Mr Williams. She rose to her feet. 'Sir, I am exceedingly grateful — '

'To hell with your gratitude,' he growled. His arms closed around her, his face was bent to hers.

She gasped. She would have protested, but he closed her mouth by swooping down upon it with his own. Desire emanated from him. And, just as before, it threatened to render her subservient to his masculine will.

Deliberately she stayed quite still, for what right had she now to resist? When his lips moved against hers, it was only natural to respond. Intuitively her mouth opened slightly in welcome, and immediately his kiss deepened. There was joy in being held so, delight in the pressure of his hands that held her body so excitingly close against the whole length of his.

He was making it seem easy and natural for her to accept that she belonged to him — but she was not yet sure. A touch of panic crept into her mind and began to build up a reaction somewhere in her stomach. The haste of the wedding, following the terror of being locked in her cabin during the battle and the threats of her fellow passengers, gave her a feeling of unreality.

Suddenly she wanted to get away from him. She tried to move her head aside, to escape from his kiss, feeling that if she did not, she would drown in the luxurious wonder of it entirely. He merely moved his head against hers, making the movement a caress, undoing her attempts to draw away from him. The beautiful shawl fell from her shoulders and lay unheeded on the floor. Moisture from his mouth was sweet on her lips and she almost swooned with the delicious taste of him.

He had unbuttoned his scarlet, gold-braided jacket, and now tucked her inside it, so that only the fine linens of his shirt and her shift separated their bare bodies. The warmth of him, as he snuggled her into his arms, drawing her close, made her arch her back, feeling the hard barrel of his chest against the soft rounded curves of her breasts.

She was intensely aware of his desire — and that she was being precipitated into giving herself to him. Had he really not heard her request when they had been interrupted by Mr Williams? He had not answered her, but it had seemed obvious that he was proposing a marriage of convenience. He had not actually made any promise to that effect, but she had believed that was what he had meant.

Wrenningham had made his reasons for wishing to take a wife perfectly clear when he had first proposed to her. Did he believe that was part of the contract they had entered into this day? Nothing was clear in her mind. Perhaps some day she would feel obligated to honour that duty — to become a real wife to him — but not now. Not so soon. Not without love. She pushed against him with her hands, making a determined effort to draw back from him. He lifted his head, loosened his hold as if afraid he had hurt her.

'What is the matter, Sarah?'

'Well — it is only — ' She broke off.

'Only what?' he asked with a sigh.

'Nothing.'

He took a short step back. His eyes raked her face. 'Come, little wife, tell me what is troubling you?'

'Well, for one thing, I am not yet accustomed to — to being a wife.'

'For that matter until this day I have never before been a husband.' He paused and watched her with a calmly speculative expression. 'Do I understand that you now have reservations?'

'Sir, I understood that ours was to have been a marriage in name only.'

'Really?' Just the one expressive word, but his eyebrows shot up, ominously. 'May I ask when you formed that idea?'

It took fortitude for her to continue. 'Sir, from the circumstances of it. What has taken place today has been so unusual, almost unreal — I know that we are indeed married — '

'That is absolutely real and true. Quite irrefutable, in fact.'

His masterful, cool, calm manner was unnerving her.

'I know — but — '

'Madam, I do not recollect giving any undertaking that our marriage should be otherwise than that which is normal.'

It seemed she was trapped. She lowered her head, and stood meekly before him. A tear rolled gently down her cheek.

'Very well, my lord, I have made my promises, and I will endeavour to keep them.' She began to talk too quickly, almost wildly. 'I know you are most anxious to beget an heir — '

He drew in his breath sharply between his

teeth, and her voice trailed away. Glancing up and she saw a look of incredulity pass over his face. She trembled, half expecting him to pick her up in fury and throw her on to the bed, but he simply stood there, watching her.

Then suddenly he threw back his head and gave a gurgling sort of chuckle. It was soft laughter — quite gentle really, and she began to feel rather foolish. She hung her head, shuffled her feet, waited for him to speak. When he did so his voice was serious.

'Why so I am, my dear Sarah.'

'I know — and — '

He placed one finger against her lips to still them. 'Hush, Sarah. Ashingby does indeed need an heir — and I shall be most willing to provide one — but that is not a decision for me to take alone.'

She gazed at him uncomprehending. 'What do you mean?'

'Why, that this heir should be conceived only when his mama wishes for that event, as much — ' He broke off, looked at her earnestly and the sensual expression in his eyes sent a shiver of excitement down her spine. There it was again, the magnetism he could so easily, and so achingly, exercise over her — so that she wanted to cry out *Take me — I am yours*. But she remained silent.

He continued, 'When this heir of which

you speak, is conceived — then it would please me if you would wish for me to make love to you as much — or perhaps I should say — almost as much — as I.'

He spoke with an assurance that made her uneasy — and then angry. Had he seduced so many women that he was confident that before long she would fall victim to his charms? Had he read her own shameful wanton susceptibility so accurately? She clenched her fists and determined that she would not give way to those distressingly primitive instincts that he was so capable of arousing in her.

Her independent spirit warned her that she must not allow him to have complete dominance over her. Her romantic heart cautioned her not to give herself fully to him without love. Harry made no mention of any such sentiment — not even when he had spoken of *making love* — for then surely he was thinking only of the sexual act. She wished he did not view everything in such a coldly practical way! To expect her to share such a heartless attitude, was asking the impossible!

'If it is left to me, my answer is simple,' she snapped. 'I say — never!'

His eyes teased her. He shook his head in mock sorrow.

'Ah! Poor unborn infant! I shall weep for him — or, of course — for her, should it be a girl, to whom you are denying the gift of life!' Then he shrugged as if it was a matter of complete indifference. 'But we have no need to trouble ourselves with that matter tonight. I have other duties to attend to.' He paused significantly. 'And, dear wife, we have a lifetime before us, have we not?'

He turned away and suddenly, infuriatingly, her eyes misted with tears. A strange stirring of wild, unleashed emotion was upsetting her. It was irrational, but overwhelmingly powerful — quite beyond her understanding. Was it some previously unforseen desire for motherhood. Or was it — her face burned at the thought — a longing for Harry to make love to her?

He walked away, but in the doorway, turned and faced her again. 'For heaven's sake, Sarah, don't look so distraught! Do you take me for some raping ogre?' The harsh note was in his voice again. 'I shall not hurry you to my bed, though one day you will be there.'

13

A week passed. Sarah continued to help the wounded, changing bandages, administering sedatives, giving hope and encouragement. Some men came to her more often than they really needed. They found comfort in having a woman to tend them. She met Harry only at meal-times. They spoke politely, never on a personal level. Yet every day she was conscious of his presence. Often she lingered on deck watching whales and dolphins playing around the vessel, but he never joined her there.

She was grateful to be away from the unpleasant company of the other passengers on *The Expeditious*. Harry seemed more remote than he had been. He had more responsibility, assisting young Mr Branley in the sailing of the ship, but it was not just that which kept them apart. He was deliberately avoiding her. The words that had been spoken on their wedding night still lay between them. She thought over that scene so often, fastened on his cool assertion that he was in no hurry to take her to his bed, but the way he looked at her belied his words. She would have been naïve not to believe he had come to her cabin with the intention of making love to her. Only her reluctance had restrained him — that and his unbending sense of honour. She should be grateful for his forbearance — so why was she feeling this strange restlessness?

A lifetime before us, he had said — how remote that sounded! Undoubtedly that was true. She told herself there was nothing she could do to change the situation — and yet she sighed and wished that somehow, in some way, she could get closer to him.

Sarah's unhappiness was in complete contrast to Lucy's ebullience. Since the day when she and Archie Reynolds had worked together, transferring things from one ship to the other, the pair had become inseparable. Any spare time they had they managed to be together and Lucy's merry laughter, and her caustic comments, were often heard ringing out over the ship. She even entertained the other sailors joining in when they danced the hornpipe, and singing in her rich, clear voice. Often Lucy repeated those melodies that reminded Sarah of the day at the seaside — did Harry ever think of that too, as he had said he would?

For several days the ship skimmed along with its vast area of canvas billowing out in splendour. Then the weather changed. The wind rose in the afternoon and orders were given to close-reef sails and prepare for a storm. The wind whistled ever louder and sharper through the rigging, the seas rose huge, towering, white-capped. By evening the ship was rocking like a cradle, and taking in so much water that the crew were forced to keep the pumps going day and night.

Sarah and Lucy hastened below, out of the way of the hardworking sailors. Soon mountainous seas were washing right over the decks and the men had to lash themselves to masts or bulkheads for fear of being swept off their feet and carried overboard. She scarcely slept at all, expecting every minute to be tossed out of her bunk. Rain and wind rattled all around, louder and more continuous than thunder. Several times during the night, she and Lucy fell to their knees and prayed for the safety of the ship, tossed, helpless as a cork on the raging, foaming waves.

'Oh, miss,' moaned Lucy. 'Don't tell me we've come through that dreadful battle only to be drowned dead in a storm!'

Sarah's mind was in a turmoil of fear — for Harry — and those other brave men struggling against the frenetic force of the storm. But always her mind came back to Harry, her husband, and her soul was filled with regrets.

At last the wind began to lessen. Soon the last squalls passed, the sun came out and Sarah was able to go up on deck. She looked around for Harry and when she could not see him, her heart seemed to shrivel inside her — until she spoke to Mr Branley and discovered that her husband was resting.

'You must be tired too,' she said.

'I had a bit of sleep early this morning,' he told her. 'His lordship insisted on that, as soon as it was certain that the weather had eased and the ship was safe. It were a bad storm an' he didn't turn a hair.'

Sarah felt a glow at such warm praise — as if her relationship was real and meaningful. Could it really be that, even though she meant nothing to Harry, she loved him? It was a bleak feeling. Her eyes roved over ocean. '*The Expeditious* has dropped behind, I see,' she commented.

'Aye. But she's catching up fast. Looks as if she's come through the storm safely, thank God. We should sight land soon,' he added.

'Really? I hadn't realized we were so close.'

'We're over the Banks. I've seen ice birds and Newfoundland petrels circling in the distance. I'm sure you won't be sorry to feel dry land under your feet again, your ladyship.'

As land came into sight she wondered what

lay ahead for her in Canada.

There was general relief and joy as the news spread that the long passage was almost over.

'Land at last, Sarah!' Wrenningham had moved quietly up behind her. 'Getting nearer home for you,' he added. 'You'll be glad of that.'

But was she? It was a reminder that they would soon be parting. Did she really want to be parted from him?

His arm brushed hers as he leaned forward. 'This is the Gulf of Saint Lawrence,' he said. 'More than a week's sailing yet to Quebec.' His hand was lying on the bulwark beside her, close but not touching. A strong shapely hand, tanned from the voyage, yet clean and neatly manicured. She had a ridiculous urge to place hers on to it — then looked up and saw that he was watching her, and colour flared into her face. She turned away. 'I've been standing here too long,' she said. 'I should go below. The men in sick bay will be waiting for me.'

He made no attempt to detain her.

★　★　★

The Expeditious was immediately behind *Dependable* as the ships anchored off

Quebec. A signal was hoisted requesting the doctor to come on board, to report on the health of passengers and crew. Fortunately there had been no infectious or contagious diseases. A great many ships were lying in the harbour. A strong fortress guarded the entrance. The two ships were tied up, so close that Sarah could see Mr and Mrs Williams. They scowled at her.

The American sailors from both ships were marched away to be interrogated and interned as prisoners of war. They looked dejected and dispirited. Sarah felt sorry for them all, with special sympathy for those young men she had cared for.

'I'll always remember what you did for me, ma'am,' one lad told her. 'You gave me hope when I thought I might just as well die.' He swung away on his crutches, and fell in beside his comrades, ready to be marched off. They were a stark reminder that but for her marriage she would have been among that forlorn band.

She walked over to where Harry stood. 'Where are they taking them?' she asked.

'A prisoner-of-war camp. They'll be well cared for.'

She hoped he was right. Several hundred townspeople gathered on the quayside, gloating over the American ship. Some shook clenched fists at the Yankee prisoners as, flanked by British redcoats with fixed bayonets, they were escorted away through the town.

Mr and Mrs Williams were disembarked followed by Miss Reader and Miss Jones.

'May we go ashore now?' Sarah asked.

'Not yet,' Harry replied. 'I have to speak to the Port Authorities with regard to handing over our prize.'

'This ship? What will they do with her?'

'Check her over and put her into service as soon as possible.'

'Under British colours.' She said it with a touch of sadness. Marriage had changed her nationality, but it did not alter her way of thinking.

'Of course.' Harry's reply was brusque. 'You must stay on board until I am free to escort you. If you have any letters they can be taken back to Britain on the next ship that leaves.'

'I'll write to Grandmama and to Corinne,' she said. 'May I send your good wishes?'

He shrugged. 'You may if it pleases you. Certainly I wish no ill to befall the foolish girl.' He strode away down the gangway.

A large proportion of the population of Quebec was French, and although they had no wish to be taken over by America, they

244

might also prove hostile to her, since their Emperor Napoleon was still at war with Britain. Rumours were spreading like wild-fire. Lucy and Archie Reynolds had a network of friends among the crew and the soldiers, and gathered up several horrendous stories and passed them on to Sarah.

Sometimes it was said that the Americans had broken through, wreaking carnage wherever they went, others said they had been repulsed. Certainly the wartime situation was menacing.

Mr and Mrs Williams disembarked and stood on the quayside talking to government officials and pointing to where she stood on board *Dependable*. She did not need to hear, to know they were passing on their distrust of her. She regarded them with a cool and disdainful expression. Presently the inspector mounted the gangway and walked towards her.

'I am informed that you are an American subject,' he said.

'I am American by birth, but British by marriage. My husband is over there — the Earl of Wrenningham.' A note of pride crept quite unbidden into her voice.

The official looked impressed but carried on with determinations 'It seems there is some doubt about the validity of your marriage.'

'There is no doubt whatsoever. You can speak to my husband, and to Captain Clibbert of *The Expeditious* who performed the ceremony.' She gave him a sweetly innocent smile. 'He is just over there.'

She pointed to the other ship and waved to the captain, to which he responded with a friendly but respectful bow. Turning back to the official, she added, 'I can fetch the marriage certificate from my cabin if you wish.'

'No need for that.' He grinned. 'You don't look like a spy to me. My apologies for troubling you, Countess.'

She watched him walk down the gangway. Mrs Williams was already seated in a carriage, whilst her ill-tempered husband waited on the quayside. The official went straight to him, and whatever he said was obviously brief and pointed. He left without listening to Mr Williams's blustering protest. Sarah could see rage reddening his face as he clambered into the carriage, bawled an order at his coachman, and was driven away at breakneck speed.

It was a triumphant moment, and yet Sarah felt humbled. Every day since her wedding she had grown increasingly aware of how greatly she was in Harry's debt. Here in Quebec, she was more conscious of that than ever.

She went down to her cabin and wrote her letter to Lady MacKenna. It was not easy to compose a sensible account of her marriage to Harry. She did not wish to cause concern to her grandmama by over-emphasizing the horror of the battle at sea, yet without putting that in, how could she explain her change of mind? But did it matter? Whatever had brought her marriage about, she guessed the shrewd old lady would be more than pleased. She had said she was a fool for refusing him in the first place. Did a special wisdom come with age? Should Sarah have relied on her judgement?

Hastily she finished the letter off, not wishing to pursue that line of thought. Then she wrote to Corinne, Mrs Forbes Thackstone. Were they as happy as they had predicted they would be? She sincerely hoped so. How far away were those days when she had first met Corinne, when they had nothing more to concern themselves with other than what they should wear, which invitations they should accept, what rout or assembly would be most pleasurable.

The letters finished and sealed, Sarah went up on deck again. The handing over of the ship was almost complete. Harry's company had disembarked and assembled on the quay with full kit. He inspected them; smart in their scarlet tunics, they stood stiffly to attention. The sergeant barked the orders and they moved as one, part of Wellington's well-trained professional army. How would the American volunteer militiamen stand up to them? How many on either side would have to die before the war was over?

The earl, their colonel, addressed the men. His message was short, his voice loud and clear. He praised them for their efforts, for their successful stand in the battle at sea, in which they had conducted themselves bravely and well. He expressed his trust in their loyalty and courage to tackle whatever lay ahead of them as they continued their journey up the St Lawrence River.

The men gave him three hearty cheers and he handed command back to his junior officers, to be marched off to the river transport boat. Then he walked smartly up the gangway towards Sarah.

'Ready?' he asked.

'Yes. And I've two letters to be sent back.'

He took them. 'I'll see they get off on the next boat out.'

Again he brought Reynolds and another soldier to carry the luggage which Lucy had packed earlier.

Reynolds had a heavy trunk balanced on his shoulder, he was not much taller than

Lucy herself. The friendly feeling between the two was more obvious every time Sarah saw them together. They continually chaffed each other, acted as if each thought the other was half-daft, yet when their eyes met it was always with warmth and a smile.

'Where are we going, my lord?' Sarah asked.

'I've arranged for you to stay on board the transport vessel and sail up the St Lawrence with us, at least as far as York,' he told her. 'When we get there I'll be in a better position to weigh up the situation. Then I'll decide whether there is any chance of your crossing Lake Ontario to get back to America. I'm afraid I shall be unable to accompany you. I have to march my men on to Fort George. It may be safer for you to stay in York — '

'Can I not go on, with you?' she asked. 'Fort George is on the Canadian side of the river, close to the Niagara Falls. Cassie's Rock is just on the other side, in America.'

'I'm aware of that. However, I think it may be easier for you to cross Lake Ontario from York. I've been told the Americans are reinforcing their fort at Niagara, probably planning an advance into Quebec province.'

'Then there will be fighting?'

'What else is war about? Even though half of America, certainly none of the New

England states, wish to be at war with Britain, the hawks have had their way. They would not have dared to declare war if Britain had not been so heavily engaged against France.' His voice was bitter.

She recalled her very first conversation with him, when she had seen tragedy in his face. He had been a professional soldier too long and was sensitive to the horrors he had seen. Yet his iron will and devotion to duty drove him on relentlessly. Deep concern for his safety made her feel hollow inside. Why could she not tell him so? Why had she built this wall between them? If only there was some way in which she could get nearer to him.

'My lord,' she ventured. 'I have heard rumours that fighting has already begun.'

'So I believe,' he replied. 'You have no need to trouble yourself about that. I shall see to it that you do not go near the front line. Come — this way.'

He tucked a guiding hand beneath her elbow and escorted her down the gangway. Side by side, they walked along the quayside to where a smaller, tubbier-looking vessel was waiting to take them further up-river. He escorted her to the door of the cabin that had been allocated to her, obviously the best available and reasonably comfortable. He left her there. The sequence of events set up on the night of their wedding had become an unspoken rule. He remained remote from her.

The ship set sail in the late afternoon and arrived at Montreal the following morning. The town was prettier than Quebec, with many handsome buildings among the usual miscellany of wooden ones. Another full day's travel took them to Lake Ontario, which was more like a sea than a lake. They hugged the Canadian shore and by the evening of the following day were nearing York. Many battles had been fought on the Great Lakes, between American and British or Canadian ships, and Sarah sensed increasing danger. Never before had she faced the thought of someone she loved going into battle. She could understand the frustration of her fellow-Americans over trade restrictions imposed unfairly by the British, and their hatred of the Royal Navy's high-handed kidnapping of sailors to man their ships, but was war the only answer?

Harry had spoken of leaving her at York whilst he went on with his troops to Fort George — a prospect that caused her great concern. She was conscious of him every waking moment, always looking for him, watching him. Her greatest happiness was when she sat beside him at meals, for then he made pleasant conversation with her. She, too, saved up titbits of gossip to relate to him.

At other times her concern for him made her quieter, even a trifle irritable. When Captain Smalley or any of the other officers attempted to divert her attention, she had difficulty in hiding her impatience. Their frivolous comments, which had previously amused her, now seemed irrelevant, childish.

Harry seemed to have grown more distant than ever and that played on her mind. She blamed herself for such an unhappy state of affairs — she ought to have been kinder, more giving after their marriage. Soon he would be going into battle, and already he bore the scars of past wars. She was sure now that she loved him and even if he could not love her in return, surely she ought to try and make up to him for his disappointment in her as a wife?

All through dinner on the evening before they were due to reach York, she was troubled by the thought that tomorrow he would be moving on — closer into the war zone. Somewhere out there American forces were waiting to attack, and the fact that they were her people made it all the more terrible. She felt a dreadful presentiment that disaster lay ahead, though exactly why she should feel that she could not have explained.

Theirs had been a marriage of convenience, brought about by the circumstances in which they found themselves, but she could not help recalling when Harry had first proposed. Then it was an act of gallantry, because she had been compromised. Then she had been infuriated by the things he had said — but he had spoken only the truth. A lesser man might have tried to pretend to have tender feelings for her; Harry had been explicit in giving his reasons for proposing marriage.

Those reasons were as apt now as they had been then. There was, she decided, only one way in which she could express some of the gratitude she felt. She must offer to provide that heir he so desired.

14

Dinner seemed interminable, Sarah could eat little. There was an uncanny change in the atmosphere, not openly expressed, never admitted, but undoubtedly all were mindful that the enemy was now not far ahead. The officers drank even more than usual, and passed the port around freely.

She could not help noticing that Harry, too, who was usually rather abstemious, had taken several glasses. The voices were becoming more strident. As the only woman there she ought to leave, but she could not bring herself to be separated from him. She lingered on, locked in her own thoughts.

Their routine of separate cabins was well established, and she had long ago insisted that it was quite unnecessary for him to accompany her to her door when she retired. She wished now that she had not been so brusque on that point, but then she had never expected to change her mind. She had never dreamed that she would long for his kisses, as she did now. That she would yearn for the touch, the feel, the warm wonder of him — that she would want to be his.

She had snapped *Never!* when he had said that one day she would be want him to make love to her. But now she did and how could she invite him into her cabin without seeming quite shamefully bold? Her mind played around with various words — should she say this — or that? Nothing seemed right. Every approach that sprang to her mind was so outrageously improper that she knew she would never be able to voice any one of them. The more she turned it over in her mind, the more difficult it became.

She sat for a long time, with her eyes downcast, clasping and unclasping her hands nervously in her lap. How could she catch his attention, without actually saying what she had in mind? He was engrossed in conversation with Captain Smalley about the relative merits of different guns. Every word she overheard added to her concern — these were lethal weapons they were discussing and preparing to use! Everyone at the table joined in the argument, and she hated having to listen.

When she looked up, Harry was watching her, she tried to smile at him, but it was a sickly effort. The conversation continued around them, across the table, opinions flung back and forth. She shuffled uncomfortably in her chair.

'Sarah,' he said, leaning a little towards her, keeping his voice low, 'I am sorry to see you so troubled. There is something I have to say to you, which may help to ease your mind.' He leaned a little towards her as he spoke. 'I must have a word with you in private.'

Her heart leapt, eagerly. Had he actually been able to read her mind? Did he really know what was troubling her? Had she made it so obvious? Wrenningham pulled back her chair. The other officers lurched to their feet. She was scarcely aware of them. Someone opened the door for her, and she swept through.

'It's raining,' Wrenningham said. 'It won't be comfortable out on deck.'

'Perhaps — in my cabin — ' she stammered, and broke off.

If he was surprised he did not show it, merely indicated with a sweep of his hand that she should precede him in that direction. She found herself walking too fast, in a state of agitation, and deliberately slowed her steps. She was concentrating, as she had been all evening, on what she would say to him, completely forgetting that he had said he wished to talk to her.

Closely followed by Wrenningham, she made her way along the shadowy passageway, checked involuntarily on hearing voices just

256

outside the door of her cabin. A man's irritated exclamation — then Lucy appeared from a dark corner, smoothing down her dress, looking flustered.

'Evenin', my lady.' She hurried to open the cabin door, bobbed a quick curtsy. 'I've laid out your best nightdress like you said — '

'Thank you, Lucy,' Sarah interrupted. 'You may wait outside until I call you.'

Inside the cabin, she was glad of the dimness of the lamplight to cover her embarrassment. She knew that Harry followed her, and heard him close the door. Then all was still apart from the creaking of the weathered timbers, and the distant shouts of the sailors, the constant sounds of the ship under full canvas. She drew in a deep breath, then turned to face him.

Harry stood braced, his powerful legs in their tight white trousers, slightly apart. So handsome, his scarlet jacket fitted without a crease, as smooth as a second skin over his muscular torso. The urge to fling herself into his arms was almost irresistible.

'Sarah,' he said, 'I think you should sit down before we talk.'

'No. I-I must stand or I will not be able to say — what I must say.'

'You have something you wish to say to me?' His eyebrows quirked up in surprise.

'Yes.'

She twisted her fingers together. Suddenly she could remember none of the words she had intended to say. If only he would step forward and take her into his arms, as he had done before when they had been alone together! Her eyes roved over his face, pleading for him to understand, to make it easy for her. She willed him to take arrogant, assured command as he usually did — but he remained exactly where he was, scarcely moving a muscle.

'Well, Sarah?' he prompted.

She swallowed, and lowered her eyes from the penetrating stare of his. 'I — I'm willing,' she said.

He still did not move. Nor did he speak, at least not immediately. Then softly he repeated what she had said. 'You're — willing?'

'Yes, Harry.'

'Willing? Er — willing for what?'

Her courage was failing her, but there was no retreat for her now. She had brought him to her cabin for one reason, and one reason only. She struggled again to find words and recalled the conversation on their wedding night.

'I-I am willing to — to give you an heir.' The whispered sentence tumbled out so quickly her tongue stumbled.

She thought then he would take her into

his arms and this whole awful scene would be brought to an end, forgotten as she drowned in his kiss. She heard him draw in his breath sharply, but he still took not one step towards her.

'How very noble, Sarah. Do I understand you are actually offering to — er — sacrifice yourself to my lust?'

She closed her ears to the note of sarcasm in his voice.

'No, not really — not noble, I mean,' she replied seriously. 'It's just that I've been thinking and I know how much you have longed to have a child — and especially a son, if it can be managed — to inherit Ashingby. And I am your wife . . . ' She faltered, and broke off.

'Why, so you are, Sarah. Indeed, you have been my wife these past two weeks or more. But tell me, for I should be most interested to know, what makes the sudden change of heart now?'

'I-I wished to show my gratitude — I really think I would have died if they'd locked me up.' Surely he could understand? 'And now there is danger everywhere — the war is very close — you're going into battle — who knows what lies ahead?'

'Ah, I see.' He stroked his chin contemplatively, and his eyes continued to regard her with disconcerting steadiness. He seemed determined to keep the conversation cool and reasonable. 'You think your Yankee compatriots will achieve what the French failed to do and kill me off?'

She drew in her breath sharply. 'No — no! Please, do not tempt fate by talking so. Take care, Harry. I'm so afraid for you.'

'Very touching, but not really convincing, Sarah.'

She had expected him to be overjoyed — eager to clasp her in his arms, as he had done before. She had had no doubt that he would take her, make love to her. What was more, she fully believed she would become pregnant immediately — her only doubt had been whether she would produce a son — but she had not worried too much about that, because he had suggested that he would be just as happy with a female heir. Now he was here in her cabin, but her gesture was not being received with the pleasure she had expected. His attitude was making it all go wrong.

'I'm sorry,' she murmured. She felt defeated. 'I know I'm not explaining myself very well.'

'Then let us attempt to get the situation absolutely clear. Because there is danger ahead for me and you are grateful for the assistance you received by our marriage, you feel you have a duty to provide me with an heir. Is that correct?'

'I-I suppose so — at least, I thought — ' She lifted her arms in a gesture of helplessness, and then allowed them to drop to her sides. 'Obviously I was wrong. Please forget that I mentioned it.'

'Oh, no — I could not possibly do that. Nor would I wish to.' He moved very slightly towards her as he spoke.

Her heart began to beat furiously and, as she read the sensuality in him, she trembled.

Another step closer. 'Your offer is far, far too tempting to refuse, Sarah.'

She did not move, even when he reached towards her, touching her face gently, running his hands down her cheeks and over her shoulders. He placed a finger beneath her chin and lifted her face, so that she had to meet his eyes. She quivered at the burning desire she saw in them. He rubbed his thumbs very gently against her jawbone.

Until then she had not moved at all. Bemused by his changing attitude, she had simply watched and waited, but his touch was working a magic on her. As if of their own volition her arms were raised, she slipped caressing hands around the back of his neck and entwined her fingers in his hair.

His response was immediate. With a soft moaning sound, he grasped her, close, urgently, almost roughly. Crushed against his chest she felt his breath warm on her face. Just before he kissed her, he whispered in her ear, 'You are so beautiful, Sarah. So very, very beautiful. It would take a stronger, more honourable man than I am not to take advantage of such a delectable invitation.'

Then his mouth covered hers, and the sensation was just as sweet as she had remembered. She gave a gasp of pleasure. Sensually his lips moved over hers, and she returned his kisses with wanton voluptuousness, opening her mouth in total surrender to his, wanting the moment never to end. The tip of his tongue slipped into her mouth, gently probed and his kiss grew more possessive, more demanding, delighting her with a flood of new sensations.

'How I have longed for this!' he murmured. 'I have desired you quite desperately from the first moment I set eyes on you.'

His lips, softly moist, held, teased and played with hers — and now his hands roved down her back, awakening a tingling sensation along her spine. She made no demur. Even when he clasped her buttocks in an entirely reprehensible manner, it was as if she was suddenly unshockable. Instinctively she arched her back allowing him to draw her body closer to his.

She felt a touch of alarm at the unfamiliar masculinity of him but seemed to have no will-power to make even the least protest. She had offered herself, with little knowledge of reality and found herself filled with wonder, not only at what he was doing but in her supine acceptance. In amazement, she realized that she had unleashed an urge in him, more powerful than anything she had ever dreamed of and, even more extraordinarily, she was responding with a quite shameless lack of restraint.

When at last he disengaged his mouth from hers, it was only briefly to smile at her.

'What an exciting, enchanting woman you are, Sarah.'

Then he began to shower little tantalizing kisses inch by inch down her throat. His chin nuzzled into the low neckline of her gown and she gasped as he began to awaken undreamed of feelings in her breasts, making her nipples stand up in peaks. His fingers felt for the fastenings of her gown — suddenly she was uncertain. She should have been in her nightgown before this.

'Harry?'

'Yes?' His voice was muffled, she felt his breath on the skin between her breasts.

'Perhaps I should call Lucy.'

'Your maid? Why?' He lifted his head. There was a soft smile on his face.

'I-I thought perhaps she should help me get ready for bed,' she stammered.

'Not when I'm here.' He strode to the door and opened it. 'Lucy,' he called.

A scuffle of feet, then Lucy's voice. 'Yes, my lord?'

'Your mistress will have no more need for you this night. You may go to your bed.'

'Thank you, my lord.'

He closed the door behind him and turned the key in the lock. Facing her, keeping his eyes fixed on her face, he unfastened and removed his magnificent scarlet jacket and tossed it on to a chair as if it was but a rag. Mesmerized she watched as his fingers rapidly unknotted his stock and that too was cast aside. The ruffled front of his fine linen shirt lay open, revealing a mat of hair on his broad chest. He moved towards her and knelt to remove her slippers, one by one. She trembled slightly as his hand slid up her leg to above her knee, found and removed her garter, then rolled down her fashionable pink stockings.

'Now, Sarah. If you will turn around I will unfasten your gown.'

He knew exactly what he was doing. Shyly

she obeyed the cool command, and stood very still, scarcely daring to breathe, glad that her back was to him, intensely aware of his fingers untying the tapes, loosening folds. With his fingers on her bare flesh, he caressed her, even as he slipped the gown from her shoulders, easing it down, allowing it to fall to the floor, with as little care as he had shown for his own jacket and stock. Lastly, he set about removing her petticoat — her only item of underwear — all with a speed that suggested he knew a great deal about women's clothing.

Within minutes, her elegant clothes lay jumbled around her feet, or tossed unceremoniously aside. She was as naked as on the day she was born, and intensely aware that Harry was standing behind her.

She drew in a sharp breath, unsure what to do. She heard a movement and formed the impression that he had moved back a step, but he said nothing. His silence became unnerving. Was he waiting for her to make some other move? Should she get on to the bed? Did he find her ignorance irritating? She remained unmoving, eyes downcast, hands clasped in front of her.

'Sarah,' he whispered.

Still with her back to him, she turned her head, and glanced shyly over her shoulder.

'You're not having second thoughts?' he asked.

'No, my lord.'

'You're still — willing?' There was the hint of a chuckle in his throaty voice.

She nodded. To prove it, she turned and held out her arms towards him.

He uttered a deep groaning cry, as of exquisite anguish. His eyes raked over her, there was no amusement in them now. He moved swiftly, tore off his shirt, tugged impatiently at its fastenings, threw it aside.

She gazed in wonder at the strength of his muscular torso, the hair that matted not only his chest but grew lower on his body, down into the loosened top of his close-fitting white pantaloons. He tugged off his boots and moved towards her, picked her up and carried her over to the bed. Carefully, as if she was made of porcelain, he set her down on it, then stood up.

For a long while he remained there, gazing and gazing, seeming to drink her into his mind from her head to her toes, as if he could not have enough of looking at her. She read on his face the pleasure that her naked body was giving him, saw his eyes linger on those most private parts and her own sensuality was rekindled. She could have swooned beneath the carnality of his expression, the audacious lust of it awoke in her a tingling sensuality of response.

Slowly he unfastened the front flap of his pantaloons and stepped out of them. Momentarily she saw him, then he was on top of her, she felt the weight of his body pressing down on hers.

Softly he whispered, 'What a lucky fellow my heir will be — to have such a very, very beautiful mama.'

Those words reminded her that there was only one reason why he was there, reminded her that it was of an heir he was thinking, as solemnly, carefully and thoroughly he made love to her. He took care to see that she was aroused, kissing and caressing her until she was in a fever pitch of excitement. When he entered her she gave an involuntary gasp of pain. He stilled her cry with a kiss, virginity lost for ever, she clung to him and gloried in the excitement that coursed from his pulsating body to hers.

Just before she fell asleep she remembered — 'What was it you wished to say to me, Harry?'

'Never mind now. It will have to wait until the morning.' His voice trailed away.

She was content to leave it at that. His arms were still encircling her, emphasizing that wonderful feeling of being his. She lay very still. Within minutes his regular breathing told her he was asleep.

★ ★ ★

When she woke she was alone in the cabin. The boat was surprisingly still. She rolled over lazily, stretched and felt a vague reawakening of the sensations of the previous night. Her hand stroked her tummy — she tried to imagine the child she was quite sure now lay there within her. The thought made her wonder what Harry had looked like when he was a little boy? She imagined him as rather a serious child, but perhaps he had been quite different then, before life in the army hardened him?

She dismissed the fantasy. There was so much she would never know about him and her mood became sad. Harry had made love to her in no uncertain manner — but how could she use that word? There had been no love in it — lust, yes, she recognized that. From their very first meeting she had been aware that she aroused a strong physical desire in him. Last night was proof of that. He had said — *I have desired you quite desperately ever since I first saw you.* She recalled the cool way in which he had discussed her proposal when she first, falteringly mentioned what she had in mind. His lack of immediate response, had so distressed her that she had implored him to forget she had ever made such a suggestion. He had brushed that aside. Had he merely been teasing her, playing with her. *It would take a more honourable man than I am, not to take advantage of such a delectable invitation*, he had said. He had known precisely what he was about, as he had undressed her.

All that she could smile about — she was less certain about that moment when his naked body had pressed down upon hers. She wished he had not then been thinking about the begetting of an heir, even though it was she who had mentioned it earlier. Passionate though he was as a lover, there was still a part of him that was calculating, a part of him that remained remote from her, the part of him that belonged to the army, that which made him a soldier, hardened by battle. She wished she did not love him so desperately. For although she had believed herself in love with him before last night, her passionate nature was now more deeply aroused.

Her heart leapt when there was a light tap at the door, thinking he might be returning, but it was Lucy who entered, bringing breakfast on a tray.

'Mornin', my lady,' she said, glancing around the untidy cabin with a cheeky grin. 'His lordship said I was to bring breakfast to you.'

'Thank you, Lucy.'

Vaguely she wondered again — what was it Harry had intended to tell her?

Lucy poured coffee and, whilst Sarah ate, she set about tidying up the cabin, as if clothes scattered around the floor was an everyday occurrence, chattering cheerfully, as she always did.

'Where is the earl?' Sarah asked.

'On deck, miss. We're anchored off York. You'll never guess who his lordship was talking to, my lady,' Lucy went on.

Sarah waited and Lucy proceeded to give the answer with the minimum of delay. 'Two Red Indian gentlemen! They come aboard this morning, miss. Gave me quite a turn, it did, when I saw them.'

'They are Native Americans, Lucy. I'm sure they are friendly.'

'Well, I ain't used to seeing people like that, livin' most of my life in Norfolk, but my friend, Archie, said as how they're scouts an' bringin' news about the enemy, so I suppose it's all right.'

The enemy — again that horrifying realization! To her they were not and never

270

would be — the enemy. Americans were her own people! Sarah shuddered as visions of battles, fighting, invasion, flashed through her mind. She'd had a taste of it in that terrible sea-battle; she would never forget the horror of those dead and wounded men. For her it was like another civil war! Her husband on one side, and her countrymen on the other.

'I hope it's all going to be all right, miss.' Lucy's eyes were wide.

'I understand many of the Indians are on the British side in this conflict, Lucy,' Sarah said, with calming practicality. 'My papa has often told me that they've been sadly persecuted by some of the settlers in America.'

'Well, there they was, in company with his lordship, and they seemed to be talking quite friendly like. Tall, good-looking bloke one of them was, dressed outlandish though, all in leather, with fringes.'

Sarah was familiar with the native people; some had visited her father's surgery, though more often they relied on their own traditional medicines. She wondered fearfully what news they had brought. She thrust her breakfast tray aside and leapt out of bed.

'I must go up and discover what is happening, Lucy,' she said. 'Help me to dress, as quickly as you can.'

On deck Sarah's eyes immediately sought and found Harry. He was alone, looking through a telescope across the huge inland sea that was Lake Ontario. She moved quietly to stand by his side, gazing over the blue water that shimmered in the sunshine as far as the eye could see. Without even glancing in her direction he seemed to be aware of her presence. Perhaps it was the light touch of perfume she wore. 'Good morning, Harry.'

He lowered the telescope and looked down at her with a quizzical expression. 'I trust you slept well?'

'Very well, thank you.' She had not even been disturbed when he left her bed.

He murmured, 'Thank you — for last night.'

She smiled, then modestly lowered her eyes.

'You enchant me,' he said. 'Would that I could dally with you all day!' He turned away and lifted the telescope to his eye again.

'My lord, may I ask what it is you are looking at?'

'Nothing. Absolutely nothing!'

She was about to protest, but a wide smile spread over his face. 'Just as I hoped. No enemy ships in sight.'

'Lucy said some Indians had come aboard. I thought they might have brought news.'

'They did.' He paused. 'I was about to tell you, last night, Sarah, but you diverted me with a temptation far too compelling for me to refuse.'

'My lord — ' she protested.

He held up his hand. 'That is the truth. Nothing would have kept me from you — once you made that delectable offer.' His voice was low, husky. He paused. 'However, in the cold light of day reality has to be faced.'

'It is bad news?' she asked.

'Not entirely. But I think it is right that you should know. The Americans under Major-General Hull have moved into the attack.'

Sarah drew in her breath sharply. 'And you? Will you be taking part?'

'I'm waiting for official notice of where to muster my troops.'

Her worst nightmares were about to materialize. She knew the hatred felt by many Americans for the redcoats. They had not forgotten the War of Independence. Seth Boyer, her childhood friend, often told her how his grandfather had been killed at Bunker Hill. He hated the British. She looked at Harry and could not help thinking what an outstanding target he would make in his scarlet, gold-braided jacket. So tall, too, and leading his men.

'Dear God! What will happen?' she breathed.

'That we have to leave to fate. We can only do our best. I've been in battle before, and with my same tried and tested men. We are professionals.'

She felt like screaming her abhorrence of it all, but remained silent.

'My main concern, Sarah, is what to do about you. I've been trying to work out a plan which will enable you to reach your home and family. I've made arrangements which I think could be suitable, but unfortunately, because of events here, I cannot escort you all the way.'

She stared at him with blank disbelief. He was sending her away from him. Even after last night, he was still anxious to be rid of her at the earliest possible moment.

'What are these arrangements?' she asked, steadying her voice.

'Those Indians your maid saw — they're scouts and on the payroll of the British Army. A couple of first-class men. I sent them to Cassie's Rock to seek news of your family. I didn't tell you about it then; I didn't want to raise your hopes, in case it proved impossible.'

'And they returned this morning? Did they see my parents?' She waited breathlessly for his reply.

'They reached Cassie's Rock, but I'm afraid they did not actually meet your father.' He paused. She watched him apprehensively. Then he asked, 'Does the name Seth Boyer mean anything to you?'

'Why, yes. I know Seth very well. We practically grew up together. He was like an older brother to me.'

Harry was watching her so closely that she blushed, recalling that Seth had sometimes said he would marry her when they grew up. Just childish nonsense of course — and certainly meaningless now.

'Do you think he is trustworthy?' Harry asked.

'Absolutely!' She had no hesitation in answering.

He nodded, yet she felt he was still doubtful. 'The scouts said that the American Militia are camped in the region of Cassie's Rock. They had to move with the utmost care. But they are resourceful men and they know the territory — the militia are amateurs by comparison. My men managed to reach your father's house. It was late at night and there was no sign of Dr Dunthorne or any of your family.'

'If it was late at night they would probably be asleep,' Sarah said.

'That's what my scouts decided. They went

to the house asking for the doctor, saying they needed medicines. It was your friend, Seth Boyer, who answered their knock. He told them the doctor was not available, that he had been called out to an emergency.'

Sarah nodded. 'It's not unusual for Papa to be called out in the middle of the night. But I wonder why Seth was there?'

'That I don't know. I'd be happier about this if the scouts had actually spoken to your father. They did the best they could. I had written a note for Dr Dunthorne, telling him that his daughter was on her way home and at present in York. They handed it to Mr Boyer. I made no mention of our marriage, since if all goes well you will soon be reunited and you can then explain to the family the circumstances in which that came about.'

'Yes. Of course.'

She kept her eyes sadly downcast. What could she say about her marriage? She who had always expounded a romantic view of marrying for love! 'How surprised my papa and mama will be!'

Harry made no further comment on that. His mind was wrestling with the problem of getting her away. 'You have no doubt as to the loyalty of this friend?'

'Seth? I would trust him with my life.'

'That's what we may all be doing, if we

continue with this plan.'

'Seth has been my friend since the days when I was first able to toddle around after him. But — must I go? Can I not stay with you?'

'Impossible.' His tone brooked no argument. 'We'll follow the procedure suggested. I'm not entirely happy about it, but if you can reach your family, you will be safer with them than here in York on your own.'

'I'd hate to be here on my own,' she admitted.

Women suffered in war, even though they were physically in less danger. It was agonizing to think that soon he would be marching with his troops into battle.

'In normal times there would be no difficulty in crossing Lake Ontario at this time of the year,' he said. 'But nothing is the same, now.'

'You think it may be possible for me to get home?' Sarah asked.

'As long as we can trust Mr Boyer.'

'Seth has been my friend all my life,' she said.

'So be it. This evening, I'll accompany you on the trip across the lake. I'd like to escort you all the way to Cassie's Rock, but that's impossible. I cannot risk my scouts' lives again on American territory, even though they say they had no great difficulty. Mr Boyer suggests we meet up at a place called Lone Pine Beach. I can take you that far.'

'I know it well. It's a few miles from Cassie's Rock. In the summertime Papa sometimes hired a wagonette and took us there for a picnic.'

'I'll have to leave you there and return to my duties immediately. From that point you will have to travel under your friend's protection.'

'I'll be safe with Seth. And I'm still an American citizen.'

'Yes. We'll have to cross the lake by Indian canoe, and I'm afraid you'll be able to take only bare necessities with you. Be ready to leave early this evening.'

15

'Oh, my lady! I don't know how you dare! I couldn't do it. Please don't ask me.'

Lucy's eyes filled with genuine horror when Sarah explained that she was about to travel by canoe across Lake Ontario. She had hoped to take Lucy with her.

'Indian canoes are safer than they look, Lucy. And the lake should be calm at this time of the year — '

'So you may say, my lady.' Lucy set her mouth in a stubborn line. 'I wouldn't set foot in one of those dreadful contraptions, not if you promised me the top brick off the chimney.'

'But, Lucy — '

'There's no but about it, my lady. My mind's made up!' She shook her head very positively. 'I'm sorry. I don't like letting you go off on your own, but since you're going back to your family, you won't really be needing me anyway, will you?'

'I really don't want to part with you, Lucy — I'll miss you. I'll always think of you as a friend. What will you do, if you don't come with me?'

Lucy's eyes twinkled. 'I'll be all right. You don't have to worry about me. My friend, Archie Reynolds, has asked me to marry him. He wants to set me up in lodgings in the town, until he gets back.'

'Oh, Lucy!' Sarah exclaimed. 'I might have guessed. But I remember times when it seemed as if the poor man could do nothing right in your eyes.'

Lucy tossed her head. 'I couldn't let him think I was chasing him, could I now?'

'You certainly didn't do that! Dear Lucy — I wish you every happiness.'

Sarah gave her maid a hug, and felt a twinge of envy. How she wished that Harry had suggested setting her up in lodgings in the town! If only she could stay near him! She hated being sent away like this, but he had refused to listen to any protest.

'I'll be right sorry to leave you, my lady,' Lucy said. 'You've been real good to me. Now I suppose I'd better start packing your things.'

'I can only take the barest necessities for the few days we'll be travelling. I'll leave almost all my clothes and things behind — you can have everything. It'll be part of my wedding present to you. And here's your money, and I'll add this extra — you're bound to have a great many expenses living here.'

'Oh, my lady! It's too much — '

'Nonsense.' Sarah swept aside her thanks.

'My lady, could I just ask one favour of you before you go?'

'Of course. What is it?'

'Could you write a letter to my ma and pa? Let them know as I'm here, and about Archie and me gettin' married an all that.'

'Of course. I'll be delighted to do that. Can your mother read?'

'No. She'll get the vicar to read it for her. I'd like her to know it's all turned out well for me.'

Better for maid than for her mistress, Sarah thought! But was it? It would not be a happy time for Lucy when her Archie went off to the front line and she was left alone in a strange land.

She wrote the letter straight away, and insisted that Lucy sat beside her to tell her exactly what she wanted to put down. She envied the uncomplicated love that shone from the girl's face as she talked about her fiancé.

'I'll ask the earl to arrange for the letter go on the next homeward-bound ship,' Sarah promised.

Then she turned her thoughts to her own affairs, for she had to make preparations as

Harry had instructed.

'It may be cool out on the lake tonight,' she said. 'I'd better travel in my warm skirt and blouse, and take a woollen cloak. Dark colours will be best.'

'I'll get them ready at once. Oh, miss, I do wish we didn't have to part like this.'

'So do I, Lucy, but we have to be sensible.'

★ ★ ★

'Very sensible.'

Wrenningham ran his eyes over her with approval when Sarah presented herself on deck early in the evening, wearing warm, dark clothing. He was waiting for her alone. Most of the soldiers and sailors had gone ashore, so that only a skeleton crew and guard had been left on board. Lucy had gone off arm in arm with Archie, filled with a mixture of curiosity and fear of the unknown, but proud and trusting, since she was with the man she loved.

As Harry stepped out of the shadows she noticed with relief that he had discarded his usual distinctive uniform, and was dressed like one of his Indian scouts. He looked less civilized, yet startlingly magnificent in a fringed buckskin jerkin which hung ragged-edged over loose trousers of the same material. Leather thonging laced up his soft-soled moccasins. He was armed with a rifle and a pistol and carried a round hat of beaver fur.

'So. The time has arrived. Are you quite ready?' he asked.

He sounded almost as reluctant about this expedition as she was. A fleeting breath of hope flared in her. As she had completed her preparations she had felt less and less willing to leave him.

'Please, Harry, can I not come with you? I have heard soldiers' wives sometimes follow their husbands to the very edge of the battlefield. The French have a lovely word for such ladies — *vivandières*. Truly, if you will take me I would be very little trouble to you — '

'Are you out of your mind! You know nothing of conditions under which soldiers live near the front line — and in a wilderness of a land such as this, goodness knows what we shall encounter. As for *vivandières* I'm surprised you even know of the name! Camp-followers! To provide for the soldiers' needs, that's what they are. Now, Sarah, let us waste no more time. The canoe waits alongside. We have only to get into it and go.'

He brushed away the vague hope, which had stirred in her heart, as if it was disgusting. The harsh note of impatience had returned to his voice; this was his plan and it had to be followed to the letter. She squared her shoulders. If that was the way he wanted it, then she was ready.

He took from her the small bundle which Lucy had packed — a change of underwear, a few medical items and bandages, some bread and cheese she had fetched from the cook. Wistfully, Sarah had slipped in a tiny phial of her favourite perfume.

'During the whole of this operation we must be as quiet as possible,' he warned.

She nodded. With his hand on her elbow Harry led her to the side of the ship. A rope ladder hung down, and below — a very long way below it seemed — she could see the dugout canoe with impressively upswept prow, carved and painted to propitiate the gods. At least a dozen men were seated therein. All were of Indian blood, ready at their paddles, still and silent as they waited.

'Shall I go first and help you down?' Harry offered.

'Yes, please.'

She began to understand Lucy's reluctance at trusting herself to such a craft.

Even getting into it from the high deck of the ship was not easy, especially hampered as she was by billowing skirts. However, it had to be tackled, and this was no time for squeamishness. Harry had swung himself over the side and was balanced on the ladder waiting for her.

Reminding herself that he had already seen much more of her than just her legs, she hitched up those cumbersome skirts and bunched them into the waistband. Carefully she placed one foot and then the other on the wooden rungs of the rope ladder and began her descent. It was a comfort to know that Harry was close below her. His words of encouragement helped her to climb down with movements which she hoped, even in these circumstances, were not too indecorous.

When at last she reached the bottom of the unsteady ladder, he took a firm grip on her hand and with courtesy and concern made sure that she was comfortably settled in the stern of the canoe. A feather cushion had been placed in readiness for her, a soft woven rug thoughtfully placed to be tucked around her.

Harry took his place beside her; he spoke to the chief of the Indians, whose name she discovered was Black Wolf. The chief gave a command in the tribe's own language and at once the canoe was pushed off and swung away from the ship. With steady raking sweeps of their paddles the Indians expertly headed their long streamlined and perfectly balanced craft out over the lake, as straight as an arrow.

They skimmed over the water, the men working together in easy unison, gradually building up to a surprising speed. Sarah glanced back and saw the ship, and behind it, in silhouette, the outline of the wooden buildings that made up the town of York. A few lights glittered intermittently, and all around was a back-cloth of tall pine trees. Ahead of them lay the dark waters of the great lake, ominous, vast and unfriendly. She shivered apprehensively. When, a few minutes later, she turned her head again everything was much smaller, already receding into the distance. The die had been cast.

The premonition of trouble ahead did not leave her. She tried to tell herself she was being ridiculous. She should be happy, excited — she was going home, returning to the familiar land of her birth. She concentrated her thoughts on her coming reunion with all those dear members of her family. Even that vision was clouded. They would not be pleased with her. She had been sent as their ambassador — and she was being sent home in disgrace. She hoped that she would be able to make her papa understand, but even he might feel that she had acted unwisely. As for what Monica and the boys would say, she hardly dared think.

Worse — much worse — than any of that, was the inevitability of parting with Harry. That it followed so closely on last night's wonderful awakening to the full glory of love, made it all the more poignant. She had thought she loved him before then, now, after the sensuous harmony of surrendering her body to his, the fullness of love enveloped her. She didn't want to be parted from him — but what could she do? Harry had given his word that she was to be delivered back to her parents, and nothing would make him back out of that. To him she was now an encumbrance.

In a surprisingly short space of time there was no land to be seen. Darkness enveloped them. In bad weather storms could whip up the waters of the Great Lakes as wild and rough as an ocean — thankfully that evening the weather was calm.

The Indians worked almost in silence, broken occasionally by a grunt. The rhythm of the paddles, and of the men's arms and shoulders, swinging to and fro, evenly and unchanging, was hypnotic and calming.

'Try to sleep, Sarah,' Harry whispered.

She smiled wryly. That was impossible. She

noticed that he did not sleep either — there was too much tension in the air.

★ ★ ★

They approached land under cover of darkness. The Indians slowed their paddling, and were edging the canoe slowly, silently forward. Harry picked up his telescope, scanned ahead and all around.

'Sarah, can you describe Lone Pine Beach to me?'

'It's a just a small bay. I don't know why it's got that name. There are many more than one pine tree, a whole forest of them at the back of the beach.'

'That's what I can see. If that's Lone Pine Beach, I don't like the look of it. Those trees could provide cover for a whole regiment. I'd like to find somewhere more open if possible.'

He consulted with Black Wolf. An order was given softly, and responding to it, the canoe was turned so that it proceeded alongside the shore. Sarah strained her eyes and noticed a movement.

'There,' she pointed. 'Just at the edge of the beach. I think I can see someone standing.'

'Yes. I've got him in the sight. Take a look through the telescope, Sarah.'

She had never used a telescope before and

it took her a little time to adjust her sight accurately. Harry waited with unusual patience.

'Can you see him? Is it your friend?'

'Yes. That's Seth.'

'Are you absolutely sure?'

'Absolutely. He's seen us — he's waving.'

Sarah waved back.

'Right. Then we'll go in,' said Harry. 'Stand ready, Sarah. You must get off as quickly as you can. You should be safe with your friend, but I've instructed the braves to turn about immediately.'

She sensed his anxiety, it had matched her own. It had been either foolhardy or extraordinarily courageous for him to come here, into enemy territory. She should never have allowed him to take such a risk; she could have deterred him if she had said she did not trust Seth — but that would have been ridiculous. Seth would never do anything to harm her.

Soon she would be with her old friend, on American soil, and Harry would be free to return to his regimental duties with no care for her. That was what he wanted. That was why she was here, ready to step ashore.

She turned to him — to this beloved man who was her husband. She couldn't bear to say goodbye. Would she ever see him again? The future was bleak and unknown. She yearned with all her heart and soul to kiss him, to be held in his arms once more, but he made no move towards her.

'Till we meet again,' she said.

'May it be in happier circumstances,' he responded crisply. 'Your friend is waiting.'

She stood up. The Indians had turned the canoe alongside. Seth had waded into the water. She saw his face, his eyes fastened on her. He leaned towards her. His arm was outstretched. She reached towards him, put her hand in his and immediately she was grasped in a grip of iron. He pulled her sharply towards him, catching her in strong arms, swinging her across to the beach. Her feet skimmed the water. In a moment he was there beside her. It all happened so quickly she could hardly believe she was actually standing on American soil. The canoe was already moving away — Harry was leaving her.

'Take good care of her, Mr Boyer.'

Harry was standing up in full view, his tall, slender frame, dressed Indian fashion was silhouetted against the silvery lake. His voice sped softly over to the water, every word clear.

Seth gave an involuntary movement. 'That's no Indian,' he snarled.

He pushed her aside and in a flash picked

up the rifle he had leaned against a tree. All in one movement he raised it to his shoulder.

'No!' Sarah screamed.

With all her might she threw herself against Seth. He fired. In an unbelievable agony of horror she saw Harry drop.

'No!' she screamed again. 'Harry-'

She rushed forward and would have waded into the water, but Seth grabbed her, held her back roughly. He jerked her round to face him.

'Who was that?'

She was too shocked to answer. He shook her. He repeated through clenched teeth, 'Who was that?'

'Harry.' Her voice was a dull whisper.

The canoe was moving away fast. She stared after it and a deathly chill gripped her, she had never in her life felt such an utter helpless desolation of misery.

'Harry? Who is Harry?' Seth was angry, demanding.

'You killed him,' she whispered in dull disbelief.

'Yup. And that's one bloody Englishman the less. I reckon that's my revenge for my grandpa who was killed at Bunker Hill. You don't need to mourn any of that lot! You're safe now, back on American soil where you belong, Sarah. But we mustn't linger here.

291

This way — hurry.'

He held out a hand to her, but she ignored it. She had no will to move. Her legs were shaking; her knees felt like jelly, they had lost all strength. She sank down to the ground, fell in a heap. Helpless, mindless, she sat there, huddled up, not weeping, just twisted in silent tearing agony.

'Hey, Sarah, come on. Get up — we gotta git goin'. You ain't got no call to act like that.' A pleading note came into Seth's voice.

In a state of shock she heard him as if distantly, his words meant nothing. She had no power to move, even if she had wanted to. She shook her head, rocked back and forth, made little moaning sounds. He put a hand on her shoulder. Locked in grief she didn't even bother to shake it off.

'OK,' he said. 'That's all right, Sarah. You just stay there. I'll fetch the horses, bring 'em down here.'

She had no idea how long he was away, did not hear him return. When he lifted her, placed her on the horse's back, she accepted it, responded like an automaton. In the dim recesses of her disturbed mind she thought that they were going to Cassie's Rock, to her family. But there was no joy in the prospect of reunion. She didn't care where he took her.

Harry was dead. Seth had shot and killed him. Those words battered and battered into her head, again and again. It wouldn't have happened but for her. She blamed herself. She was guilty. She should have thought how Seth hated the English. She wished he would shoot her too. She wanted only to die, to go with Harry.

Riding was like second nature, she sat in the saddle, responded mechanically to the movement of the horse beneath her. Seth mounted and led her, quite slowly at first, then seeing that she was responding sufficiently well, he set the horses trotting. She took no notice of the tracks they took, saw no trees even when the forest became denser, making the night darker, closing in on them. Time meant nothing. On and on. Where they were meant nothing. Nor did she care where they were going. Life meant nothing. Harry was dead.

Seth stopped the horses outside a roughly built log cabin. He dismounted, held up his arms and helped Sarah down. Then at last she began to look about her. This was not home. They were in the depths of the forest.

'Where are we?'

'It's all right. It's my cabin, Sarah. I'll make some food, we'll carry on tomorrow.'

'I don't want anything to eat.'

'Come inside and rest anyway.'

'I want to go to Cassie's Rock. I have to get home.'

'So you shall — tomorrow. I'll take you home tomorrow.'

He tried cajoling her, talking to her in a softly persuasive voice. When she refused to move, and stood stubbornly still, seeming not to know what he wanted of her, Seth lost patience.

'Get inside, Sarah — stop this nonsense.'

He tied up her horse, then propelled her forward. His hand was hard and heavy on her shoulder, he pushed her through the door. She felt as helpless as a child, mindless, with no will to resist. What did it matter where she was? She stumbled into the cabin. He settled her into a rocking chair and she slumped down on the soft cushions. She felt his hand brush over her hair and turned her head sharply away.

'I'll light the lamp, and make coffee,' he said 'That's what you need, Sarah, coffee with a slug of bourbon in it.'

He moved about, busily, talking as he did so. The yellow glow of the lamp revealed the sparsely furnished room. He talked to her as if she was a child who had suffered some slight mishap.

'There, isn't that better? Don't you fret, Sarah, I'll look after you.'

She watched him with hatred in her heart. Didn't he know what he had done? A few dry sticks on the hot ashes in the stove made it blaze up.

'You're safe now, Sarah. Coffee won't be long. You just tell me what's the matter, eh? I'll take care of you.'

'You — shot — my — husband.'

The words came out, very slowly and deliberately. It was as if speaking them brought her mind back into focus. Seth stood very still. All the hatred in her heart was in her eyes as she glared at him.

'Why, Seth? Why did you do it? You pretend to be my friend, but you're a murderer. You murdered my husband. I can't stay here — '

She pushed herself out of the chair and would have run to the door, but Seth was there before her.

'Your husband? That bloody Englishman!' he shouted. 'Why in hell's name would you marry an Englishman?'

'I love him.'

'We're at war, don't you know that? The English are our enemies — how could you have married one of them?'

'What has war to do with love?'

'People get killed in wars. You'll forget him — '

'Never. Never.' Her voice was rising to a scream.

'You're going to marry me, Sarah. You know that. That's what we've always planned. I'll look after you — '

'Then take me home, now, Seth.'

'Can't do that, Sarah. You just settle to stay here, an' you'll be all right.' He pushed home the bolts on the door. 'You're mine, my sweetheart. We've always been meant for each other.'

'Seth — please! Take me back to Cassie's Rock — to my family.'

'They're not there,' he growled. 'They've left.'

'Left? What do you mean?'

'Gone down to Boston, to stay with your uncle, for the duration of the war.'

'I-I don't believe you! Not Papa. He wouldn't leave his patients.'

'Well, no. Not the good doctor.' There was a hint of sarcasm in his voice. 'He's been commandeered to serve in the militia. He's too old really, but they're short of doctors. He wouldn't leave your mama and the other children in Cassie's Rock alone, that's why he sent them down to Boston.'

'But that wasn't the message I received.'

She was listening to him now, hearing him

clearly — and was beginning to understand. Her mind was reacting with anger to what he was telling her, but she was having difficulty in believing it was true.

'I said what was best for you, Sarah, honey.' Seth's voice was soft, friendly, but she no longer trusted him. 'They'd never have brought you back to me, if I'd told them your folks had all gone.'

'I don't understand.' Her suspicions grew with everything he said. 'Why were you there, in our house?'

'When those Indians came? I was getting the place set up ready for the militia to take over. It's been requisitioned. They're goin' to billet headquarters staff there.' He had remained with his back to the door.

Then it must be true. None of her family was in Cassie's Rock. She stared at him in fear and horror. What was she to do?

'Come here, Sarah.'

He held out his arms, but there was menace in his voice. His shoulders were hunched as he advanced towards her. She backed away, glanced around desperately, for a way of escape. The night was pitch black outside the uncurtained window.

'You're mine, Sarah. I will have you, whether you want to or not. I've waited too long — '

He reached out for her and she darted away. The immediate danger brought her sharply back to her senses. Instinct for survival was strong — and not just for herself. She had another life beside her own to fight for. She had lain with Wrenningham and to her mind it was reasonable to suppose that his heir was already conceived within her womb. She began to plead with him.

'Seth — please — be calm. I'm with child.'

He drew in his breath sharply. 'So. That too! You're a whore, Sarah Dunthorne — or should I say Mrs Something-or-other?'

'I am now a countess — the Countess of Wrenningham,' she said. Absurdly she thought the name and the title might have had some steadying influence on Seth. Its effect was quite the reverse.

'Huh!,' he snorted in disgust. 'A countess! Pah! So you've sold yourself for a bloody English title. Well, that don't cut no ice with me, Sarah Dunthorne. We grew up together — remember? I know you're no better than I am.'

Slowly he moved forward, cat-like, ready to spring as soon as he got near enough to her. She backed away, keeping her distance, never taking her eyes from him. She darted behind the table. It was homemade and heavy. He followed. They were moving, slowly, all the time.

'Seth, be reasonable. Of course, I haven't forgotten — we were such good friends.'

She forced herself to keep talking even as she was backing away. Step by step, she kept moving sideways around the table keeping him on the opposite side of it. 'We were such good friends, Seth — '

'We were kids then,' he interrupted. 'That's not enough for me now, Sarah. I want you as a man wants a woman — and you *are* my woman.'

Inexorably he moved after her, taking his time, certain of himself.

She kept just that bit ahead of him. She had almost completely circled the table, changing their positions. Seth was on the opposite side of it. The door was behind her, about two or three yards away she calculated. That gave her hope, yet common sense told her she could never escape that way. She had watched him draw the two heavy bolts across, fastening it top and bottom. The moment she turned towards the door, even before she could shift the bolts, Seth would be round the table.

With his strength he would easily over-power her. She had the impression he was actually waiting for her to make such a move, goading her, enjoying her desperation, wanting an excuse to grab her, brutally. Her terrified thoughts were whirling.

Then she remembered his gun. He had stood it up by the wall just inside the door. Slowly, eyes narrowed and calculating as an animal stalking his prey, Seth took another step towards her. Her only hope was to move swiftly.

She swung round, saw the gun, picked it up, lifted it and without another thought fired. A look of disbelief flashed on to Seth's face; slowly his body twisted around. With a bloodcurdling scream he fell to the floor.

She dared not look at him. She had no idea whether she had killed or wounded him. Her one thought was to get out of the cabin — to get away. She threw herself at the door, wrenched back the bolts and flung it open. Without a backward glance she rushed over the threshold — out into the night — breathing deeply of the pine-scented air.

16

Outside the log cabin Sarah stopped, looking wildly about her. A night bird screeched. How could the world be so peaceful and normal after what she had just done! Had she killed Seth Boyer? What should she do now? She had to get away, but where was she? Which way should she run?

The silence of the black night was broken by the snap of a twig. It was followed by a rustling sound. Fear prickled up the back of her neck. Someone was out there, in the woods. More than one — she heard scuffling feet. Every muscle in her body was alert now, tensed, listening. She picked up the whisper of voices.

Instinctively, she moved to one side, pressing herself close to the cabin wall, glad of her dark clothes, keeping in the shadows.

Slowly she edged towards where the horses were tethered. Who could be coming? She heard a groan from inside the cabin. Seth was alive; that added an extra edge to her fear. The voices grew louder, Americans. She heard the familiar cadences. A little group of them. Four or five. She caught a brief glimpse of them now. Militiamen, comrades of Seth, She held her breath, alert, listening.

'Seth?'

'What the hell's he doin' here?'

'Is he alone?'

Thankfully, all the other men crowded through the door. Sarah sprang into action.

She had only minutes, perhaps seconds, before Seth told them about her. As soon as he explained what had happened, how recently he had been shot, the militiamen would be out. She could all too easily imagine them. They would burst out of the cabin and spread out, searching for her, trigger-happy with those guns. Their minds would be set on revenge — she would have no chance to explain — she had shot their comrade: she could expect no mercy.

The patrol had been on foot, that was to her advantage. Moving fast, she unhitched the reins of both horses, swung herself up into the saddle of the nearest one. She had to ride astride and pulled up her voluminous skirts. She paused momentarily and gave the spare horse a slap on the rump. It reared up, then plunged away into the forest. Gathering up the reins, she dug in her heels and sent the animal on which she was mounted springing forward along the track. Bending low to avoid overhanging branches, she kept up the speed.

She glanced behind once, saw one of the militiamen in the doorway. He lifted his rifle to his shoulder; she heard a shout, but no shot. Had he decided not to waste his ammunition? Had someone from within ordered him not to shoot? She had no way of knowing.

It was but a temporary respite, danger remained all about her. When she looked behind again the cabin was hidden from view. She kept going as fast as she could, hampered by the roughness of the track and by the low branches of the crowded trees. It was a matter of life and death to put as much space as possible between her and that cabin.

She had no idea where she was going. What should she do? Could she find her way alone to Cassie's Rock? If what Seth said was true, her family had moved to Boston. Would there be any way she could find her papa, if he was in the militia?

Had Seth told her the truth? She had no reason to believe him — not now, not after his treachery. Not after his vile attempt to take her by force. If she went to Cassie's Rock there would surely be some people left there — but would they, too, call her a traitor for marrying an Englishman? Would this dreadful war make them think of her as an enemy?

Her mind was filled with panic. She

couldn't think straight. She believed she was heading back in the direction from which she and Seth had come but she couldn't be sure. Even if she arrived back at Lone Pine Beach she had no means of crossing the lake. Harry was dead and the Indians had paddled away within seconds of that fatal shot being fired. There was no one near to help her.

Her horse's hooves were muffled by the pine needles carpeting the track. How peaceful the forest would be, if she wasn't in such torment! Just a slight soughing breeze in the branches. The moon cast intermittent ethereal light wherever it could penetrate the shadowy darkness of the trees. She wasn't afraid of the night, nor of the forest. To her, those things were part of the real world, the good, honest true world.

It was men she had to fear, for human sounds that her eyes and ears were alert. The horse plodded on. Suddenly — darkly ghost-like, a figure loomed up at the side of the track. She stifled the scream that built up in her throat. Huge he seemed, as he emerged from the trees, this shadowy monster — big, brown-clad, but pale-faced. She gasped as he sprang forward, she would have spurred her horse on and away, but he flung himself at the animal's head and caught hold of the reins. 'Sarah!'

The low-key voice was sharp — and immediately recognizable. Her heart seemed to stop beating. A ghost! Oh, dear God! Who or what was this — this thing in human shape — like a shadow of the man — so familiar, the man who had been shot before her eyes. She shook her head, trying to clear her vision. It couldn't be Harry — Harry was dead! She was seeing things — her overwrought imagination must be playing tricks!

The horse pranced about, tossed its head, nostrils flaring. Then, held by the man's firm restraining hands, using soft-voiced orders, the animal responded and calmed down. It was no ghost.

'Harry?' Sarah whispered tentatively.

She reached out a hand to touch him, to assure herself that he was real, but he was not quite close enough.

'Yes. I'm here.'

Then she believed at last, even though she could not understand.

'Seth shot you — I saw you fall.'

'Black Wolf saved me. He acted like quicksilver — pulled my feet from under me. I heard the bullet whistle past. It was the closest shave I've ever had!' His voice was cool.

She drew in a quick breath. 'I was sure you were dead — I didn't think I'd ever see you again.'

'I got the impression that Mr Boyer was not as friendly as you believed him to be.'

That cool British understatement! Wrenningham's touch of irony was not lost on her.

'He — he — Oh Harry! I can't tell you how awful it's been! I didn't know what to do. Seth says my folks have all left Cassie's Rock and gone to Boston.'

She heard him draw in a sharp breath. 'Just as well we turned back.' His voice held a grim note.

'I thank God you did! For I don't know what I'd have done otherwise.' She was beginning to regain a modicum of composure.

'I was afraid for you, Sarah. I had to investigate. We landed a bit further along the shore. Black Wolf volunteered to accompany me. He had no difficulty in following the tracks of your two horses — until they were crossed by five or six militiamen, on foot. Then we had to take cover —'

'Those must have been the men who came to the cabin — where Seth took me. Oh, Harry — I-I shot him. It was the only way I could escape — they may be following me —'

She gasped as a figure rose from the forest, then with relief, recognized Black Wolf. He moved with uncanny silence, put his finger to his lips and spoke softly.

'Enemy. Men coming. You ride.'

Harry leapt up behind Sarah, grabbed the reins and set the horse moving forward. Black Wolf loped along, with fluid speed. Occasionally he would pause, hold up his hand and listen. Sometimes he knelt and put his ear to the ground. Then she found herself holding her breath, not daring to move a muscle, until with a beckoning wave, fleet-footed and strong, he darted forward again. With as little sound as possible they followed. She neither heard nor saw those signs that Black Wolf was reading from broken twigs, from indentations on the forest floor, from the movements of the birds, to him it was like a map.

Dawn was breaking when he led them down to the shore of the lake. The water stretched wide and empty for as far as she could see. Black Wolf put his hands to his mouth and made the trilling sound of a song bird. As if by magic, the canoe emerged from the cover of a cluster of fallen tree trunks.

Harry dismounted. He held up his arms and she dropped into them. Even with the underlying danger, she felt secure as he kept her in his arms, carried her across to the water's edge and set her in the canoe. Harry and Black Wolf stepped in, and without a moment's waste of time, with scarcely a word spoken, the Indians dug their paddles into the water and began to propel the canoe rapidly out over the lake.

Seconds later, the American militiamen burst out of the woods. They raised their rifles — she closed her eyes and prayed. The bullets spat up the water a couple of feet behind them. The canoe was just out of range of their fire. The Indians paddled on stoically, the rhythm of their movement totally undisturbed, as if the incident had never happened.

Sarah felt guilty at having been the cause so much trouble. 'I'm sorry, Harry. I never expected Seth to act like that.'

He shrugged. 'We all make mistakes.' His voice sounded as weary as he looked.

She longed to be able to make amends, tried to explain. 'Looking back I can see I should have known. He hated the English because of his grandpa being killed at Bunker Hill. Something seemed to snap in him when he heard your voice.'

'That was obvious!' His tone was curt.

Then she whispered softly, 'I'm so grateful that you came to look for me.'

'What else could I do! I couldn't leave you there in the wilderness with a man who was either completely ruthless or deranged — or both! Don't keep apologizing. I accept that you were not to blame for what happened.'

He gave a wry smile. 'At least not intentionally.'

'I can't understand how Seth had changed — '

'There's no point in discussing it any further. What happened is past — let it rest. The moment we get back to York I shall have to move off with my men. I've been away longer than I expected. We're both tired. Try and get some sleep.'

He stretched an arm around her shoulders and pulled her head down to rest with delicious comfort against the soft leather of his Indian jerkin. She relaxed against his living warmth. When he moved off with his men, she was determined to accompany him. Even if she could not have his love, she could put up with anything, as long as she was with him. Quietly content, and very, very tired, she closed her eyes.

★　★　★

'I am at a loss as to what arrangements to make now,' said Harry.

The canoe had drawn up alongside the boat half an hour previously. Sarah had climbed up the rope ladder, much relieved to be back on the familiar deck. The troops and crew were all on board; they had been ready to sail for the past six hours, had been held back, waiting only for his return.

'What do you mean — arrangements?' she asked.

'I intended to find lodgings for you, here in York,' he said. 'Now we've wasted hours on that wild-goose chase, there's no time for me to look around.'

'You surely don't mean to leave me here, alone!' she exclaimed in horror.

'I have to, Sarah. We're marching to the battle zone. Whilst I've been away, word has come through of Yankee troop movements heading towards Queenstown and Fort George. Reinforcements are needed there immediately. You'll be safer in York — your maid is already there, is she not?'

'It's all right for Lucy. She is British by birth,' Sarah pointed out. 'I'm American. I'll be looked upon as an enemy.'

'Nonsense! You're the Countess of Wrenningham. You bear my name — that will ensure your safety.'

'But it won't, Harry. Terrible things happen in war. Seth tried to kill you just because he could tell by your voice you were English.'

'That was different. I'm a man.'

'Being a woman didn't save me from persecution when we were on the ship, Harry. Just think what could happen to me if Mr Williams heard that I was in York, alone.'

'But we left him in Quebec.'

'That's not so far. The boats sail every day. The fact that I am the Countess of Wrenningham, would make me noticeable. Word might reach Mr Williams — you saw how he distrusted me. He might find out I am here. Can't you see, Harry? I dare not go ashore unprotected — let alone live there!'

Her fear was genuine, and she was spurred on also by her heart's desire not to be parted from him. She was distressed and angry when he dismissed her reasoning.

'In normal circumstances I might agree with you, Sarah. But this is no trip for a lady, we're going to the battlefield. It's a matter of choosing the lesser of the evils. You are exaggerating the situation.'

'I'm not, Harry. Truly I'm not!'

He sighed. 'If only I could have gone ashore and found good lodgings — then I could have made sure you were in the care of someone I could trust. Now there's no time for that. I can't hold up the men any longer.'

'Please, Harry, allow me to come with you. I assure you I shall be no trouble — never stand in the way no matter what happens.'

'You really are so determined?' His voice still expressed doubts.

'I am. Totally.' She was pleading as if for her life.

He looked at her, long and hard, deliberating. Then he nodded curtly. 'Very well.'

He turned away and strode off to attend to more urgent duties. Within a short time they set sail. Sarah was accommodated in the same cabin as on the trip from Quebec. She missed having Lucy there, both for her company and for her helpfulness, but as she was the eldest of a far from wealthy family she was accustomed to doing things for herself.

The boat hugged the coast of Canada as they sailed further westwards along Lake Ontario, towards Hamilton. There they disembarked and continued overland, crossing Stoney Creek. Horses were hired for the officers and for Sarah.

Harry assigned Reynolds to ride alongside her, and meekly she obeyed any order that was given. For hour after hour, she followed close behind the winding line of troops. Sometimes she talked to Archie Reynolds, quizzing him about where Lucy was staying. She was pleased to hear that he had found accommodation for her with a pleasant family where there were several children.

'Lucy seemed to like that,' he said. 'She was teaching them singing and dancing games when I left.'

'I can well believe it,' Sarah smiled.

'We're going to be wed, as soon as I get back from the front,' Archie said.

'You're a lucky man. Lucy is a fine young woman.'

'I think so,' he said, with simple sincerity.

On and on they went, with only occasional, very brief rest halts. Sarah was grateful she was not on foot, heavily laden with equipment as were the soldiers. Although the journey was long and tiring, she was determined to give Harry no cause for complaint. He seemed to be scarcely aware of her, as he rode at the head of the column.

17

Fort George stood on a height overlooking the Niagara River. It was surrounded by high wooden ramparts, spiked at the top and heavily fortified to repel attack. The walls enclosed several acres of land used as parade ground and exercise yards, with a multitude of buildings, towers and look-outs. Close by, but outside the walls was an Indian village, for the fort was a trading post as well as a defensive position.

Wrenningham and the commander of the fort saluted each other, then shook hands. They talked in friendly fashion, as they entered one of the buildings.

Archie Reynolds came to Sarah and assisted her to dismount. She was greatly relieved to slip her aching body from the back of the horse, for it had been a long hard ride. It was late at night and she had been in the saddle for so long her legs felt wobbly and painful.

'His lordship instructed me to see you installed in his quarters, my lady,' Reynolds explained. 'He will join you there later. This way, if you please.'

Accommodation for the officers stood three storeys high, with verandas all around the wooden building. There were smaller cabins for the men, constructed of logs cut from the surrounding forests.

Reynolds carried a candle to light her way up the wooden stairs, and showed her into a room on the second floor. He placed the candle on a table.

'I'll bring up your luggage, my lady,' he said. 'Then I'm to fetch you something to eat from the cook-house.'

'Thank you, Mr Reynolds.'

He left and Sarah looked around the room, seeing it but dimly in the flickering light of the candle. It was quite spacious, but bare and spartan, dominated by a double bed, well supplied with pillows and woven blankets and a counterpane. Although that summer night was pleasantly mild, it would be bitterly cold in winter. There were two or three chairs and a wash-stand with jug and basin. Rugs were scattered on the bare planks of the floor.

Reynolds returned with the small amount of personal luggage she had been able to bring with her, stuffed into a pannier which had been carried on one of the packhorses. Quickly she took out her soap and flannel and set about washing herself. That done she felt much refreshed, found her phial of perfume and splashed a little on her throat.

Before long Reynolds returned yet again, this time with a tray of food.

'Will there be anything more, my lady?' he enquired.

'No, thank you, Mr Reynolds. I am sure you are in need of food and a rest yourself.'

'I won't deny as I am pretty weary, ma'am. As indeed are we all. If there's nothing more I can do for you, I'll be glad to get myself a bite to eat and turn in.' With a bow he left.

The meal he had brought was simple but adequate, and Sarah was surprised to find she was hungry enough to eat almost all of it.

Time ticked by. Her watch showed it was after midnight. She sorted out the piled-up bedding, grateful that it was clean, and made up the bed. She undressed, slipped into her chemise, blew out the candle and climbed into bed. She had every intention of staying awake — hoping that Harry would soon join her, but she had no idea when — or indeed whether he would. Sheer physical weariness overcame her. She slept — until sounds in the room woke her.

'Harry?' she said.

'Yes. Go back to sleep.'

She was wide awake now. 'What news is there?' she asked.

'Not good, I'm afraid. Indian scouts have

reported that the American Army, under General van Rensslaer, is planning an invasion across the river.'

'Here? Oh, Harry — '

'I don't think there's any cause for concern, Sarah. Perhaps I should not have told you, but it seems we have only just arrived in time. At break of dawn we are to move into forward positions.'

'So soon!' There was anguish in her heart.

'The sooner we get there the better, for we must be in position ready to repulse the attack.'

His voice was dull, wooden. She could tell that he had no relish for what lay ahead. The wide window let in a shaft of moonlight and she watched as he removed his clothes. Her mind was a whirl of alarm. She could think of nothing to say to him. She was consumed by the awful knowledge that they had only a few brief hours before he would leave her. He looked so tired. Was he really fit for the battle ahead? Wearily he undressed, unbuttoning and taking off his jacket, tugging at his neckcloth, pulling his shirt over his head. His shoulders drooped, but the rhythmic mounds of muscles, biceps and pectorals, were visible, though relaxed. His skin gleamed, a pale creamy colour. His broad chest was covered with hair, brown, a shade lighter than that on his head, she noticed. He sat down to pull off his boots, then stood with his back to her whilst he removed his trousers. When he turned his loins were revealed, with their wealth of hair. She threw back a corner of the covers and moved over in the bed to make room for him. A moment later he dropped into the bed beside her. Instinctively she opened her arms to him.

'Sarah?' He spoke her name as if it was a question.

'Yes, Harry — ' She was about to add the words 'my dearest' but he covered her mouth with his, as she enfolded him in a warm embrace.

She was eager to hold him, and to feel his arms closing tightly around her. Willingly she returned his kiss and pressed her breasts against the hard wall of his chest, delighting in the warmth and the smell of his flesh. His weariness seemed to peel away. She was thrilled to have unleashed an urge in him, such as she had never dreamed of. His strength and power was like an unstoppable driving force, almost frightening in its passion.

His hands worked up under the thin material of her chemise, pushing it away from her body so that his mouth could take possession of her nipple. The craving she felt

318

from his body demanded a response from her, and the loving intensity of her nature had only one wish — to please — to give — to be possessed by him. She clasped him close as he reached a shuddering climax. Almost immediately he seemed to crumple, to lie still for a moment, then roll aside.

'Thank you,' he murmured.

She watched him with a smile on her face. A moment later she realized he was asleep — so utterly exhausted that she marvelled that he had found the energy to make love. She lay very still beside him, still holding him in her arms.

It pleased her that, weary though he had been, he had found her irresistible. Briefly the intensity of his desire had endowed him with an almost superhuman force, carrying him beyond the natural capability of his own being.

The thought had a humbling effect. She was also saddened, remembering what he had said about going to the front line at dawn.

She fully expected to remain awake, content just to lie beside him, with one arm lightly over him. For this night at least, or what was left of it, she would watch over him. By so doing she felt that she was absorbing some of his being into hers.

★　★　★

He was almost fully dressed when she awoke. It must be very early for it was still dark. She sat up quickly. He was already buckling on his sword.

'Harry.' Just to say his name was a pleasure. 'Is it time for you to go?'

'Almost. I'm glad you're awake, Sarah, for there are things I must say to you.'

She smiled. Anything, as long as he kept talking; anything rather than wish her goodbye.

'You should be safe here in the fortress.'

She nodded, mutely. She hated having to stay behind, but it was impossible now for her to accompany him. All she could do to help him was force herself to face the parting bravely.

'I shall wait here, until you return,' she said.

'God willing.'

Two simple words — that brought death to her mind. She thought of leaping out of the bed, throwing herself into his arms, but modesty was inhibiting her again. Modesty and uncertainty — still unsure how he really felt about her. Everything was so different now, his mind was on military matters.

She thought bitterly that she might just as well have been one of those *vivandières*, of whom he had spoken so dismissively. She willed him to make a move towards her — if she meant anything to him, other than as an object of desire, and as the prospective mother of his child, then surely now he would murmur some words of tenderness.

Instead she realized he was giving her instructions. His words were coolly thought out and precisely delivered. She held back the tears that pricked behind her eyes forcing herself to listen.

'Whatever the outcome of the battle, you should be safe, Sarah,' he said. He paused very slightly, cleared his throat, then continued, 'However, in the event that we are unable to withstand the attack, and the Americans manage to cross the river and take this fort, you must immediately make it known that you are American by birth and demand to see their commanding officer.'

She could not trust herself to speak, for if such circumstances arose — Harry would either be dead or a prisoner, and she found it almost impossible to imagine him surrendering!

'As one of their countrywomen I am sure you will be well received,' he continued. 'Ask for their assistance to rejoin your family. On no account tell them that you are married to me.' His face was serious, almost stern. 'Do you understand what I am saying?'

'Yes, of course — I'll do whatever you say.' She didn't want even to think of that, had only half listened. 'But you'll come back, Harry, I know you will. You must come back for the sake of your child.'

He started. Then shook his head, that quizzical smile twisted the corner of his mouth and wrenched at her heart.

'You can't possibly know, not so soon. Now, I must go.'

Still he stood, gazing at her. Her eyes scanned his beloved face, imprinting every feature more deeply into her memory. She hoped he would say something more and waited with bated breath, but he turned sharply and without another word, marched away. His back was ramrod straight, his head held high, his bicorn tucked beneath one arm, the other hand on his sword.

She remained motionless for some time, staring blankly at the door that he had closed silently behind him. Then she got out of bed and threw her cashmere shawl around her shoulders. She could not bear to go out on to the veranda and watch him leave the fort. She sat down in a rocking chair, dry-eyed but moaning in utter misery. From outside she heard commands yelled out, the stamp of heavy boots, and then the rhythmical tramp

— tramp — tramp that told her the troops were leaving.

Vividly she visualized him, riding at the head of the long column, straight and tall in the saddle, proudly wearing his scarlet, gold-braided jacket, recklessly exposed to any enemy marksman. The tears she had held back before he left ran unchecked down her pale cheeks. There was so much she wished she could have said — was it now too late — for ever?

★ ★ ★

The days that followed were the most awful of her whole life. The knowledge that Harry was in danger was with her every waking hour. Even in the night she would waken in a cold sweat, certain that he had been killed or badly wounded. Sometimes she imagined him calling for her and could not shake off the feeling of dread. She told herself that was ridiculous! He cared nothing for her. It was unlikely he would give even a fleeting thought to her, especially in a time of stress and peril.

Then one sad grey morning she awoke to the realization that she was not pregnant. It was a great shock for she had been so sure. With simple innocence she had assumed that their union would be fruitful, convinced that she would immediately be with child. She felt doubly bereft, as if one disaster was following another. Harry so wanted an heir, that had been the reason he had made that first offer of marriage — and she had no doubt it had also played a part in his second proposal. Conversely it had also been one of the reasons why she had refused him that day when he had come to her in the arbour at Ashingby. How shocked she had been at what he had said! How her opinion of him had changed as she had grown to know him better!

Now she knew that she loved him, and that changed everything. She would always love him and with a passion so fierce it almost unnerved her. Even if he never came to love her in the same way, she would never change. Perhaps there was a coolness in his nature that prevented him from loving anyone with great passion, or perhaps it was just something about her personally that did not really stir him. Whatever it was she would try to accept it, for quite certainly she could never be happy without him. Wherever he was, there she wanted to be.

Her agony of longing had deepened since he had gone into battle. The belief that she was carrying his child had been her only positive link with him, a prop to hold on to, to live for. He had so wanted a child, an heir for Ashingby and she had dared to think that if she gave birth to a boy-child, Harry would really fall in love with her.

If he should be killed, her life would be meaningless, she knew that quite definitely. The belief that she was carrying his child had given her a sense of closeness with him; she had cherished the idea that a part of him had been entrusted to her. This illusory infant had been a talisman, as if somehow it would bring Harry back. He had discounted her belief that she was with child — *you can't possibly know* he had said — but she had seen hope lighten his face. Now she was devastated; it had been nothing but wishful thinking. Without that comfort, she felt empty and useless.

★   ★   ★

There were a few other women living in the fort. Two were of French descent, who spoke only a little English and chattered together incessantly in their own language. There was also one Scots lady, several years older than Sarah, but she suffered from ill-health. She was often confined to her room, and made it clear she preferred to be alone. One of the officers had an Indian wife and Sarah sometimes spoke a little with her, but in truth there was no one with whom she could really communicate. She passed a great deal of time alone, reading or playing on the rather tinny spinet that a previous commandant's wife had brought out with her.

Shortage of clothes was a considerable difficulty, for she had given almost everything she had to Lucy, before she had set out on that dreadful voyage across Lake Ontario to meet Seth Boyer. She had taken with her only a single change of underwear, and had worn a warm blouse and skirt. The quartermaster at the fort had given her a soldier's shirt and she had skilfully adapted that to fit herself, but it was a relief when a pedlar called with a horse-drawn covered cart. She bought several lengths of material, some lace and ribbons, needles, sewing cottons and silks. The material was mostly plain cotton and flannelette, but he had one piece of quite pretty Indian spotted muslin, which she hoped to make into a gown for evening wear.

For many days she was occupied with sewing and she blessed her early training, when she had been expected to make garments for herself and also for the younger children. Although she was clever with her needle, she could not help a sigh of regret as she recalled the wondrous fashions Grandmama had had made for her — especially that pale apple-green gown — but what did clothes matter when Harry was away from her and in danger! The deft movements of her fingers never diverted her thoughts from him for more than a few moments.

From time to time messages came back to the fort. The officer in command tried to be helpful. He assiduously passed on any information that came in but often it was confused, sometimes one word contradicted another. At first it was said that the Americans had landed and were advancing. Then the news was that the British had crossed the river and were heading towards Fort Niagara. No one was sure which was correct.

More positive information seemed to come from the other battle front, much further away, to the west. There the advance of the American Governor William Hull had been successfully countered by Major General Brock, who with a force made up of Canadian Militia, British Regulars and Indians, was driving the Yankees back. There was tremendous rejoicing in Fort George when they heard that the British had captured Detroit.

Sarah found herself unable to enter wholeheartedly into the celebrations. She walked to the wall of the fort and stood for a long time, looking away into the far distance, trying to come to terms with her mixed feelings. She welcomed anything that would help to bring the war to an end, yet her American patriotism could not be entirely suppressed. For her there was no pleasure in the British victory over her fellow countrymen.

The only outcome she could definitely welcome was brought by an Indian messenger a few days later. A small force had been left under British command to hold Detroit, whilst Brock and his main army were returning to reinforce Harry's contingent facing the enemy across the Niagara River. They were still valiantly holding out against the attempted American advance into Canada. Reinforcements were desperately needed.

★　★　★

'They're bringing in Yankee prisoners of war!'

Sarah threw aside the shift she was working on, hurried to the veranda. It ran along the front of the first-floor rooms that had been allocated to Harry and which she now occupied alone. She leaned forward eagerly, looking down. Was the fighting over? Were the troops also returning?

There was no sign of that distinctively tall figure in the scarlet tunic. A motley rabble of defeated humanity shambled into the fort, lightly guarded by British infantrymen. Some of the Americans were barely sixteen years old, others twice that age and more, men who had left homes and families to fight for a cause they had been persuaded was just and right. They walked by, in ragged ranks, not bothering to keep in step, many of them with heads bent, feet shuffling. The sadness of their defeat communicated itself to her, but their sorrow could not really be hers. For them the war with all its dangers was over — Harry was still at the front, facing the danger of bombardment and fighting.

The British guards returning with the prisoners brought news.

'We're holding the Yankees at bay.'

'Those that have ventured across the river have paid the price!'

'We sent over a raiding party and picked up these men.'

Nothing was said that gave Sarah comfort — except that there had been few casualties. Both armies had been playing a waiting game. The American Militia was reluctant to cross the river whilst the British on the northern side were well dug in, ready to repel any advance.

About thirty prisoners were marched in. They were mustered in the parade ground, given a hunk of bread and had their water-bottles refilled. Then they were ordered to sit on the ground to await interrogation by the officer who would demand their names, regiments and any other information he could elicit.

Sarah was about to turn away when her attention was drawn to one of the prisoners, older than most, a man in his mid-fifties. He was standing stooped as he carefully tended a wound on the head of a fellow militiaman. She caught only a brief glimpse of his face — but it was sufficient.

Scarcely able to believe her own eyes, she ran down the veranda steps and threaded her way through the knot of men who were sitting or lying on the ground. Every step of the way she kept her gaze fixed on that one she had recognized. It was as if she felt that he would vanish if she took her eyes off him for a second. Just before she reached him he turned and she was able to see him fully. She had not been mistaken. He was about to move away but she cried out, 'Papa! Papa!'

At the sound of her voice the prisoner looked in her direction. Disbelief gave his haggard face a blank expression. She threw herself into his arms.

'It's me. Sarah.'

He hugged her tight, then drew back to gaze at her, long and hard, puzzled, disbelieving. 'My darling girl — what in heaven's name are you doing here?'

'Oh, Papa, that's such a long story! So much has happened to me since I left home. I'll tell you later.'

Love beamed from one face to the other.

'I still don't believe it's really you, Sarah! How are you, my dear? Are you all right? You're not a prisoner, are you?' He regarded her anxiously.

She shook her head. 'I'm fine, Papa — '

'A letter came from your grandmama, just before they enlisted me into the militia. I gathered from it she was not best pleased with you.' He tried to look sternly disapproving, but he kept hold of her hands and could not suppress the wide smile of welcome on his face.

'I was foolish, I suppose. I'll try and explain — and I think by now Grandmama will have forgiven me. But what about you?'

'A different man now I've seen you, my darling. I confess I am a little tired. I'm too old for this military life, but they needed a medical man and there was no one else.'

'Lady Wrenningham.'

Neither Sarah nor her father had noticed the officer until he called her name. He touched Dr Dunthorne's shoulder reprovingly and her father's mouth dropped open — his bewilderment patently obvious.

Sarah turned towards Captain Wishaw, who was regarding her with an expression of stern disapproval. 'Lady Wrenningham,' he repeated, 'I must ask you not to communicate with the prisoners. Please be so good as to return to your quarters immediately.'

'I beg your pardon, Captain Wishaw. But, you see, this gentleman is my father, Dr Dunthorne.'

The stunned expression on the young officer's face would have been comical in other circumstances. He swallowed, looked from one to the other, then said, 'I think you had better speak to the CO about this, my lady.'

'I will, most certainly.'

'Sarah, what does this mean?' Dr Dunthorne asked. 'Why does the captain address you as — Lady Wrenningham?'

She had no alternative but to tell him and there was no time to lead up to it.

'I'm married, Papa,' she said, very simply.

'To a British officer?'

His face was an expressionless mask; it

distanced him from her. That remote, displeased look had made her tremble in childhood. She experienced something of the same feeling, and longed to tell him all — to make him understand.

'Please, dear Papa, don't be angry with me. I would dearly have liked your permission and advice, but I had no opportunity to seek it. I'll explain as soon as I can, but just now I must go and see the commanding officer. Perhaps he'll allow you to stay in my rooms — so you can have a good rest. You look so tired! I'm sure you shouldn't be here in this state. Oh, Papa — how dreadful is this war! How I wish it was all over!'

'All wars are dreadful and this one should never have happened. By all means ask your commanding officer if we may be permitted to talk together later, Sarah, but do not make any special arrangements for me. I shall stay with the men; some are ill and others seriously wounded — they need me here.'

She knew it would be useless to argue with him. He was a man of high principles; he would not take the easy way and desert those who needed his medical skills. She felt immensely proud of her papa for she could see the high esteem in which he was held by the troops.

Captain Wishaw escorted her to the CO's

office. Sarah had spoken to General Waters on several occasions since she had been at the fort. He had told her more than once how he admired her husband, what a fine soldier he was, and the awards for bravery which Harry had won. Every anecdote he quoted had made her more proud than ever to be the wife of such an outstanding man — but those tales had also been heart-rending. Always General Waters told of Harry being in the thick of the worst fighting — never expecting his men to undertake anything he would shy away from himself.

He greeted her warmly, as always, kissing her hand and expressing pleasure at the sight of her. He listened in amazement as she told him that the American doctor who had been brought in with the prisoners was her father.

'Good gracious! Most extraordinary! Of course, I've always known by your accent that you were American, Lady Wrenningham, but I'd never have believed this!'

Once he had recovered from the surprise of Sarah's revelation, however, he willingly granted permission for Dr Dunthorne to visit her in her rooms every afternoon, giving them the opportunity to talk together in private.

★　★　★

Sarah's excitement knew no bounds, as she waited in the parade ground for her dear papa and led him up to the privacy of her room. There she hugged him, and kissed him and made tea for him. She fed him with tasty titbits she had scrounged from the officers' mess hall.

'I can scarcely believe it's you, Papa!' she exclaimed. 'Especially as you've always been a man of peace.'

'And so I am still, my dear. I had no thought of joining the militia, but there was no one else available. The other doctor in Cassie's Rock is even older than I am. I couldn't let our young men face battle without medical aid.'

His explanation was typical. 'You're not old, Papa,' she chided him fondly. 'I've thought of you all so often — tell me about Mama and the rest of the family? How are they?'

'Well. All in the best of health. I arranged for them to stay in Boston with your uncle for the duration of the war. But now, Sarah, no more prevarication,' he said seriously. 'It's time you told me something about yourself. I must say I'm surprised — even a little shocked — that your Grandmama should have arranged your marriage without consulting me.'

'There was no time to ask anyone. You see Grandmama did not actually arrange it — in fact she didn't know anything about it.'

'Good heavens, Sarah!'

'But I know she would have approved,' she hurried to assure her astounded father. 'Because Harry asked me to marry him earlier on, just after Corinne eloped, and that was what Grandmama was so cross about when she wrote to you. And we were married on the ship — '

'Why on earth did you do that?' He looked thoroughly disapproving now.

'It was a terrible time — our ship was attacked — and there was a great deal of trouble. I was locked in my cabin and so frightened — and — '

'Hush, Sarah. You're making me more confused than ever.' Dr Dunthorne took hold of her hands and pressed them tightly. 'Let us sit down here. Now, when you have composed yourself, start at the beginning and tell me slowly and logically exactly how this extraordinary state of affairs came about.'

So that was what she did. She told him too about her attempt to get back to Cassie's Rock, and the terror of her meeting with Seth.

'I'm not entirely surprised,' her Papa said. 'I've had my doubts about that young man for some time. I was never very keen on your friendship, especially when you grew up — that was one of the reasons why I wished you to get away to England.' He paused, then added, 'It seems that this husband of yours is a brave and resourceful man.'

'Yes, Papa. He is.'

'Good,' he smiled. 'It was a love match between your mama and me and I've always hoped it would be the same for all our children.' He patted her hand benignly, warmly showing his pleasure.

Oh, if only it was the same for her! Throughout her childhood she had been aware of the love that pervaded the house. She could not bear to disillusion him — she let him go on thinking that Harry loved her.

'From what you've told me, I think I'm going to like my new son-in-law,' he said.

They talked together for another half-hour or so, then he stood up. 'Now, dear girl, I must go. I have a meeting with the British surgeons. It's been suggested that we should work together as a team, for the good of all the wounded. I think that's an excellent idea and we're going to discuss it further.'

'You'll come back and see me tomorrow, won't you?'

'Of course.'

★ ★ ★

More groups of prisoners of war were marched in almost daily and even more sadly came the stream of wounded from both sides, British and American. The medical men were all involved together, doing their best for each and every one, no matter what their nationality. As their numbers increased, Dr Dunthorne had less time to talk with her; every day he was on duty in the room that served as an operating theatre. More men arrived, mostly in small groups, carried in on horseback, on the backs of carts, then moved on stretchers for treatment.

Sarah waited and watched with deepening fear, for she received no word from Harry. Every day she spent a great deal of time on the veranda in front of her apartments, from which there was a good view in the direction from which soldiers came and went. She was torn between yearning to see him yet fearful — for she had no way of knowing how he was.

Then at last she saw him. He was on horseback. His faithful batman, Reynolds, riding pillion, held his master in the saddle. The torn, blood-darkened sleeve of Harry's scarlet jacket, hung empty at his side, his arm was across his chest, supported by an even more bloodstained sling. Sarah caught her breath as she saw his face, ashen with pain and loss of blood. Two soldiers caught him as valiantly he tried to dismount from his horse.

'Harry! Oh my beloved!'

She rushed forward and would have clasped him in her arms, but at the sight of him, stopped in dismay. She could not even be sure whether he had seen her as they lowered him on to a stretcher. At once they carried him inside — into the room used for major surgery — for amputations. Would it come to that? She knew how few of those operated upon recovered from the shock!

18

They carried him into the medical room. Sarah would have followed, but an orderly stepped forward smartly, barring her way.

'Begging your pardon, my lady, only medical staff are allowed in here,' he said, firmly closing the door.

Helplessly she stepped back. She began to walk backwards and forwards outside that closed door, needing to remain as near to Harry as possible. Up and down, ten paces one way, ten back, uselessly, restlessly, alternately gnawing at her knuckles or wringing her hands, deep despair in her heart. He had looked so ill! He, who had been so vigorous, so vital, had not even had the strength to dismount unaided. If only she could give him some of her own strength, some of the blood that pulsed so potently in her own veins, some of this energy that would not allow her to rest!

She tried to comfort herself with the knowledge that her papa was in there — she had waved to him from her veranda early in the morning, long before Harry had been brought in. She clung to the recollection that, only the previous day, her father had praised the skill of the British surgeons. But no matter how she tried to keep calm, to hope, to believe in the future, her mind always slid back to the fear — what were they doing to him?

Would they amputate? Would he survive? A deep bellowing scream from within the room, was like a knife being plunged into her stomach and twisted. It might not be Harry — there were other wounded men in there — she quickened her pace. Walked and walked.

Captain Wishaw came to her, suggested she should go to her room and wait there, but she would not leave.

'I have to be here, so that I can hear any news immediately. Could you not ask them to let me in, please? For pity's sake! Just to see him, if only for a minute — '

'I'm afraid that's quite impossible, Lady Wrenningham. But I'll look in myself. Perhaps I can have a word with Dr Dunthorne — I'll ask if he can step outside and see you.'

'Oh yes, please. If that's possible, but you mustn't disturb him if — if — '

'No, of course. I won't even speak to him if it's not convenient. Stay here, Lady Wrenningham. I'll be back in a minute.'

She forced herself to stand still, waiting,

woodenly immobile with her eyes fixed on the door. Waiting. Waiting. Suddenly it opened.

'Papa!' She ran to him and he caught her in his arms, held her close, comfortingly. She stayed there, very still for a moment, taking comfort from the love that shone from him. Then she lifted her head and looked straight into his tired, sympathetic face.

'Have you seen Harry?' she whispered.

'Yes, yes. There, there!'

'Is he going to be all right?'

'There is hope, my dear. They're doing all they can.'

'He — he looked so ill — so weak.'

'He has lost a lot of blood, but we don't think he will have to lose his arm. With careful nursing — '

A joyous relief burst over her. 'I can nurse him.' What more could she ask? 'I'll devote myself entirely to him — I'll do anything.'

'Yes. Yes, I know. I'm sure you will.'

'He — he will — get better?' She searched his face as she waited for him to answer.

'I believe he will, Sarah. It's good that we have not had to amputate, for I doubt if he would have the strength to withstand that. But he will need devoted care and attention.' Dr Dunthorne spoke in serious, measured tones, that told her as much as his words did. There was hope but recovery was not absolutely certain.

'When can I see him?'

'Soon, quite soon. If anyone can heal him, it will be you. You must make him want to live.'

How she wished she had that power! Would she really be able to help him, when he thought so little of her?

'It was an old wound, reopened,' Dr Dunthorne continued. 'In my opinion he should never have been allowed to come back into a fighting unit.'

'The war must be over for him now,' she said quietly.

'It's over temporarily for all of us. Our brave American forces have retreated to their side of the river, wisely in my opinion. The British may try to take Fort Niagara some time in the future, but before then they need some time to consolidate.'

'Then the fighting is over?' That was a heartening thought.

'For the time being, thank heavens! We don't expect many more casualties in now. Your husband stayed with his men to the very last, even though he was wounded. He refused to leave until he knew the outcome of the battle. That's the reason he lost so much blood. If he had come back here sooner — '

He raised his hands expressively and

dropped them to his sides.

'Oh, if only he had!'

'You would feel like that, being a woman. He is a soldier. He did his duty.'

'Did you talk to him, Papa? Did he know you are my father?'

'Of course.' He held her hands and looked down into her upturned face. 'We have introduced ourselves. He's a good man, Sarah.'

'I know.'

'Go to your quarters and make them ready to receive him.'

Hope had returned. She had something to do, things to prepare. She remade the bed with clean linen, ordered hot water to be ready on the stove in the cookhouse and personally supervised the making of a nourishing broth. What a relief it was to be busy, and to know that there was still hope. Her father had given her to understand that Harry's recovery would depend to some extent upon her — if that was so, then he would get well again. He must. She would not let him die!

She was shocked to realize how fragile was his hold on life when, about an hour later, Harry was brought in on a stretcher, carefully carried by Lucy's husband, Archie Reynolds, and another soldier. The earl moaned heart-rendingly as they carefully transferred him to the bed. Almost immediately they left, for there were others needing their assistance.

Fear gripped Sarah as she stood back and regarded him properly, this man she loved with all her heart! His skin had the waxen pallor of death. His eyes had briefly flickered open as that groan escaped his mouth when he was placed on the bed, then as if he had not even the strength to keep them open, the long-lashed lids had fallen back. His beautiful, damaged body had been put into a clean nightshirt, his arm was heavily bandaged. His lips moved, but no sound came from them. He was delirious.

Her emotions were in chaos. Almost out of her mind to see him in such a state, she wanted to smother him in loving attention, but at that moment there was not one single thing she could do. Rest — peace — quiet. No doubt that would do more to aid his recovery than anything else. She drew up a chair, seated herself beside the bed and prepared for her vigil.

★　★　★

For two days there was little change. When Harry woke up briefly she fed him with small spoons of beef-tea, steamed fish, coddled eggs, anything she could think of to tempt his jaded appetite. The amounts he took were scarcely enough to keep a bird alive, yet every minuscule mouthful she could persuade him to swallow was a triumph.

Reynolds and another orderly came every morning and helped her to change the bedlinen.

'I pray night and morning, for his lordship's recovery,' Archie told her.

'Thank you, Mr Reynolds. We can only wait and hope.' She knew he meant those words wholeheartedly.

The surgeon inspected once a day. Her father visited morning, noon and night. Both those highly skilled medical men pronounced themselves well satisfied with the progress that Harry was making.

'Now, Sarah you must take more rest yourself,' her father told her.

'I'm all right,' she assured him quickly. 'I sleep well enough. I lie on the sofa there; it's perfectly comfortable.'

'You should go into the next room and lie down properly. I'll sit by the bed — '

'Certainly not! You need rest much more than I do. Besides, I like to be here — I wouldn't rest at all away from him. I wake up the moment he stirs, but he sleeps so much, that really it's no problem for me.' She paused. 'And he is getting better, isn't he, Papa? You can see it too, can't you?' She pleaded for reassurance.

'Yes, my dear. I really think he is.'

The very next day, Sarah woke up sharply, as she always did when sounds of movement came from the bed. In an instant she was on her feet and padding across the room to where Harry was struggling to rise. He was speaking, too, in a funny, croaky sort of voice, faint but audible.

'Where am I? Sarah?' For the first time he seemed to recognize her, though doubtfully. His brow knitted, his face was frowning, troubled.

'Yes, my lord.' She tried to reassure him, but he wouldn't listen.

'What am I doing here?' he interrupted. 'What is this place?' He tried to toss back the bedcovers.

'They brought you back to Fort George. You were wounded — I've been looking after you.'

'The battle — my men — what happened?'

'My lord — please be calm. The battle is over. The American forces have retreated back across the river. You need rest — '

'I must get up — '

Again he struggled to rise, feebly threshed about for a minute or so, clutched at the sheets with pale, thin fingers, then fell back, exhausted even by that small effort. It hurt her to see him in such a state, this vigorous man who had been so strong, so vital, so capable.

'I don't seem able to move. Help me, Sarah.' His voice was a moan.

'No, my lord. Please — lie still,' she pleaded. 'You've been very ill.'

'I'm — so weak.'

'You lost so much blood — but you're getting better; you'll soon get your strength back now. I'll bring you some broth.'

'Not broth — real food. I'm starving.'

'Of course you are.' Tear-brimmingly wonderful to hear him say that! 'I'll bring you a good breakfast. I'll be back in two shakes of a lamb's tail!'

Sarah sped away to fetch a tray. From that moment there was no doubt about his recovery. What joy it was to see his health improving! An answer to prayers! It was for this that she had devoted herself entirely to him, nursed him through the days of delirium, without thought for herself. Now she delighted to tempt him with delicious food, cooking it herself so that she could be sure none of its nourishment was wasted.

She attended to his physical well-being in every possible way, and every service was a token of her love. Yet part of her held back, for she felt that she had failed him in the one thing that he most wanted from her. She shrank from the moment when she would have to tell him that she was not after all carrying his child. When they spoke it was with that same hideous formality they had adopted on the voyage.

As he regained strength, the British surgeon ceased his visits, but, of course, Dr Dunthorne continued to call in regularly. It pleased her that he and Harry became good friends, for they each held the other in great respect. She told herself that she had so much to be grateful for. If only she could shake off those doubts and fears that continued to hang darkly over her future! If only Harry would give her one sign, say one word that would suggest — even in the most tentative way — that he had some tender feeling for her! There was no pleasure in this comedy of cool friendship — proof, if proof were needed, that a marriage without love could only be a desolation for her!

Caring for him when he was ill and weak had brought its own satisfaction, but as he gained strength she faced the fear that soon he would need her no longer. What then?

Her distress deepened when, within days of his being up and about, the earl arranged an interview with General Waters. It tore her heart as she helped him to don his uniform, to see how loosely the brilliant scarlet and gold jacket hung on his wasted frame. She watched from the veranda balcony as he walked off, making a brave effort to resume his customary straight-backed, smart-stepping assurance. She was sure he would insist upon returning to his company, volunteer his services, for the lull in the fighting had been temporary. Skirmishes were taking place daily along the border between America and Canada. The war was far from finished.

She could settle to nothing whilst he was with the general. When he returned, his expression was grim. He dropped into the armchair, haggard and dispirited.

'I'm told I'm no longer fit to be in the army.' There was a bitter note in his voice.

Sarah's heart leapt with relief, but she tried not to show it. 'You've done more than your share for king and country.'

'I'm to be sent back to England as soon as transport can be aranged.'

Her mouth felt dry. Why did he not say 'we'?

'It will be good for you to be back at Ashingby,' she said.

'That is my one consolation.'

He sat quietly for a time. His face was thin,

lined from suffering. She poured wine for him and set it with biscuits on a small table at his elbow. She poured a glass for herself too, needing a stimulant. Instinctively she knew he had more news to deliver and was dreadfully certain it would be momentous for her.

'When I was with the CO I took the opportunity to speak to him about the prisoners of war,' Harry said. 'I put in a special plea for your father to be repatriated, now that the fighting is over.'

'He won't go whilst he has work to do here.'

'I know. But many, like me, are recovering from their wounds. Some have already rejoined their fighting units. The British Army surgeons will be able to attend to those that remain.'

She watched his face — it told her nothing. She said, 'Mama will be overjoyed to see Papa again, if it can be arranged.'

'Naturally. You've told me what a devoted couple they are.' He paused.

In the silence she could feel a pulse throbbing in her temple.

The earl cleared his throat and continued. 'I think it would be a good idea if you were to go with him, Sarah.'

The words flew at her — an arrow piercing her heart.

'No — oh, no!' she protested fiercely. 'I

cannot leave you. You're still in need of careful nursing.'

'Rubbish!' he interrupted. 'I'm grateful for the devoted way you've attended to me, Sarah, but I've had enough of mollycoddling. I have to get on with my own life again.' His voice was sharp.

Dully she looked away from him. 'You don't need me any more!' she whispered. She wasn't sure if he heard her.

He was pursuing his own line of thought. 'I wronged you when I persuaded you to marry me. I can see that now. It's clear to me that you're not happy. I've thought about this long and hard — you should go back to your old life and forget that you ever met me.'

She could not do that — not ever!

He was still speaking — and so calmly and rationally! 'I believe it's possible for a divorce to be arranged, though I know it won't be easy — '

Tears started into her eyes. 'Oh, no, my lord. Not that! I know I'm a dreadful failure as a wife, and I'm sorry — ' She broke off, choking over the words and pulled a little lace handkerchief from her sleeve.

'For goodness sake, Sarah, don't look like that.' He sounded both anguished and impatient. 'I never meant to hurt you. I've told you I'm grateful.'

She brushed that aside, wiped her eyes and made a great effort to control her emotions.

'I don't want your gratitude. All I want is to be a good wife, to be with you always — I know I've let you down — '

He stood up, walked towards her chair and held his hands out to her.

'Sarah? What are you saying?' His voice was suddenly uncertain, gravelly. 'It's not *you* that's let *me* down.'

She hesitated to put her hands into his, though they were outstretched towards her, and she longed to clasp them.

'But it is!' she stumbled on, miserably. 'I know how greatly you wanted an heir for Ashingby — and I-I should be with child . . . and I'm not.'

She could not bring herself to look at him, kept her eyes downcast. Then, amazingly his hands closed over hers, and his grip tightened and, although she was reluctant, he pulled her to her feet.

Still she did not lift her gaze, fearing to see his condemnation, until his fingers lifted her chin so that she was obliged to look straight at him. Then the expression she saw in his eyes made her tremble and she experienced a most peculiar weakness in her knees.

'Does that matter?' he asked very softly, very gently.

'My lord! How can you say that!'

'Nothing matters, Sarah, if you really mean that you are willing to stay with me?'

'Willing!' she breathed, scarcely able to believe it.

'Dear wife, don't you know how much I love you?' His voice held a note of impatience.

She gazed at him in disbelief. He had spoken those words that she had never expected to hear, and his tone and the glow in his eyes reflected the truth of them.

'Oh, my lord!' she breathed.

She was unable to say more for his arms closed around her. Her slender body, in its home-made cotton gown, was gathered tightly to his chest and held there with a strength that was really quite amazing — particularly in consideration of the wounds from which he had not yet fully recovered.

Nor was there any sign of weakness as his lips covered hers and he kissed and kissed her until she was breathless.

When at last he released her sufficiently so that she could look up into his eyes there was such fire in them that she thought he must be running a high temperature.

'Have a care, Harry, you must not get too

excited,' she warned.

'Who gives those orders?' he responded.

'I do and I'm your nurse — you've been very ill. Please, my dear one, I must insist that you sit down.'

'Why, certainly — but with the proviso that you must sit on my knee.'

He moved just a few steps away, settled himself in a large armchair, and reached out a hand towards her.

'Come, Sarah.'

Hesitantly she moved a step towards him.

'Nearer,' he ordered. 'Or do I have to carry you?'

'You mustn't — '

'Balderdash!'

Since it was necessary to prevent him from straining himself, she hastily moved to stand beside him and placed her hand in his.

'On my knee, Sarah.'

His fingers closed over hers gently pulling her towards him, until with smiling acquiescence she obeyed. She sat lightly, even a little primly, but nevertheless she placed her arms around his neck and lifted her face for his kisses.

After a time, with his lips close to her ear, he whispered, 'When they brought me back to the fort, after the battle — you were there, weren't you?'

'Yes.' She shuddered at the memory. 'I'd been watching out — every day.'

'I wasn't sure — but — I thought you called my name?'

'I was shocked to see you so badly wounded.'

'And then you said something else, do you remember?'

She smiled, for she remembered very well. 'My beloved,' she whispered.

'Then it wasn't a dream.' He heaved a sigh. 'Those words made me fight to get better, Sarah. You gave me hope — made me feel I had something to live for.'

She smiled softly. 'But that is what you are, my most beloved husband.'

Musingly he continued, 'Later I thought it must have been a delusion caused by my own disordered mind. You were so cool and I knew you didn't really want to marry me. You had rejected me most positively when I first asked you.'

'But then, my lord,' she told him, with a mischievous touch of coquettishness, 'it seemed that you had no great desire to marry me, either.'

'On that point you are wrong, sweet lady. I've been consumed with desire for you from the very first moment I set eyes on you.'

He was looking at her in such a way that a

delightful warm feeling swept over her, making her cheeks flame rosy red. She tried to wriggle away, for she was beginning to worry about his health, feeling sure her weight must be too much for him.

'My lord, you must allow me to stand up. You are not yet fully recovered.'

'Are you calling me a weakling?' he growled.

He clasped her closer, refusing to allow her to escape and he set about kissing her even more fervently than before.

Still she worried about those half-healed wounds and with great determination she managed to release herself from his hold. She struggled off his knee and, smoothing her disgracefully ruffled skirts, looked down at him sternly.

'I can see you are indeed a great deal better, but — '

'Don't think you're married to a husband so feeble he will make no demands upon you, Sarah,' he interrupted. 'In fact, I think it's high time I carried you over to that bed. I've been lying on it — quite abominably alone — for far too long.'

'Harry!' she protested. 'You will never recover if you do not behave — '

'How little you know of men, dear wife! I assure you, most categorically, that making love to you will do me more good than all the medicines in the world.'

He made to put his words into action, and advanced, prepared to scoop her up in his arms. At which she gave a little scream, for truly there was no mistaking his determination. So, although she stepped quickly aside, she moved in the direction of the bed and lay down with a smile on her face and her arms outstretched in welcome.

There was no doubt then that the Earl was indeed making a quite remarkable recovery — nor about his devotion to his beautiful young wife, as tenderly he undressed her and kissed her. He wooed her with soft seductive words and gazed at her with love and mounting passion. He caressed her with his hands and his mouth and his tongue, till Sarah wanted only to drown in the final ecstasy of his love-making.

Afterwards he slept, with a little smile on his lips, and she watched over him, and thought of the wonder of the life together that lay ahead for her — for them both — secure now in each other's love.

19

By late September preparations had been made for Sarah and the earl to make the return journey to England, together with those other wounded men who were considered fit enough to undertake the long journey and trans-Atlantic crossing.

Shortly before the day of their departure, they bade farewell to Dr Dunthorne, whose repatriation orders had been granted. Sarah thrust upon him letters and such small gifts as she could make or buy, for her Mama and for each of her brothers and her sister. She wished she could have seen them, visited them, no matter how briefly, but that was impossible. War still divided their two countries.

'They will be delighted for your happiness, Sarah,' Dr Dunthorne told her. 'Just as I am. A marriage founded on love, that's what your mother and I have been blessed with, and when I see Harry and you together, I know it is so for you also.'

'It is, Papa. I am more fortunate than I deserve.'

'Nonsense. You were a lovely child, Sarah,

and over the past few weeks you've developed into a fine young woman. I'm very proud of you. I shall have so much to tell them when I reach Boston. We've spoken about you every day since you left Cassie's Rock, and you'll be in our thoughts no matter where you are. You must write to us often — long letters, mind.'

'I will, Papa — I'll write every week — pages and pages.'

'Good. As soon as this terrible war is over I shall bring your mama to stay with you, and if possible arrange for Monica to visit her grandmama. The foolish girl has been eating her heart out with jealousy since you went to London.'

'It will be a great joy to me to have her company and to introduce her to the *ton*. Let us pray that this dreadful war will not continue for very long.'

'Amen to that.'

Dr Dunthorne shook hands with his upstanding and handsome son-in-law. 'I know you'll take good care of my sweet girl,' he said.

'You may be assured of that, sir,' the earl replied.

Dr Dunthorne clasped his much loved daughter in his arms and hugged her. Then, with a final wave, he stepped on to the boat that would take him over to the American side of the Niagara River. He was happy to be returning to his adopted homeland and as eager as a young man to be reunited with his dear wife.

The earl put an arm around Sarah's shoulders. 'Do you wish you were going with him?' he asked.

She shook her head. 'I hope it will be possible for all of us to meet together some time — but I know where I belong, from now on.'

'And where is that?'

She had no real need to answer, their eyes told it all, but she said, 'With you, my beloved.'

★   ★   ★

Two days later the small contingent left Fort George. Archie Reynolds was there to see them leave. He was unable to accompany them, for he had become indispensable to the surgeons, having developed first-class nursing skills, caring for the men in the camp hospital.

'My lady, may I ask a favour of you?' he asked, deferentially.

'Of course, Mr Reynolds,' she replied. 'You wish me to take a message to Lucy, I'll be bound.'

He nodded eagerly. 'I'd be greatly obliged

if you would let her know that I'm well and that I'll come to her as soon as I'm no longer needed here.'

'I shall most certainly do that. I shall also tell her what excellent work you've been doing for the sick and wounded. And, Mr Reynolds, I must tender you my heartfelt thanks for all you did to assist my husband. Without your help, in bringing him back to me, I fear he might have died on the battlefield.'

'He's a good man, is the earl. There's not many like him,' said Reynolds.

Sarah nodded. 'On that point we are most certainly in agreement.' She looked at him questioningly. 'Is there any other message you would like me to convey? Some extra little words?'

'I don't think so,' he said shyly. 'Besides — she'd only laugh.'

He explained exactly where Lucy's lodgings were, then it was time for Sarah to mount the horse that was to carry her on the first part of the trek.

'I shall seek out Lucy as soon as we reach York, Mr Reynolds.'

'Tell Lucy I love her,' he called after her, suddenly overcoming his diffidence.

★　★　★

Arduous though the journey was, Sarah found it much less tiring than it had been previously, for this time Harry was never far from her side, always ready with a loving smile to give her assistance and encouragement.

On their arrival in York, the earl engaged accommodation for them in the best hotel in town, close to the wharf. They had a few days to wait before boarding the boat that would take them up Lake Ontario towards Quebec, where they would be able to find a passage on a ship bound for England.

York was quite large, a bustling business centre for the area, proudly aware of its own importance to the local community, and the outlying districts. The surrounding forests had provided the timber from which its ever-spreading houses, shops, hotels and warehouses had been built along wide, dusty streets. The government buildings were impressive as befitted the town's status. It was defended by strong fortifications, including a main magazine chock-a-block with ammunition, as well as a garrison of several hundred men. Autumn was already splashing the background of forests with vivid yellows and reds.

On the morning after their arrival, Sarah planned to seek out Lucy's lodgings, not only to deliver the messages Archie Reynolds had entrusted to her, but also because she was herself eager to see her maid again. She had for a long time thought of her more as a friend than a servant. She even hoped to persuade Lucy to accompany her back to England, though she was aware that might not now be possible, since Archie was not yet able to rejoin her.

After Sarah and the earl had breakfasted together, she spoke of her intention to her husband.

'By all means,' he said, agreeably. 'But I have urgent messages to deliver to the general at the fort which will occupy me for most of the morning. I would prefer that you wait until after lunch, so that I may accompany you. If you have any difficulty in locating the house where Lucy is staying, I could perhaps be of assistance.'

Since that seemed eminently sensible, and she always enjoyed her husband's company, Sarah readily agreed. As the earl left, she noticed, with great satisfaction, that his scarlet, gold-braided jacket no longer hung loosely upon his shoulders. Indeed he was beginning to look much more like the handsome buck she had taken him for when she first saw him at that grand London ball.

Whilst he was away she passed the time,

quite happily, attending to small alterations to her homemade clothes. It was late morning when there came a tap on the door of her room.

'Come in.'

A chambermaid apeared in the doorway.

'If you please, ma'am, there's a lady downstairs, asking fer you.'

Sarah was surprised. 'Did the lady give her name?'

'I never thought to ask, ma'am, but it must be all right, for she's a real lady, very finely dressed. I've asked her to step into the best parlour.'

'Very well. Thank you. I shall come down.'

Sarah surveyed herself in the mirror, conscious of the short-comings of her attire. She really must have some more fashionable clothes made as soon as possible. Who could the unexpected caller be, she wondered, as she descended the stairs? Perhaps the earl had arranged for the general's lady to call upon her.

'Here's the countess, my lady,' the chambermaid announced, flinging the door open to admit Sarah, and curtsying deferentially.

Then to the chambermaid's obvious amazement, the finely dressed lady, whom she had shown into the best parlour, bobbed a curtsy to the plainly clothed young woman who had followed her down the stairs.

'Lucy!' Sarah gasped with delight.

Her erstwhile maid was beaming all over her pretty, fresh-complexioned face — and she was indeed finely dressed! She wore the most beautiful of the morning gowns which Sarah had given her, just before she set off for the ill-fated meeting with Seth Boyer. It was no wonder that the chambermaid had taken her for a fine lady, for she looked most elegant, with a befeathered hat perched on the front of her head and carrying a frilly pink parasol that had once been Sarah's pride and joy.

'I am absolutely delighted to see you!' Sarah held open her arms.

'My lady!' cried Lucy, rushing forward to embrace her mistress. 'I couldn't hardly believe it when I heard as how his lordship had arrived in town, and I just hoped that you might be with him, so I took a chance and came along to the best hotel and asked for you.'

'I'm so happy you did. The earl would have accompanied me this afternoon, so that I might seek your lodgings. Mr Reynolds — '

'Is he here here too?' Lucy interrupted eagerly.

'I'm afraid not, but I have messages — and

he said to tell you he loves you.'

Lucy blushed. 'He's allus foolin',' she said, with a happy smile. Then anxiously, 'But is he all right? Not wounded or anything?'

'I assure you, he was in excellent health when we left him, and he deeply regretted that he was unable to accompany us. You have reason to be very proud of him, Lucy.'

Sarah went on to explain why Archie had been obliged to remain at Fort George. She ordered refreshments to be brought to them, and Lucy listened eagerly, for she did not even know that the expedition Sarah had made across the great lake in the Indian canoe had been unsuccessful.

Then Sarah asked, 'But what about you, Lucy? How have you fared, here in York, on your own?'

'I've done well enough, my lady, thank you.'

'I was hoping that you might like to come back to England with me. There'd be a place in the household for Mr Reynolds too, for I'm sure he would be able to follow you before very long.'

'It's kind of you to ask, my lady. But I think I'll stay here, if you don't mind.'

Sarah was somewhat taken aback.

'I would not expect you to return on the same terms,' she said. 'I'm sure the earl would agree an increase in your wages, Lucy, and there's a nice little cottage on the estate you could have, when you are married.'

'I dare say there is, my lady, and I won't deny that in some ways it'd be very tempting, fer I'd dearly like to see my ma and pa and all the lit'luns again. But you see, I've done quite nicely for myself, since I've been here.'

'You mean — you've found another position?'

'Well, not exactly another position. If I was going to be a lady's maid, I wouldn't want to work for no one but you.' Lucy paused. Then quickly continued, 'You know as how I like to sing a bit?'

Sarah nodded, puzzled, wondering.

'An' you give me all these fine clothes, didn't you?'

'Yes.'

'Well, one day I dressed myself up all fine, like, and I sang and danced about a bit. I only did it fer bit of a lark an' to entertain the family where I was staying, 'cause they was good to me. Well, I had to do something to keep my spirits up — 'cos you weren't there, my lady, and neither was my Archie.'

'Yes?'

'You'll never believe this, my lady — '

'Oh, Lucy — pray do not keep me guessing any longer.'

'Well, there was a gentleman happened to

call in, an' he owns a hotel in the town. Not this one, but it's the next best, I reckon. Anyway, he offered to pay me to sing for his guests. So I did — an' they liked it. They liked the way I looked, too. I don't think I'd have had the courage to do it, but for the clothes you give me, my lady. They made me look so diff'rent — and I felt special, somehow. Mr Murphy — that's the gent's name — he reckons I bring in a lot more custom than he used to have.'

'And you like doing it,' Sarah said.

'Oh, yes, my lady. I really enjoy it. An' I've saved up enough money, so's I'll be able to buy Archie out of the army, and then, if he wants to, I thought we might be able to set up our own place. I reckon we'll do better in this country than we would in England. You don't mind, do you, my lady?'

'Dear Lucy — I wish you every success. I'm so pleased things have turned out well for you.'

'Who'd have thought all this would have happened — you remember how I cried, how miserable I felt, when the ship set sail? I was so scared, then.'

'I remember very well. I, too, was quite miserable. But that is past and it seems we may both have a good future to look forward to.'

They talked on until the earl returned and he arranged to take Sarah that evening to see Lucy's performance — and at his special request she sang 'The Raggle-Taggle Gypsies', which Sarah and he had sung as a duet, when she was staying at Ashingby.

'All together, now,' Lucy boldly invited her audience to join in. Voices were raised lustily and there was no doubt of the young singer's popularity.

There were tears in both Lucy and Sarah's eyes as they made their farewells. Both knew it was unlikely they would ever meet again.

'Do you mind how you go, my lady,' said Lucy, in her broad Norfolk accent.

'You too, Lucy. Take good care of yourself.'

'I will. An' I'd take it most kindly if, when you get back to Ashingby, you'd let my ma and pa know that I'm all right.'

'I most certainly shall, Lucy. It will be a great pleasure to me. I shall be sure to visit them myself and tell them of your good fortune.'

★   ★   ★

Two letters were waiting for Sarah in Quebec, replies to those she had dispatched when she first arrived in Canada.

Grandmama MacKenna's precise hand

conveyed somewhat ironic congratulations over the knowledge that Sarah had come to her senses in time and had married Harry.

I found it extremely difficult to comprehend that a granddaughter of mine could behave as foolishly as you did, she wrote. *I have never known a young woman do so little to capture the most eligible and elusive bachelor in the whole of London society. I am still not entirely convinced that you deserve to have done so — but I am overjoyed nevertheless.*

Beatrix was agog when I passed the news on to her. She set off at once to make sure that Mr Rawlingson heard of your marriage and, true to form, he produced the most amusing cartoon. It may be slightly risqué but I am not displeased, for he does not take note of people unless they have really arrived.

She ended the letter on a most affable note, with news of current happenings in the *ton.*

The other letter was from Corinne. She was fulsome in her good wishes.

It was certainly high time that Harry found himself a wife, and I'm so absolutely delighted that it's you, dear

Sarah. Now we're cousins as well as friends!! And I can never thank you enough for the help you gave me when Forbes and I eloped. What bliss it is to be Mrs Thackstone!!

And I've such news to tell!! Can you imagine me as a Mama??

Her scribbled style with a surfeit of exclamation marks emphasized her excitement and joy as much as her words.

Yes. I'm going to have a baby!!! she wrote. *Forbes is just as delighted as I am, and the trustees of my estate are going to release more of my money, so that we shall be able to move into a larger residence more appropriate to bringing up a family, with a nursery and a garden.*

She continued with descriptions of the prettiness of the baby clothes she had already begun to purchase.

Sarah showed the letters to Harry. He chuckled as he read of the Rawlingson cartoon. 'Lady MacKenna seems to approve,' he said, drily. 'I'm glad of that — she can be a most formidable adversary if she is crossed.'

'As I know all too well!' Sarah agreed. 'But Grandmama is a very wise old lady,' she said, seriously. 'She is quite right, too — I don't really deserve to be the Countess of Wrenningham.'

'That is a matter entirely for me to decide, and I have not the least doubt about it, for I know I am the most fortunate man in the world. As for my eligibility — I always felt privileged to own Ashingby; it's a magnificent house and a wonderful place.'

'I believe Grandmama was referring not only to your wealth and position but also to you as a very fine and honourable gentleman,' Sarah said. With wonder and humility she added, 'You could have married almost any young lady you chose.'

'But it was you that I fell in love with,' he murmured. 'That makes all the difference. Now I look forward to sharing all that I have with you. What more could I wish for?'

He kissed her tenderly. Sarah looked down demurely and sighed with happiness.

After a moment she raised her head and regarded him speculatively. 'The other letter is from Corinne.'

She watched as he read, his face was impassive. When he had done, he handed the letter back.

'She appears to be as harebrained as ever!' he commented.

'But still so much in love!' she whispered.

'True. I have to admit that. Perhaps I misjudged Forbes Thackstone.' He paused, then, lifting one expressive eyebrow, he added, 'If it would please you we could, I suppose, invite them to visit us at Ashingby.'

'Oh, yes, Harry!' Sarah clapped her hands in delight, for she knew then that he had forgiven his young cousin. 'I should like that immensely.'

'You really are fond of her, aren't you?'

Sarah nodded.

'Then I suppose I shall have to tolerate her foolishness.' He chuckled. 'You know — I really cannot imagine Corinne as a mama!'

'Can you imagine me?' she asked softly.

He reached out his hands and clasped hers, his expression was gentle, questioning.

'It's too early to be sure,' she admitted. 'But I believe, this time — '

He placed a silencing finger on her lips. 'I meant it when I said it didn't matter, Sarah. Having you for my wife is the only really important thing in my life.'

'I know. And for me — you are my life, dearest Harry,' she smiled, resting her head against his shoulder.

Before they reached the shores of England, she knew that the heir to Ashingby was definitely making the journey with them.

We do hope that you have enjoyed reading this large print book.

Did you know that all of our titles are available for purchase?

We publish a wide range of high quality large print books including:
**Romances, Mysteries, Classics
General Fiction
Non Fiction and Westerns**

Special interest titles available in large print are:
**The Little Oxford Dictionary
Music Book
Song Book
Hymn Book
Service Book**

Also available from us courtesy of Oxford University Press:
**Young Readers' Dictionary
(large print edition)
Young Readers' Thesaurus
(large print edition)**

For further information or a free brochure, please contact us at:
**Ulverscroft Large Print Books Ltd.,
The Green, Bradgate Road, Anstey,
Leicester, LE7 7FU, England.
Tel:** (00 44) **0116 236 4325
Fax:** (00 44) **0116 234 0205**

A FAIR PRETENDER

Janet Woods

Alone in England, a strange and cold country, and without means of support, Graine Seaton impersonates Evelyn Adams simply to survive. Her new identity comes with a fortune, and betrothal to a man of letters. This is the respectability Graine has always craved, for her past history is not something she can be proud of. But she doesn't count on falling in love with Saville Lamartine, the master of Rushford House. Nor does she envisage becoming involved in opposing the very trade that earned her fortune in the first place — that of slavery. With her pretence exposed as a lie and her life under threat, will Saville come to her rescue?

DANGEROUS LEGACY

Shirley Smith

When Sir Thomas Capley inherits a fortune from his great-uncle, he returns to Wintham determined to restore the family seat to its former glory. In somewhat unusual circumstances, he meets the proud and beautiful heiress, Miss Helena Steer, who has decided never to marry and, instead, devotes herself to her widowed father and her two young sisters. However, aided by Thomas's mischievous grandmother, the couple fall in love. There are many dangerous adventures for both of them, but will Helena find happiness with the passionate Sir Thomas?

ARROWS OF LONGING

Virginia Moriconi

When Gretchen decides to spend a year on the south-west coast of Ireland she knows that she is entering a world quite different from that of her strict Pennsylvania childhood. To her parents, Ireland is teeming with alcoholics and slipshod Catholics. To Gretchen, it is the native home of mystery and rapture. It does not take her long, however, in the dilapidated grandeur of Dufresne Hall — where squalor rules and nothing works — to change her views. But she finds a new direction for her feelings in a personal involvement that surprises and overwhelms her.